Praise for Ellie Alexander's Bakeshop mystery series

"Delectable."                    —*Portland Book Reviews*

"Quirky . . . intriguing . . . [with] recipes to make your stomach growl."                    —*Reader to Reader*

"Delicious."                    —*RT Book Reviews*

"This debut culinary mystery is a light soufflé of a book (with recipes) that makes a perfect mix for fans of Jenn McKinlay, Leslie Budewitz, or Jessica Beck."
—*Library Journal* on *Meet Your Baker*

"Marvelous."                    —*Fresh Fiction*

"Scrumptious . . . will delight fans of cozy mysteries with culinary delights."                    —*Night Owl Reviews*

"Clever plots, likable characters, and good food . . . Still hungry? Not to worry, because desserts abound in . . . this delectable series."                    —*Mystery Scene* on
*A Batter of Life and Death*

"[With] *Meet Your Baker*, Alexander weaves a tasty tale of deceit, family ties, delicious pastries, and murder."
—Edith Maxwell, author of *A Tine to Live,*
*A Tine to Die*

"Sure to satisfy both dedicated foodies and ardent mystery lovers alike."                    —Jessie Crockett, author of
*Drizzled with Death*

# Catch Me if You Candy

Ellie Alexander

St. Martin's Paperbacks

This is a work of fiction. All of the characters, organizations, and events portrayed in this novel are either products of the author's imagination or are used fictitiously.

First published in the United States by St. Martin's Paperbacks, an imprint of St. Martin's Publishing Group.

CATCH ME IF YOU CANDY

Copyright © 2023 by Katherine Dyer-Seeley.
Excerpt from *A Smoking Bun* copyright © 2023 by Katherine Dyer-Seeley.

Town map by Rhys Davies.

All rights reserved.

For information, address St. Martin's Publishing Group, 120 Broadway, New York, NY 10271.

www.stmartins.com

ISBN: 978-1-250-85440-7

Our books may be purchased in bulk for promotional, educational, or business use. Please contact your local bookseller or the Macmillan Corporate and Premium Sales Department at 1-800-221-7945, ext. 5442, or by email at MacmillanSpecialMarkets@macmillan.com.

Printed in the United States of America

St. Martin's Paperbacks edition / September 2023

10  9  8  7  6  5  4  3  2  1

*For the real George*

to Emigrant Lake

Oregon Shakespeare Festival

Lithia Park

The Merry Windsor

Ashland Police

THE GREEN GOBLIN

The Green Goblin

A Rose By Any
Other Name

Puck's Pub

Ashland

to Crater Lake

# Chapter One

They say that things are not always what they seem. For a long time, I might not have agreed when it came to my idyllic hometown of Ashland, Oregon, where neighbors helped neighbors and there was a strong sense of community spirit. But my perspective shifted a few days before Halloween this year when a strange turn of events left me unsettled and made me question whether I was sugarcoating the details of my life in our little corner of the Siskiyou Mountains.

The first sign that something wasn't quite right started amid the pre-holiday frenzy. We had been preparing for the upcoming ghoulish festivities at Torte, my family's bakeshop. Halloween in Ashland was like stepping onstage at one of the most elaborate productions in the Oregon Shakespeare Festival (known locally as OSF). Perhaps it was due to the creative and artistic types drawn to the Rogue Valley or that OSF had an entire warehouse dedicated to costumes ranging from Greek and Roman times to the Renaissance era, full military regalia to 1960s beehive headpieces, and everything in between. The company rented costumes to theaters of all shapes and sizes as well as for film and TV. Living in a thespian mecca meant that All Hallows' Eve might be the biggest holiday of the year.

Kids and adults alike would spend hours crafting unique and clever costumes for the celebration. That was my favorite part of the Halloween parade—*everyone* participated. In fact, to call it a parade didn't really do the event justice. It was more like a costume street party. And Torte was right in the mix.

We would close shop to join in the revelry and then, as soon as the parade spilled into the plaza, reopen to serve sweets, coffee, and snacks late into the evening. Trick-or-treaters would receive special Halloween goody bags, a longtime tradition at Torte. Mom and Dad had started the trend back in the bakeshop's early days. They had partnered with other family-owned businesses in town to offer a safe space for little witches and pumpkins to traipse from storefront to storefront in search of treats. Every business in the plaza embraced the experience. Next door to Torte, at A Rose by Any Other Name, Janet would hand out bunches of colorful lollipops tied with silky ribbons to resemble a bouquet of flowers. Puck's Pub offered red-and-white-striped bags of cheesy and spiced popcorn. The bookstore gave every youngster a free comic. There was always a long line at the Green Goblin at the end of the block, where servers roamed the sidewalk with trays of their signature garlic fries and lemon aioli dipping sauce.

At Torte we packaged hundreds of Halloween treat bags filled with our classic sugar cookies designed to resemble candy corn, ghosts, and spiders. We also included cider spice mixes, Frankenstein and eyeball cake pops, and mummy munch—our Halloween take on trail mix, with crumbled pieces of shortbread, toasted nuts, coconut, pretzels, and orange and black M&M's.

In addition to the treat bags, our pastry cases would be stocked with chocolate cupcakes featuring fluffy buttercream ghosts, tiered cakes with festive Halloween sprinkles, and cauldrons filled with decadent custards. Many customers had already put in special orders for parties, but the parade and subsequent street fair would bring in thousands of costumed tourists to our little hamlet, and we wanted to be prepared to keep them fed and happy throughout the evening.

On a blustery late October morning, I made my way along Main Street while the last of the stars flicked overhead. As was typical, I had snuck out of bed while Carlos was still sleeping. After pulling on a pair of jeans, tennis shoes, and one of our new Torte hoodies, I tiptoed downstairs and left him and Ramiro a note letting them know that I would see them later. Ramiro had been living with us since August. He was doing an exchange year at Ashland High School and, unless he was a master of deception, seemed to be fitting in seamlessly. His classes were going well, his soccer team had qualified for the state championships, and he had a date for homecoming.

I had been nervous about whether the transition from Spanish to American schools would be difficult and whether things between us would feel awkward or forced. I wanted Ramiro to know that he was welcome and would always have a place with Carlos and me. Fortunately, his easygoing attitude abated my fears. It was as if he had grown up in Ashland with the way he had almost instantly made friends and learned his way around the Alice in Wonderland trails that connected from our house to Lithia Park and all the way to Mount A. Watching him compete in his red and white Grizzly gear brought back many happy memories of my time at Ashland High School, running cross-country and helping build sets for our theater projects. Ramiro had yet to experience an Ashland Halloween, though. He had looked at me skeptically when I told him that the entire town plus a few thousand extra visitors would be in costume. I'm sure he thought I was exaggerating. He would have to see for himself.

Neighbors had already decked out porches with carved jack-o'-lanterns, black and orange twinkle lights, and skeletons. If Ramiro had doubted me, he need only take a stroll through the plaza. Downtown, with its vintage Tudor-style homes and buildings, the Halloween theme continued. Scarecrows, bats, and creatures that go bump in the night were propped in front of restaurants and shops. Silky gold banners announcing the parade hung from the antique lampposts that lined the street. There were window displays with retro candy, advertisements for a midnight showing of *The Rocky Horror Picture Show* at the movie theater, and jewel-toned masks for sale at the costume shop.

I was glad for my hoodie as the breeze kicked up leaves on the sidewalks. A faint hint of woodsmoke lingered in the air. There was nothing like Ashland in the fall. To be fair, there wasn't a bad time of the year to visit our village nestled amongst the endless mountain ranges of the Rogue Valley, but autumn put on a glorious show of color. Every tree in the plaza looked as if it had been painted by hand. Deep maroon, mustard yellow, and burnt orange leaves glowed under the dimming starlight. I drank in the view and the early morning calm as I crossed the street in front of the police station and headed toward Torte.

Our family bakeshop sat on the corner of the plaza. Its cheerful red and teal awning and large bay windows always brought a smile to my face. I paused for a minute to take in the Halloween window display that Steph, our cake artist and a recent college grad, and Rosa, our dining room manager and part-time baker, had created. They had turned the bakeshop's front windows into an inviting and slightly spooky scene. Black and white bunting and twinkling lights hung from the top of the window, below which hung a six-foot-wide spider's web. Steph and Rosa had stretched fake webbing from it in each direction, creating a gauzy effect. Cake stands at the base of the window displayed skull-shaped Bundts, and red velvet cakes pierced with bloody knives. Somehow, they had managed to strike the right balance of whimsy with just a touch of creepiness.

The vibe on the plaza was the same. At this early hour, fading moonlight illuminated the trees, casting moving shadows on the ground. The Lithia bubblers gurgled steadily. A crow circled overhead, cawing its morning greeting. Most of the other storefronts were still dark, except the Merry Windsor Hotel, which looked like it should have been named Hotel Transylvania instead, with its crumbling faux-stone façade and dusty windows. Nothing about the dilapidated exterior, however, was an effect for Halloween. The owner, Richard Lord, just refused to spend a dime modernizing the hotel.

I made a mental note to tell Steph and Rosa how much I loved their display as I continued downstairs, unlocked the basement door, and went inside. Being the first person in the kitchen helped set the tone and center me for the day. My first task was to light a fire in our wood-burning pizza oven. Almost immediately the basement began to warm and the scent of applewood wafted into the workspace. Mom and I had designed the commercial kitchen with stations for baking, decorating, and making our savory breakfast and lunch items. I loved our modern revamp with bright overhead lights for the painstaking task of piping detail work on cakes and the easy flow between baking and prep stations. Prior to expanding downstairs, our entire operation had been crammed into the original kitchen upstairs. By far my favorite thing about the basement space was the exposed brick wall and wood-burning pizza oven that our contractor had unearthed in the remodeling process.

After hanging up my coat and turning on the lights, I didn't bother to brew a pot of coffee, because I knew that Andy, our head barista, would be arriving soon. Instead, I washed my hands, tied on a fire-engine–red Torte apron, and gathered the ingredients I needed for devil's food cupcakes. I wanted to get a head start on our specialty bakes. We had multiple orders for dozens of custom Halloween cakes, cookies, and cupcakes. The baking was relatively easy, but the task of piping dainty bones or devil horns would be much more arduous. If I could get all of the baking done before Steph and Bethany arrived, that would give the cupcakes and cookies plenty of time to cool before they began to work their buttercream and royal icing magic.

I began by incorporating vegetable oil and sugar into our industrial mixer. Then I added vanilla and eggs. I sifted flour, baking powder, salt, and dark chocolate in next, alternating with a splash of buttermilk and espresso powder. Once a thick chocolate batter had formed, I scooped it into cupcake tins lined with blood-red and ghostly white wrappers. We would use the devil's food cupcakes for a variety of Halloween designs, including actual devils made with a chocolate ganache glaze and pieces of red licorice for the horns. White meringue ghosts would top some of the cupcakes, and others would get drizzled with melted white chocolate spiderwebs.

As I was sliding the first batch of cupcakes into the oven, Andy came in through the basement door, the howling wind following after him. He clenched his stocking cap and tried, unsuccessfully, to smooth down his unruly hair.

"Whew, it's really kicking out there." His youthful cheeks were flushed from the wind. He yanked off his coat and hung it on the rack near the door. "If it keeps up like this for the rest of the week, the trick-or-treaters might get blown away."

"Somehow I don't think they'll mind." I smiled and then turned to the pantry to get the ingredients I needed for our pumpkin cream cupcakes. "As long as there's candy, right?"

"Fair point, boss." He licked his index finger and pressed down a strand of wild hair.

Andy had taken to calling me boss instead of Jules or my given name, Juliet Montague Capshaw. I didn't mind. I knew it was a term of endearment, and quite honestly, growing up with such a Shakespearean moniker had its own issues. These days I appreciated that my namesake was arguably the most romantic heroine in all of literature, but there had been a time when I was convinced that I was destined for a life of unrequited love, thanks to my name.

"When I was a kid I didn't care if it was pouring rain on Halloween," Andy said, coming into the kitchen. "Give me the candy, and I'm good."

"Same here." I set pumpkin puree and a trio of spices on the counter. "What's on the coffee menu?"

Andy had been roasting his own beans lately. After much deliberation, he had decided to take a break from college and football to focus on his passion—coffee roasting. Mom and I supported him by sending him to regional training and serving his specialty roasts. Part of me worried about him giving up the stability of a college degree, but then again, I had followed my dream of going to culinary school and becoming a pastry chef. That choice had sent me around the world and landed me back in Ashland. I'm a firm believer in living authentically and pursuing a passion. Andy had won a number of roasting competitions and installed his own setup in his grandmother's converted garage. He was definitely on his way to something bigger, but in the meantime, I was so glad that we were the beneficiaries of his quest for the perfect brew.

"I'm not going to give anything away yet, but let's just say that I have a few tricks up my sleeve." He winked and rattled the container of beans he had brought from home before heading upstairs.

"Am I going to get to taste these tricks?" I called after him.

"You know it. Hang tight, I'll be down in a few with my mysterious brew."

While he went upstairs, I returned my attention to the pumpkin cupcake batter. No Halloween pastry case could be complete without pumpkin on the menu. For these, I whipped butter and sugar together until the mixture was light and fluffy, then incorporated the pumpkin puree, spices, eggs, flour, salt, baking powder, and sour cream to give the cupcakes a slight tang. Once the cakes cooled, we would core out the centers and fill them with our cream cheese frosting. These would be finished with cinnamon buttercream and topped with pumpkin-shaped candies.

While I waited for Andy's coffee of the day and the rest of the team to arrive, I managed to finish a vat of the day's batches of dough for sugar cookies and snickerdoodles as well. There was nothing quite as satisfying as checking off tasks on my morning to-do list.

Sterling and Steph showed up about thirty minutes later. They had been living together for a while, and I was curious about what would be next for the young couple. Sterling had worked as our sous chef, and his skills continued to blow me away. Steph had graduated from Southern Oregon University in June with a degree in design. Buttercream had been her muse lately, but I had a feeling that like Andy, they were destined for their own culinary adventures. I wasn't sure what that meant, but I knew I had to appreciate every moment with them.

"I love the new tattoos," I said to Steph. "They're perfect for Halloween."

She tapped a skull cupcake on her forearm and then shot Sterling a triumphant grin. "That didn't even take a minute. I win. You're making dinner tonight." Her violet hair was styled in two braids tied with black rubber bands.

"I always make dinner," he countered.

"We had a bet how long it would take for someone to comment on my temporary tattoos," Steph said to me.

"Those are temporary? They look so real." I leaned in to get a closer look. Steph's left arm sported a collection of tattoos, both baking and Halloween themed. An anatomically correct heart with tendrils of purple and red veins with tiny heart shapes stretched from the top of her right shoulder to her elbow. "Wow, that heart is incredible."

Steph's eyes sparkled beneath a layer of black and violet eyeshadow that perfectly matched her hair. "I was going to save this reveal for Bethany." She patted her arm. "I wear my heart on my sleeve. Get it?"

"Well done. Well done." I clapped.

Sterling rolled up the sleeves of his hoodie to reveal his collection of skin art. "I told her once she goes temporary, she's going to do the real thing."

"Never." Steph made a slicing motion across her neck. "Just the thought of a needle makes me want to pass out."

"It's not that bad. You hardly feel it," Sterling replied.

Marty came in to save Sterling and Steph from their tattoo debate. "Happy almost Halloween," he called out as he joined us around the island. "It sure feels like a good morning for bread," he said with a broad grin. "Warm bread, hot soup, a fresh-from-the-oven cookie, what could be better on a cold autumn day?"

"Coffee," Andy interrupted, coming down the stairs, balancing a tray of diner-style mugs in one arm. "Always coffee."

"Do we get to know what your roast is before we try it?" I asked, wiping my hands on my apron.

Andy set the tray in the center of the island. "I'm calling it Burial Grounds, get it?" He waited for a reaction. "Burial *grounds*."

"Oh no." Marty rolled his eyes. "Where's Bethany when we need her?"

"Still on the road with her celebrity crush." Andy's normally lighthearted tone turned a touch bitter, like a coffee that had sat in the pot for too long.

Bethany had landed an opportunity to partner with a celebrity chef, Jeremy DeSalt, who discovered her on Instagram, thanks to her witty captions and artistic eye for styling food photos. Jeremy's roving kitchen, *Pass DeSalt*, was hugely popular. He had rolled into the Rogue Valley with his decked-out food truck for a few weeks and then invited her to continue the journey, traveling to Portland, Bend, Seattle, and BC with him. She was due back on Halloween, and I knew I wasn't the only one excited about her return.

"What's the roast?" I changed the subject.

Andy passed around coffees. "It's my darkest roast ever. Like pitch-black, strong, and spicy, but so smooth that it will fool you going down. Fair warning, there's enough caffeine in this beauty to keep you kicking, so this one is a slow sipper. Unless you're wanting to fly high all morning."

"Yikes." I grimaced in anticipation of taking a sip. "Does it need to come with a warning label?"

"Probably." Andy held character, keeping his eyes narrowed and his brows furrowed. "It's dark, deadly, and delicious."

Marty pushed up his sleeves and took off his watch. "It sounds like this is going to have us howling at the moon."

"That's the goal." Andy raised his mug in a toast. "Let's see who's brave enough to handle these grounds."

"I feel like we need to make some graveyard pudding cups to accompany this," I said, taking a tiny sip. I half expected his highly caffeinated fuel to be bitter, but Andy was right that the coffee was smooth and easy to drink. I tasted notes of black tea and molasses with a spicy finish.

Sterling pounded his chest like a gorilla. "This will put hair on your chest, man."

"Or turn you into a werewolf," Marty countered.

"That's the goal. It is Halloween week, after all. We've got to keep the thrills and chills coming." Andy tipped his mug to take a large gulp.

"Hey, on that note, I know we've closed Scoops for the season, but I was wondering what you think about offering a couple of Halloween concrete specials?" Sterling asked.

Scoops, our summer pop-up ice cream shop in the railroad district, had been a hit with locals and tourists. We didn't serve an extensive menu at the outdoor spot, but rather stocked it with to-go options like sandwiches and cookies for picnics as well as daily "concretes," thick, creamy ice cream made with seasonal fruits and berries.

"We could turn our dark chocolate concrete even darker by adding extra cocoa powder and charcoal, and serve it in waffle cones with chunks of candy bars," Sterling continued. "And we have to have something pumpkin. Everyone loves pumpkin ice cream this time of year. I can level it up with chunks of piecrust and cinnamon crumble topping."

"I love it," I replied. "What are we thinking for lunch today?"

Marty leveled flour to add to his sourdough starter. "I was planning to make batches of breadsticks to serve with Sterling's soup of the day and for our annual mummy dogs."

Mummy dogs were a favorite amongst adults and kids. We wrapped natural organic Angus beef hot dogs with our breadstick dough to mimic mummy bandages. Then we baked them in the pizza oven and finished them off with mustard eyes and house-made ketchup for dipping.

"I'm doing a black bean stew with fresh avocado and cilantro," Sterling said, as he tied an apron around his waist. "I was also thinking of mac and cheese with toasted herbed bread crumbs in ramekins to go with the mummy dogs."

"Can it be lunchtime now?" I gave the clock a wistful glance.

"If nothing else, I can have tastes ready soon." Sterling tossed a dish towel over his shoulder and prepared his workstation.

We went over the rest of the schedule and custom cake and specialty treat box orders. Soon the kitchen was alive with energy. As much as I enjoyed my early solo baking, I thrived on collaborating with my staff as we blasted a Halloween playlist and went to work on our individual tasks. Running a bakeshop was like choreographing a scene for the stage. We each had our own marks to hit, but once everything came together, it was a fluid display of edible art.

By the time we were ready to open the front doors, the pastry case was filled with purple, orange, neon green, and black stacked cakes; sweet and savory breakfast pastries; hot-from-the-oven cookies, scones, and muffins; and loaves of freshly baked bread.

My phone dinged as I took a spin through the dining

room to make sure everything was in order. The text was from Mom. She and her mahjong group were meeting at her friend Wendy's house later. She had forgotten that she was supposed to bring dessert and wondered if she could reserve a Halloween treat box.

I could do better than that. I could deliver a box to Wendy's house personally. It was only a few blocks from the plaza, and it would be fun to see Mom's gaming crew. She and her dear friends Wendy, Janet, and Marcia had been playing mahjong for as long as I could remember. Their weekly gaming sessions were really an excuse to get together for a long lunch and an afternoon of catching up.

I shot her a text back to let her know that I would swing by later and then went to open the bakeshop. The next few hours were a blur of activity as Andy and Sequoia managed the continual line at the espresso bar, doling out orange spice lattes and cups of Andy's Burial Grounds roast. Rosa and I rang up orders for ham and Swiss croissants, pesto egg breakfast sandwiches, and toasted almond pastries. Within thirty minutes of opening, every table upstairs and downstairs was filled with customers sipping from steaming mugs and enjoying leisurely breakfasts.

I couldn't contain my happiness watching friends linger over Earl Grey tea while the trees shed their leaves outside. The blustery winds bending branches and sending orange and yellow leaves scattering like confetti made it feel like Halloween. I still had plenty of work to finish in the kitchen and a costume to put together, but it was impossible to ignore the palpable excitement of the upcoming holiday. We were going to be in the center of the action, and I couldn't wait. What could be better than our entire community parading in costumes down our charming Main Street? I wasn't worried about ghosts, ghouls, or things that go bump in the night. This was Ashland, Oregon, perhaps the most idyllic place on the planet. Nothing could go wrong.

# Chapter Two

The morning flew by. Sterling's black bean stew and Marty's mummy dogs were so popular that I must have logged twenty trips up and down the stairs delivering orders. Everyone chatted about their costume ideas for the parade and noshed on our oversized snickerdoodles. Once the bulk of the lunch rush had died down, I used the opportunity to package a box of desserts for Mom and her friends.

"I'm going to head out on a quick delivery," I said to Steph, who was piping a spiderweb pattern onto a four-layer cake draped in black fondant. "Need anything while I'm out?"

"Nope." She steadied the piping bag with one hand. "We're good."

It was true. My team could run the bakeshop in their sleep. I prided myself on the fact that we had built such a solid and diverse crew at Torte.

I wished I had brought a coat as I stepped out into the plaza. It wasn't that cold, probably in the mid-fifties, but the wind cut through my hoodie, sending shivers up my spine. I passed A Rose by Any Other Name, where a CLOSED sign hung in the window. That was probably because Janet was at Wendy's. Flyers posted at Puck's Pub advertised a special midnight show with the band the Rolling Bones.

I chuckled at the name as I passed my old apartment above Elevation, the outdoor equipment store.

Wendy lived a few blocks away in a cottage not far from Lithia Park. Even with the wind assaulting my face, I enjoyed getting out for some fresh air and a walk. I scurried past the Merry Windsor, fortunately avoiding a run-in with Richard Lord. He owned the aging Shakespearean-themed hotel and had made it his mission to make me miserable ever since I had returned to Ashland.

Lithia Park was breathtakingly beautiful. I passed a herd of deer grazing on the green grass beneath a brilliant currant-colored Japanese maple refusing to give up its leaves. Ducks bobbed on the waves caused by the wind in the pond. Tourists and joggers meandered the walking and running trails that led deep into the forest.

I soaked in the autumnal light filtering in through the canopy of deciduous and evergreen trees. How lucky I was to get to live in such a stunning place. How lucky to have seasons again. That was one thing I had missed desperately in my years on the *Amour of the Seas*. Sure, sailing from one far-flung port of call to another had its own benefits, like seeing every part of the world and immersing myself in different cultures, but endless azure waters and sun-drenched skies had nothing on Ashland. I had come to appreciate following Mother Nature's cycles. The crisp air and sepia tones of fall, snowy winter nights in front of a crackling fire, the pinkish light of spring in bloom, the warmth of summer on my skin.

I came to a fork in the pathway that cut through the park and up to the network of running and biking trails. I turned toward a grouping of houses on the edge of the park's boundary. Wendy's cottage was the last one on the street. It was easy to recognize with its snowy white paint and forest green trim. I unlatched the picket fence and walked past a group of apple trees that the deer had already eaten clean. Two rockers sat on her wraparound porch along with yet-to-be-carved pumpkins.

"Come on in, it's unlocked," someone called when I knocked on the front door.

I was immediately greeted by Wendy's dog, who came running to meet me. "Well, hi, to you, my sweet, furry friend." I bent down to pet a yellow Lab with a goofy pink tongue hanging out of the side of its mouth.

"Sorry," Wendy said, clapping twice as she came to the door. "Cooper, come here." She reached for the yellow Lab's collar. "It's a total doghouse around here today. What am I saying, it's always a doghouse here. Cooper pretty much runs this place."

"I didn't even think about it, I should have brought dog treats." I pointed to the pastry box.

Wendy waved me inside. Her cottage was warm and cozy, with a stone fireplace and an open living and dining room. There were bookshelves everywhere stacked with books, art, and pottery. I was transported back to my childhood. Wendy and Mom had been friends for as long as I could remember, and I had spent many afternoons here playing board games and making homemade strawberry jam in the summer. "Come in, come in," Wendy said, tugging Cooper's collar. "We have food, snacks, bubbles."

"Thanks so much for coming, Juliet." Mom waved me

toward the dining room table. "Everyone wanted to meet King George, and we didn't coordinate who was bringing dessert today."

"King George?" I scrunched my nose and glanced around the living room. "Is Lance coming in costume or something?"

Everyone chuckled.

Wendy tapped her head with her index finger. "Now, why didn't I think of that?"

I approached the table. An ornate mahjong box, tiles, and racks were already set up. The game, said to have originated in nineteenth-century China, is almost like cards, but played with enchantingly artistic tiles. The women had been playing once a week for decades. They spent as much time chatting and eating delectable food as they did playing. "Where should I put these, and who is King George?"

Wendy motioned for Cooper to sit. Wendy was a year or two older than Mom. In her sixties, I would guess, with white-blond hair. I had known her most of my life, since attending preschool with her daughter. "Jules, it was so kind of you to bring us dessert." She patted my arm and motioned me into her attached galley kitchen. "All of the food is in here. You know where everything is. Help yourself and come join us."

Their lunch spread wasn't merely sandwiches and chips. There were pasta salads, hummus and veggies, crackers, cheese, salami, fresh fruit, dips, and little bowls with nuts and popcorn. I made a space for the pastries and grabbed a handful of cashews.

"You look like you have enough food for the entire neighborhood," I teased.

Janet, Thomas's mom and a second mother to me, gave

me a sheepish grin. "You know us. We like to snack as we play. But no looking at each other's tiles when we get up to refresh our plates, right, ladies?"

Mom covered her tile rack with a hand. "Never."

"Hey, no judgment from me when it comes to snacking." I popped a couple of nuts in my mouth and took a seat next to their fourth player, Marcia. Marcia was a newer addition to the group, as in ten years new. She had joined the weekly game when she moved to Ashland from Santa Cruz and met Wendy at the dog park.

"It's so great to see you, Juliet." Marcia reached over to give me a half hug. "Your mom was telling us about all of the exciting things happening at Torte. You have really created an empire."

I could feel heat start to rise in my cheeks. "I don't know about an empire, but it's been fun to expand and try some new things."

"She's too self-effacing," Mom said to Marcia before catching my eye and winking.

Sunlight streaming in through the sheer drapes illuminated the colorful collection of tiles and score sheets. I started to study the bone and bamboo tiles on the table when a tiny yap drew my attention in Marcia's direction. I hadn't noticed it when I sat down next to her, but there was a large basket with two blankets and an adorable pug wearing a silky red king's robe and a gold crown. "Let me guess, this must be King George?"

Marcia beamed with pride. "Isn't he the cutest? He's my newest fur baby. He's two years and eight months old today and the smartest pooch on the planet.

"She's not biased," Wendy interjected with a friendly grin.

"Me? Never." Marcia patted her heart. "I was so sad after I lost my last dog, and King George has filled a hole in my heart. We're trying to figure out which costume will be best for his grand appearance in the parade." She reached down to grab a sewing bag at her feet and then held up a Superman costume. "What do you think is better, the royal robes he's wearing now? Or Super-George?"

"King," all three friends answered together.

"He's going to be in the parade?" I munched on the nuts.

"He's the grand marshal this year. Can you believe it?" Marcia patted George's basket. "He's just auditioned for a huge role at OSF next season. I had just been about to tell everyone about George's surprise before you got here . . ." She paused and glanced around the table. "Are you ready for some news?"

Wendy stacked tiles in the center of the table. "Did he get it?"

"He did." Marcia clasped her hands together. She turned and cooed at George. "Aren't you going to be a star? He's landed a role in *A Play About a Dragon*. It's a delightful farce set in the Middle Ages where a troupe of actors is under the assumption that they're performing a play about a dragon to impress their king when in actuality they're being sent to slay a real dragon. And George here has the role of the king."

Mom had gone into the kitchen for a coffee refill. She poked her head out of the door. "Wait, did I hear you correctly, George got the role?"

"We're in the presence of royalty, Helen. I don't know if we'll be invited back to play now that George is going to make his debut onstage," Janet responded, giving

Marcia a friendly wink. She raised her coffee mug. "Would you mind topping me off while you're up?"

Mom deftly filled everyone's mug. "Juliet, coffee?"

"Sure." I turned to Marcia. "Wait, I need more information. Did George actually audition for a part?"

She reached into her purse for a dog treat, shaped like a miniature bone. "Of course. The entire cast has to audition, including canines. It's an OSF production, and I have to say the entire process was quite grueling. George was a trouper, but don't get me started on the audition process. It was an utter fiasco."

"I didn't realize there was an audition process for animals," I admitted.

Marcia gasped. She looked at me as if she was shocked that I didn't know this. "Uh, yes. And let me tell you, I have nothing good to say about what poor Georgie here had to go through to land the part. I have some feedback to share with Lance about his staff, mainly Newell Taylor, who claims to be the casting director in charge of canines."

"Claims to be?" Mom interjected.

Marcia broke another piece of a dog treat into a tiny bite for George. "He's been assigned as the animal performer coordinator, but he also helped cast the roles. It was pure chaos. There's a poodle—now George's understudy, who tried to steal the part right out from under George's nose, but we wouldn't let that happen now, would we?" She nuzzled the pug's head.

"That sounds intense," Wendy said.

"It was. Jax, the poodle's owner, was tossing around threats like you wouldn't believe. She is completely unhinged. Although I suppose it's a glimpse into what's in store for us this upcoming season. You should see his call sheet. He'll be in rehearsals with Newell, his dresser, and the understudy twice a week." Her face was serious. "The good thing is that George has been doing private training lessons with Anton Dudley for the past year to prepare for his audition, so hopefully he won't get too worn out with rehearsals and daily performances."

"I'm sure I should know this, but who is Anton Dudley?" I glanced around the table for help.

All of the women laughed, including Marcia.

"Oh no, dear, I wouldn't expect anyone outside of the dog world to know Anton." She fed George the treat and then gathered her tiles. "He's the best trainer on the West Coast. It took forever to get in with him, didn't it, Georgie?" She addressed the pug before returning her attention to me. "George has absolutely thrived under his direction, but I was just telling everyone before you arrived that I'm about ready to throttle that man."

"Be careful, Marcia," Wendy warned. "This group does not tolerate violence. Do I need to remind you of the hand-slapping incident?"

"Hand-slapping incident?" I wrinkled my brow. "I need to know more about this, and apparently, I need to come to mahjong for the gossip."

"You really do." Janet bobbed her head in agreement. "When we first started playing, we used to keep score, but we're too competitive. One of our former members slapped Wendy's hand when she reached for a tile out of turn."

I gasped and put my hand over my mouth. "Oh, the humanity."

"Don't mess with our tiles." Janet scooted her stack of

the bamboo tiles closer. "Marcia has stabbed us in the heart on more than one occasion with her killer moves."

"I can't promise that I won't resort to violence when it comes to Anton. He's on my hit list at the moment," Marcia said with disdain, giving George a pat on the head. "After all the work George has put in and all the money we've paid Anton, he actually had the nerve to take on Pippa as a client even after Jax made a tremendous scene at auditions."

"Dare I ask, who's Pippa?" I made a face.

Marcia sighed. "Pippa is the poodle who now has the role as George's understudy. She is the most pampered and unruly toy poodle you've ever met. She and her owner, Jax Woofard, made a farce of this whole thing. They prance around town in matching pink costumes and prance around the stage like they own the place, but Pippa is not well trained. She can't keep her mark. She doesn't do a single trick on command, but she weaseled her way into getting an audition. I'm convinced that Jax is having an affair with or has dirt on someone at OSF."

"But she didn't get the part?" Mom confirmed.

"No." Marcia shook her head in disgust. "Pippa might have the breeding pedigree, but she cannot follow a single command—sit, stay, bark, roll over. I'm not even exaggerating when I tell you that she doesn't know any stage directions or follow cues. How could she possibly land a role that requires dancing onstage, even as an understudy?"

"Dancing?" Janet chuckled. "I'm stuck on the fact that her owner's last name is *Woof*ard."

"Well, it sounds like everything worked out." Mom kept things upbeat. "We'll all be there to cheer George on in the parade."

"Thanks." Marcia gave her a dismissive wave. "Enough about me. Wendy, show us the new set that you found." She fluffed George's blanket and offered him another treat.

Wendy stood. "You won't believe it. When I was wandering through the hospice retail shop, I nearly fainted. It's in my guest room. Help yourself to food. I'll be right back."

"She found an antique mahjong set from the late 1800s, imported from China," Mom explained to me. "They're extremely valuable and rare."

"Here?" I asked.

"Yes, at the hospice shop. Such a lucky find." Janet stirred cream into her coffee before setting her drink on a hand-painted coaster. "Would you like to stay for lunch and play a round with us?"

"I'd love to, but duty calls. We're baking up a storm before Halloween."

A look of concern crossed Mom's face. "Should I come help?"

"No, not at all. We have it under control. Plus Bethany will be back on Halloween," I assured her. "I do want to see Wendy's treasure before I head back, though."

Wendy emerged from the hallway a minute later, carrying an ornately carved wooden mahjong box like it was a newborn baby.

Mom and Marcia made space on the table.

"Isn't it exquisite?" Wendy ran her hand over the lacquered wood, which had been hand-carved with Chinese characters and writing. "I haven't had a chance to do much research yet, but I have a feeling that Camille, the new owner of the hospice shop, didn't charge me enough. I told them that when I purchased it, but they insisted that it was a fair price."

She proceeded to open the top drawer to show us the bone and bamboo tiles. The first row contained tiles with hand-painted birds in deep reds, blues, and yellows. Each "bam," as the women called them, was like a miniature art piece. There were hawks, parrots, and cranes perched on globes and tiles depicting entire village scenes.

"Wendy, these are stunning," Mom said. "We can't play with this set, though. I would be too worried that I'd spill coffee on it."

"Yes, I think I'll keep this one for show," Wendy agreed. She carefully tugged on the rounded handle of the next few drawers to let us see the unique tiles. "This last drawer has my favorites—the dragons."

Everyone oohed and aahed over the delicately painted designs. Red, white, green, and blue dragons looked like they belonged in the pages of an illustrated book. As Wendy started to close the bottom drawer, it stuck. She jiggled the handle twice.

"It won't go back in."

Mom stood to help her. Wendy pulled the drawer completely out. Mom knelt to get a better look. "Is that a piece of paper jammed inside?"

Wendy squinted. "You're right." She gently reached into the drawer and freed a tightly folded piece of paper.

"What is it?" Janet asked.

"A secret love note?" Marcia suggested.

"I have no idea." Wendy examined the paper. "It looks new. It's not faded or yellowed, so it can't be from the original set."

"Open it," Janet suggested.

Wendy's eyes widened, and her mouth fell open a bit as she read the note.

"Are you okay?" Mom asked.

Wendy tilted her head to the side. "I don't know. It's a bit odd, unsettling. Or maybe uncanny timing is a better word."

"What does that mean?" Marcia continued to pet George as she spoke.

I noticed Wendy's fingers tremble ever so slightly as she read the note out loud. "It says, 'If you're reading this, then the dragon is dead. Heed this warning—the dragon is dead.'"

George let out a yap, causing all of us to startle.

"I wonder what it means." Wendy flipped the paper over as if trying to see if there was more to the note. "It's odd timing, don't you think? We've been talking about plays about dragons and then a note about a dragon is stuffed inside this vintage mahjong set."

"Can I see it?" Mom asked.

Wendy handed her the paper. "The dragon is dead. Heed this warning—the dragon is dead. You all don't think that this set is cursed or something? Could the note be some kind of warning?"

"No." Marcia responded first. "What kind of warning would be hidden in an old mahjong set?"

Janet agreed. "It's probably something to do with the tiles. An inside joke about the dragons in the game."

"Yeah." Mom gave the note back to Wendy.

Wendy nodded and returned to her seat. "I'm sure you're right, it's just weird. But have any of you ever gotten goosebumps like this?" She held out her arms to show little bumps erupting on her skin. "It feels like a premonition or a curse. I mean, don't get me wrong, I'm likely overreacting. I've read too many Agatha Christie novels and spent too many hours watching those village mysteries on the BBC, but isn't there something ominous about the note?"

"Steer clear of rehearsals for *A Play About a Dragon* at the Bowmer, and you'll be fine," Marcia teased.

"Yeah, yeah, you're right." Wendy carefully refolded the note. "I'm just telling you right now, ladies, that if I bump into a dead dragon, I'm never going to let you live it down."

# Chapter Three

Finding the mysterious note had seemed to rattle Wendy, but the rest of the game group convinced her it was probably a prank and to play on. I made my exit, promising to come back another time when I could stay longer.

I didn't think Wendy's rare set was cursed, but I had to agree that finding the note was a coincidence in terms of timing. *A Play About a Dragon* sounded like a great show, and Janet was probably right that the note had something to do with the dragon tiles and nothing to do with being a real warning.

Fitting for Halloween, I thought as I made my return trip through Lithia Park. A warning note hidden in a compartment of an expensive vintage mahjong set had the writings of Shakespeare all over it. Lance would love this.

As the thought came to mind, I heard his distinctive telltale voice call out, "Well, well, well. If it isn't the one and only Juliet Montague Capshaw."

I looked up to see Lance strolling down the Shakespearean stairs. In true Lance fashion, he was dressed in a sleek black suit with a crisp white shirt and a pumpkin orange tie.

"I was literally just thinking about you," I said, greeting him with a hug.

He kissed both of my cheeks. "Of course you were. Isn't that the norm? There's not a single second that I shouldn't be top of mind."

"Right. My mistake." I laughed. "You're looking particularly dapper and in the Halloween spirit today."

"Ah, yes, I have next season's cast announcement later this afternoon. I wouldn't want to disappoint my fans."

"Certainly not. I just met one of your cast members."

"Do tell. Who?" Lance looped his arm through mine as we left the park and headed toward Torte.

"A very special cast member, King George."

Lance tilted his head back and moaned. "Oh, the drama. The drama amongst our four-legged actors, who could have thunk it?"

"Thunk it?"

"Darling, do not get me started. The show is literally going to the dogs."

"I heard that auditions were intense."

"If that isn't the understatement of the century. Kill me now." He pretended to use his tie to choke himself. "I made the mistake of hiring an unknown animal performer coordinator, Newell, who is more skittish than anyone I've ever met. He gives new meaning to the phrase scaredy cat. The guy is terrified of his own shadow and cowers when any of the dogs so much as let out a little bark. How he's going to control the canines or their owners is a mystery to me."

He paused to wave hello to a tourist who recognized him and asked to take a selfie. As artistic director for OSF, Lance was Ashland's version of royalty. Theater patrons returned year after year not only to take in productions of *The Tempest* under a blanket of stars but also because of Lance. His naturally endearing personality and his pure passion for the stage made him as popular, if not more popular, than the rest of the company. His monthly brunch and lunch chats where he shared mimosas and inside secrets about productions routinely sold out within minutes. People queued up early to listen to his preshow introductions during the season, and he could often be spotted lingering in the lobby after performances to mingle and autograph playbills. It wasn't an overstatement to say that Lance and OSF were synonymous.

I offered my picture-taking services before we continued on.

"Now, tell me, why was I on your mind?" Lance asked, extending his arm.

"You're going to love this." I proceeded to tell him about Wendy's mahjong set and the hidden note.

Lance stopped in midstride when I finished. "Did you get it?"

"Get what?" I caught a whiff of pizza from a couple of shops away. My stomach growled in response to the aroma.

"The note." Lance threw his hands up in exasperation.

"No, why?" I glanced at the display in the front windows of the mountain shop as we passed by. They had swapped their rafting gear and swimsuits for snowshoes and winter boots. It was hard to believe that as of this weekend, the holiday season was upon us and it would be a whirlwind of baking from now through the end of the year.

"Isn't it obvious? We should take the case."

"The case of what?"

He rolled his eyes. "The case of the dragon. I wouldn't be so quick to dismiss this as a prank. It could be that there's a dragon out there in desperate need of our services."

"What exactly would our services entail?" I teased.

"Our superior sleuthing skills, of course." He leaned back and ran his hand over his tie.

"Right, how could I forget our superior sleuthing skills." We made it to A Rose by Any Other Name, where one of Janet's staff members was refilling galvanized tins on the sidewalk with bright orange poppies.

"You laugh now, but how terrible will you feel if you see a headline in the next few days about a dragon meeting an untimely death?"

"Terrible. So terrible." I pretended to dab my eye.

Lance released me and shook his finger in my face. "Fair warning, Juliet, I'll be keeping my eye out for any flying, fire-breathing dragons on the loose, and you should do the same."

"Will do." I made an X over my heart.

"Before I go, how are the costumes coming for the parade?" Lance asked.

"Good. Ramiro is so excited to get to experience an American Halloween."

"Have you given any thought to my offer?"

I cringed. "Thanks, but no thanks. Carlos and I have it covered."

"Are you sure? I have my suggestions reserved for you."

"Hard pass, but I love you." I leaned in to kiss him on the cheek. "What about you and Arlo? Are you doing a couples thing?"

"You'll have to wait and see, darling. Everything shall be revealed shortly."

"You're such an international man of mystery."

That made him bow. "Why, thank you. I mustn't dally, but I shall be seeing you soon. Ta-ta."

He crossed the street toward the Lithia bubblers. I imagined how uncomfortable I would feel in his costume suggestion. He had come by the bakeshop a few days ago to offer to reserve matching Jasmine and Aladdin costumes from OSF's warehouse. I politely declined, since neither costume left anything to the imagination when it came to showing skin. I had seen the Jasmine costume in a production of *Aladdin* a few summers ago, and there was no way I was joining the parade in a glorified skimpy bikini.

Inside Torte, things had slowed. A handful of customers waited for lattes at the espresso bar. There were a few tables taken too, but otherwise, the dining room was in a sweet, lazy afternoon haze. I snagged a second cup of Andy's Burial Grounds, knowing that I might regret it later, and went downstairs to check on how things were going in the kitchen.

Steph had completed dozens of Halloween cakes that she was boxing and labeling for pickup and delivery. Sterling and Marty were wrapping up lunch orders, and Rosa was bringing a new tray of cookies and cupcakes upstairs for the late afternoon crowd.

When there was a lull in the activity, I called everyone to the island for a quick team meeting. "Great work today. I know things are winding down, but I want to touch base about the parade and Halloween."

"I'm ready." Marty twirled his rolling pin. "My costume is set."

"What are you going as?" Sterling asked.

"A butcher, a baker, and a candlestick maker." He emphasized each word by pointing at himself.

"All three?" Steph wiped black frosting from her hands with a dish towel.

"You know it." Marty held the rolling pin in his left hand. "This hand will have a rolling pin, and the other will have a candlestick."

"What about the butcher?" Sterling asked. "You only have two hands."

"Ah, that's where the fun comes in." Marty set the rolling pin on the island and reached down to the built-in shelves. He proceeded to put on a traditional white chef's hat with a fake cleaver stabbed through the center.

"That's pretty good." Steph gave him a nod of approval, which was high praise for her.

"I can't wait to see everyone's costumes," I continued. "On that note, I'm assuming everyone wants to participate in the parade?"

The yeses were unanimous.

"Great. That's what I figured. Let's plan to close the bakeshop by about two to give everyone time to get changed and congregate at the library. Then anyone who wants extra hours is welcome to work the evening shift. Andy already said he wants to run the espresso counter. Sequoia is taking the night off for a party. Obviously, we won't be baking anything extra, so we can run with a skeleton crew."

"Nice pun, Jules." Sterling forced himself to stifle a laugh.

"I didn't even mean it." I tried to wink and contorted my face into a goofy grin. "If you want to be here to help hand out treat bags and serve walk-in customers, I'd love to have you, but don't feel any pressure if you have other plans."

"Count this butcher and baker in," Marty replied.

Sterling nodded and looked at Steph. "I think we'll come help at least for an hour or so. How late are you going to stay open?"

I shrugged. "Usually we play it by ear. The first hour or two after the parade tends to be a mob scene, but then people head to restaurants and bars for dinner and the kiddos head to their own neighborhoods for more trick-or-treating."

"Kiddos?" Steph raised her eyebrow.

"Is that not how I'm supposed to refer to kids these days? Am I that out of touch?"

Her lips, which had been lined with purple and filled in with black lipstick, actually formed a real smile. "No. Well, yeah, you are getting up there, but I meant that we're going to see just as many adults trick-or-treating."

"Fair point." It was true. Ashland didn't have age limitations when it came to going door to door for candy. If you were wearing a costume, odds were in your favor that neighbors would hand you treats whether you were six or ninety-six. "Anyway, I can't imagine staying open late. We'll all want to enjoy the festivities too."

After we finalized our plans, we returned to baking. Halloween was only a few days away, and if Torte was going to be in the center of the activity, we had a lot of work to do. By the time the day was over, I was exhausted. Carlos picked me up and suggested we stop to get falafels on the way home. As much as I enjoyed cooking, grabbing takeout sounded dreamy.

When we got home, he started a fire and opened a bottle of wine. Ramiro finished soccer practice and joined us in front of the crackling fire for dinner.

"You are going to be with the team for the parade?" Carlos asked.

"Yes. Instead of costumes, they want the entire team to wear our uniforms. Coach is going to get us funny Grizzly hats and red and white glow sticks." Ramiro polished off one falafel and went in for seconds. "If it's okay with you, after the parade I've been invited for dinner and thrasher movies with the team too. We're getting pizza. I'm supposed to bring something to share."

"Sí, you must do this." Carlos swirled his wine. "You will have a real American Halloween."

"Complete with thrasher flicks," I added. "I remember one Halloween my friends and I did the same thing, and I spent the entire night watching the movies with one eye open from beneath a blanket. I'm such a chicken when it comes to horror films."

"Boo!" Carlos tried to startle me.

I punched him in the arm. "Be careful, or you'll end up sleeping outside with bears."

"Now, that is something to be scared of," Ramiro said.

"I'm sorry your mom can't be here. Hopefully, they'll be able to visit for the holidays." Originally Ramiro's mom and his family from Spain had been intending to spend a week with us for Halloween, but their plans changed.

"It's okay. I told her I would livestream the parade, and they are excited to do an American Thanksgiving."

Ramiro's voice turned nasally when he pronounced *American* without his accent.

I reflected on my own growth and progress. When I had first learned about Ramiro, I had been shocked and even jealous, but now I was genuinely eager to extend our family.

We finished mapping out our costumes. Carlos and I were going as peanut butter and jelly. He had found a photo online, and Mom had offered to sew them for us. We just needed to finalize our accessories.

I didn't make it up very late. I drifted off to sleep dreaming about Halloween, curses, and dragons as a storm kicked up outside. Little did I know that another kind of storm was brewing too.

# Chapter Four

Halloween morning dawned bright and sunny, albeit cold. A storm had ushered in the first freeze of fall, sending temperatures plummeting. Anticipation of what was to come drew me from beneath the down comforter on our bed and downstairs to make a pot of coffee. I lingered over the strong brew, watching deer graze on the frosty grass in the backyard. We had already decided that Carlos would bring our costumes and meet me at Torte later, so I bundled up for the walk into town and left him and Ramiro sleeping.

Unlike earlier in the week, the holiday had shopkeepers up early. City workers were posting no-parking signs along Main Street and Siskiyou Boulevard, and setting out cones to block traffic from the parade route. I blasted our Halloween playlist as I whipped up batches of pumpkin scones and apple muffins. It didn't take long for the bakeshop to start humming.

Andy arrived first, dressed as an iced coffee, complete with a two-foot paper straw. Steph had her face painted like a Day of the Dead sugar skull. Sterling and Marty sported matching fake butcher knives, which worked perfectly with Marty's butcher, baker and candlestick maker costume. Rosa came as a gothic dancer, and Sequoia as a garden fairy.

"Boss, where is your spirit?" Andy demanded at our morning meeting.

"I didn't know everyone was going to dress up for the day," I said, with an apologetic smile. "My costume doesn't really work without Carlos."

Bethany showed up at the moment to save the day. "Happy, happy Halloween, my bakers." She danced into the kitchen in a spider costume with eight furry legs sticking out her back. "I'm so excited to see everyone. I've missed your faces so, so, so much." She blew us kisses and then proceeded to heave a tote bag onto the island and start unpacking T-shirts and Pass DeSalt tchotchkes. "I brought you all gifts—swag."

"Tell me everything. What have I missed? I feel so out of the loop." She passed around swag bags and offered me some of her extra fake spider rings and a temporary face tattoo. "Jules, do you want some of my spiders for the day? Like Andy said, you're not looking very trick-or-*Torte*-ish."

Sterling groaned.

Andy and Marty applauded.

"All is right with the world," Marty said, reaching across the island to give Bethany a high five. "Our punster is back."

"We should call tonight Trick-or-Torte." Andy kept his gaze on Bethany. "Steph, maybe you can make a banner for the front."

"Absolutely." I tugged one of Bethany's plastic rings onto my finger. "It would feel like a waste to let a pun that clever pass us by."

Steph and Rosa agreed to make some tweaks to the chalkboard menu, and Andy and Sequoia decided to put their heads together to create a Trick-or-Torte special for the day.

Bethany gave us a recap of her time on the roving reality food show as we loaded the ovens with buttery croissants and pumpkin custards. The mood upstairs when we opened was buzzing with anticipation. At least half, if not more, of our customers arrived in full costume for flat whites and ham and cheddar biscuits. As promised, Steph had sketched out a Trick-or-Torte menu on our chalkboard. Rosa had added an interactive chart at the bottom for everyone to vote on their favorite Halloween candy. At the moment, Milky Way bars were the runaway winner.

Sequoia motioned me over to the espresso bar after I placed my vote for Reese's Peanut Butter Cups. "Are you ready for a taste of Trick-or-Torte? This one is pure Andy."

"Uh-oh." I bit my bottom lip. "Is this like his Burial Grounds?"

Andy was steaming milk while chatting with a customer at the other end of the bar, but that didn't stop him from turning to me and raising his eyebrows in puckish amusement.

Sequoia topped my drink with purple whipping cream and Halloween sprinkles. She moved in fluid, fairy-like motions when she worked. I enjoyed watching the way she made her job as a barista look like an interpretive performance. "I would call this saccharine, but I did get to put my spin on his sugary bomb."

I took a timid sip, getting notes of vanilla, raspberry, and matcha. "It's good."

"You sound surprised." She shook sprinkles onto another drink. "We went for our take on cotton candy. House-made vanilla and raspberry syrup was Andy's idea."

"Let me guess, you added the matcha."

"For color and to ground the drink to earth, you know?" She planted her feet firmly on the floor and pressed her index fingers and thumbs together. "Coffee is rooted in the earth, so that should be part of the drinking experience."

I appreciated Sequoia's mystical approach to coffee. She brought a different presence to the espresso bar, one that balanced Andy's buzzing energy with her meditative movements and desire to infuse our artisan roasts with unique natural ingredients.

"Is the whipping cream flavored too?" I asked.

A slow smile spread across her face as she pointed to a canister behind the bar. "Some beetroot powder and blackberry syrup for a touch of color and magic."

"It works for Halloween." I raised my mug in a toast and went outside to see how progress was coming for the parade.

The plaza was equally alive with activity. Speakers were being set up across the street by the Lithia bubblers for music for the annual *Thriller* showcase put on by the local dance team. More orange cones and signage blocked areas that were off-limits for cars, and nearly every business had sandwich boards touting Halloween specials and encouraging trick-or-treaters to stop in after the parade.

The rest of the day passed in a whirl of activity, and by the time Carlos arrived, I had barely had a minute to sit down, let alone eat anything. Of course I had consumed the Trick-or-Torte latte and at least three cups of Burial Grounds, so I was highly caffeinated.

"Julieta, you look pale." Carlos studied my face with concern. "Are you feeling okay?"

"I'm fine, but all of a sudden I'm so hungry." I glanced at the kitchen clock; it was after two.

"Sit. I will make you something."

I didn't argue. It was good to take a minute to rest, knowing that I would be on my feet again for the parade and the evening shift.

Carlos returned with a turkey and Swiss panini, apple slices, and our house-made salt and vinegar chips.

"Thanks. I don't think I realized how late it is. The Halloween rush is real." I took a bite of the sandwich.

"Sí. The streets even up by the college are already filled with cars. There must be at least a few thousand people already gathering at the library. You told us that the parade was big, but I did not think I realized it was this big."

"Oh yeah. Just wait." I polished off my lunch and changed into my jelly costume.

"OMG, you two are peanut butter and jelly." Bethany reached for her phone. "I have to put this on Instagram. Scoot closer and say cheese—or, wait, peanuts."

We posed for her photo and then left with everyone to join in the fun.

Families camped out on either side of Main Street. The late afternoon sun hit the trees lining the street at just the right angle to give the effect that they were glowing with sepia-toned color. Vendors selling light-up wands, bat ears, and balloons strolled through the street, which was completely closed to traffic. Jugglers and acrobats did backflips for the crowd. There were dozens of drummers who would lead the march and people in costume everywhere. Professor McGonagall handed out black-and-white-striped packets of licorice ropes in front of the bank. Inflatable dinosaurs, Ghostbusters, unicorns, skeletons, and aliens packed into the street on our way up to the library.

"My eyes do not know where to focus." Carlos's mouth hung open at the sight of so many people in our little town. "The costumes are like nothing I have ever seen."

Giant stilt walkers passed us, followed by a magician doling out tricks, and a trio of dogs in costume. King George wasn't part of the pack, but a young woman dressed as Elle Woods in her pink bunny suit from *Legally Blonde* carried a poodle with a matching pink costume and pink rhinestone collar. That had to be Pippa, the dog that Marcia had claimed was George's understudy and nemesis.

"I bet you anything that's the dog," I whispered to Carlos as we passed by. I had filled him in on meeting King George at Wendy's. Like me, he had been incredulous that the animal cast members had to go through such a rigorous audition process.

Pippa's owner looked like she had her own entourage. She was with a thin man in his thirties or forties dressed in a velvet suit and top hat, who I assumed must be Newell Taylor, the animal performer coordinator at OSF. I wasn't sure what he was supposed to be dressed as, but Lance had nailed his personality. Newell practically leaped out of his chocolate velvet suit when the woman dressed as Elle Woods held her poodle up to his face for a kiss. He bent so far away from the dog that for a minute I thought he was going to do a backflip in the middle of the street. Was he showing off, or was he revolted by the poodle? That wouldn't make sense, given his role with the company. Maybe it was an inside joke.

Newell and Pippa's owner were accompanied by another man about the same age. I didn't have to guess who he was. His costume was a dead giveaway. He had a cardboard bathtub and grooming shears attached to his body and was passing out business cards and dog treats for his pet grooming and accessory shop—Wizard of Paws. His aqua and purple spiky hair matched the colors on the Wizard of Paws logo. I wasn't sure if the flashy, chromatic crest was his natural style or if it was part of his costume.

The last member of their group made me freeze. I tried not to gape.

"Carlos, look." I grabbed his arm. "It's a dragon."

A full-fledged dragon costume. The person's face was obscured by the red dragon head with fake plastic flames shooting from the mouth. Their tail dragged on the pavement as Newell and the other members of their group guided them on where to step. The full-body suit spared no detail. Gold scales covered the dragon's chest. Wings protruded from the back. Claw mitts and shoe covers added to the ferocious medieval design.

My thoughts immediately went to Wendy's mahjong set and the warning note.

*It has to be a coincidence. This is Halloween, after all. There are probably going to be plenty of dragons in the parade.*

For the briefest moment, I considered stopping the dragon, and then what? Warn them that they might be in danger? The thought was ridiculous.

"That is a very realistic dragon," Carlos commented,

unaware that my active imagination was spinning wild stories in my head.

Suddenly, a commotion broke out. I watched as Marcia approached the group, King George in tow. She went straight up to Jax and began waving a finger in her face. "I know you did this," she shouted.

A hush fell over the crowd.

"Someone is going to pay for what you did to my King George," Marcia screamed.

The dragon tried to step between her and Jax to break up the fight, but Marcia threw an elbow. King George yapped as Marcia scooped him up.

I'd never seen Marcia so angry.

The guy in the Wizard of Paws tub managed to maneuver between them. Newell and the Dragon dragged Jax and Pippa away.

"What was that about?" Carlos asked.

"I'm not sure." I watched Marcia's hands fly as she pointed from King George in his silky royal cape to Jax and her pink poodle. I didn't know what was going on between them, but Wendy's warning about the dragon note being an ominous premonition came rushing to my mind.

I pushed the thought away as we continued up the street to the Carnegie Library.

Police gathered at the south end of town in front of the library's lush green lawn. They would kick off the parade, followed by the drum line, and then everyone and anyone in a costume would join in. It was more like a giant mosh pit than a traditional parade.

Like Carlos, my eyes drifted in every direction. There was so much to take in. Our Torte crew gathered at the edge of the library lawn. Mom and the Professor had come as

Benedick and Beatrice from *Much Ado About Nothing*. He was dressed in a tan muslin shirt, a muted blue vest, and knee-high boots. Mom's cream bodice and thin veil complemented his traditional Elizabethan attire perfectly. The Professor looked at ease in his costume, like he was ready to perform at the Globe. He had garnered his nickname because he could—and often did—quote nearly any sonnet or soliloquy from Shakespeare's canon at will. As Ashland's longtime lead detective, he had managed to blend his love of the Bard, his ability to create community, and his commitment to bringing justice to the world. I was thrilled that he and Mom had found each other and selfishly happy to be able to call him my second father.

"Love the costumes," I said to Mom, giving her a hug. "And thank you so much for your hard work on our PB&J. We're getting lots of compliments on them." She had outdone herself on sewing swaths of felt together to create jars of jam and peanut butter with slats for our arms and lettering on the front.

"My pleasure." Mom lifted the edge of her long skirts and gave me a curtsey.

"Helen, I love the commitment to character." Lance came up behind Mom. He was dressed as a garden gnome with a toadstool and a long white fake beard. Arlo had cleverly opted to come as a garden. Felt carrots, rhubarb, and tomatoes grew out of his hat. Trowels and garden tools hung from his belt. Seed packets and sprouts had been fastened to his jacket.

Mom turned to greet them. "A garden and a gnome! You two might win the couples costume contest."

Lance made a tsking sound and shook his head. "I don't know. There's some stiff competition out there. Did you see Bob Ross and his painting? Or my favorite is the Netflix and Chill couple." He bowed in admiration to the Professor. "Benedick, it's an honor."

The Professor bowed in return. "As with my fair Gnome."

Lights flashed on the police vehicles, alerting the crowd that the parade was about to begin. A siren wailed, and the drum line took their positions. Directly behind the drummers was a royal horse-drawn carriage where King George and his human actor were perched, ready to offer parade goers their regal waves.

"That's our cue," I said to Carlos, linking my hand through his.

"I'm nervous. This is my first parade. What do I do?"

Lance clapped him on the back. "Not to worry. You'll be as smooth as peanut butter. Fall in step and enjoy the street soirée."

With that, we merged into the swarm of costumes. The beat of the drums led the march down Main Street. We waved to spectators and danced from group to group. People stopped to take selfies and pose for pictures with participants and onlookers. It took nearly a half hour to shimmy our way from the library to the plaza. We watched zombie dancers perform *Thriller* and spent time taking more pics and checking out the creative costumes on display, like Barbie and Ken dolls in pink cardboard packaging and two giant ice cubes pushing their baby in a stroller with shirts that read ICE, ICE BABY.

I caught sight of Ramiro and his teammates a few times. They had their phones in the air, streaming as they shuffled along the street in their soccer uniforms and fuzzy Grizzly hats.

The back of my neck dripped with sweat. My cheeks hurt from smiling and my hands were red from clapping along to the beat of the drums, but I wouldn't have had it any other way. It was impossible not to get swept up in the magic and delight of seeing our immensely creative community. The air smelled of crisp leaves and popcorn. Music and laughter reverberated through the plaza as the sun slowly sunk.

Once the bulk of parade goers had found their way to the center of the activity, I decided that it was a good time to open Torte for trick-or-treaters, or as Bethany had coined—Trick-or-Torters. From the moment we re-opened the bakeshop's front doors, there was a constant line of kids waiting for treat bags. I couldn't contain my grin as I handed out the fruits of our labor to Torte's youngest guests. The kids' costumes were just as creative and elaborate as some of the adult costumes. One of my favorites was a little girl dressed as a jellybean dispenser with balloons blown up to resemble the sweet candies.

Carlos appeared to be having as much fun as me passing out Torte treats and filling plastic pumpkins with chocolates. Every time a new kiddo would enter the bakeshop, he would bend down to their level and ask them questions about their costume.

Watching him interact with the littles made my heart flop more than once.

*Are we ready?*

*Is it soon going to be time to have a baby of our own?*

There wasn't time to dwell on the thought, because the line didn't let up. Andy kept the adults caffeinated with his Burial Grounds roast and spiced lattes. He was very impressed with one toddler's Albert Einstein costume and a young couple who had bundled their baby up like a burrito.

"You said that the costumes would be incredible, but I had no idea," he said as he boxed up the last of the ghost cupcakes.

"It's impossible to comprehend the scale until you experience it firsthand." I was glad that Mom had cut armholes in my jelly costume; otherwise, it might have been challenging to maneuver through the bakeshop.

Ramiro stopped in with his soccer friends shortly before we were ready to close for the night. Most of the little kids had filled their treat buckets, and adults and college students trickled into neighboring bars and restaurants to continue the festivities. The soccer team looked like a cohesive group in their bright red shorts and jerseys and furry bear hats.

"Wow, this is amazing." Ramiro's cheeks were flushed with color, and his eyes lit up like the glow sticks hanging around his neck. "You said it would be cool, Jules, but this is so cool."

I grinned. "We were all just saying the same thing. I'm so glad you're having fun." I glanced at the pastry case, which had cookies and Halloween macarons left. "Do you want to take the rest of our treats to your friend's house? I saved a few extras downstairs for you too."

"Sure." He waited while I packed up the goodies. "I can get a ride home later, so you don't need to wait around for me."

Carlos kissed the top of his head. "Okay, but do not get too scared of these horror movies. If you do, text and we will come to get you. Pero mantente a salvo, vale?" He slipped into Spanish. I loved listening to them speak in their native tongue, even though I could typically only make out a few words.

"Está bien, no te preocupes." Ramiro hugged him back. I was always impressed by their ability to show affection. Some teenagers might bristle at being kissed or hugged in front of their friends, but not Ramiro.

He gave me a hug too, thanked us for the treats, and vanished into the darkness outside. I sent the rest of the team home while Carlos and I gave the bakeshop a quick once-over.

"Are you ready for dinner?" I asked him after I had wiped down the espresso bar and done a sweep of the basement. "Lance and Arlo promised to save us a seat at the Green Goblin."

"Sí. We must take our peanut butter and jelly out to join in the fun." He looked to the front window. Darkness had settled over the plaza, but there was nothing dark about the evening. Music pulsed from every restaurant. I could feel the beat in my chest. Even the front windows rattled in response. People milled about the center of the plaza and continued to dance in the street. It was going to be a late night for sure.

I took one final spin through the dining room, turning off the lights and making sure that everything was ready for tomorrow. "Let's do it," I said, following him to the front door and making sure to lock it and turn the sign to CLOSED.

We ventured out into the festive atmosphere. The crowd had thinned some, but costumed people milled about in every direction. There were queues in front of all of the restaurants and a kids' light-up dance party going on in front of the bookshop a few doors down.

I was about to head down the sidewalk toward the Green Goblin when I noticed that someone was slumped up against Torte. Not just someone, but someone in a dragon costume—the same elaborate dragon costume I had seen earlier in the parade.

"Carlos, look." I tried to ignore the rolling sensation in my stomach.

"It looks like this dragon has already had too much to drink." Carlos bent down to nudge the person.

An unwelcome tingling feeling spread from the nape of my neck as I watched Carlos gently shake the person.

*The person in a dragon costume.*

*No way.*

*This isn't happening.*

They didn't respond.

Carlos shook them harder. "Wake up. Wake up. Are you okay?"

I felt an impending sense of doom as Carlos looked from me and then back to the dragon. Even in the dark, I could see the veins in Carlos's neck bulging.

This wasn't good.

Carlos tugged off the dragon's head.

I clutched my stomach as my breath came in short gasps.

"Julieta, call for help. I think he is dead."

# Chapter Five

While Carlos tried to revive the guy in the dragon costume, I dialed 911 and raced across the street to the police station. The lights were on, and given the Halloween activity downtown, I had a good feeling that someone would be there.

I burst open the door. "Help, come quick."

Kerry stood organizing a stack of police badge stickers that they handed out to kids. She drew her eyebrows together. "What's wrong, Jules?"

"Someone is passed out in front of Torte." I pointed to the phone. "I'm on with 911. They're sending an ambulance."

She tossed the stickers on the counter and sprinted outside. I followed her while keeping the dispatcher abreast of what was happening.

Kerry took over for Carlos while I stayed on the phone with the paramedics. A small crowd began to form.

"Keep them back," Kerry directed after I hung up. "Call Thomas and the Professor."

Carlos motioned for everyone to give her space while

I called for more help. Within minutes the ambulance arrived, followed shortly by Thomas, the Professor, and Mom.

I couldn't steady my hands as I watched them try to resuscitate the man. A man in a dragon costume.

*This can't be happening.*

*A dead dragon.*

*It doesn't make sense.*

Mom hurried over to me and wrapped me in a hug. "Are you okay?"

"I guess," I lied.

"I know what you're thinking," Mom whispered in my ear. "The dragon."

"It's weird, isn't it?" I tucked my arms through the holes in my jelly costume.

"I would say that it's certainly a strange coincidence, but I wouldn't try to assign more meaning to it than necessary." Mom's tone was reassuring. "I'm sure there were dozens of dragons in the parade this afternoon."

"Right, but how many of them passed out in front of the bakeshop? And days after we found the warning note in Wendy's mahjong set. What if the warning was real? What if this is *the* dragon?"

Mom secured her arm around my waist. "I know, honey. I admit that it's unnerving and has me a bit rattled too, but I can't imagine how a random note in a mahjong set could be connected to this."

I nodded, but I wasn't sure I agreed. "Wendy bought the set here in Ashland, though."

"She did," Mom agreed, keeping a firm grip on me like she was making sure I was staying upright.

I didn't think I was in danger of passing out, but I could

tell that my breathing was shallow, and I didn't exactly feel steady on my feet.

The EMS and police activity had drawn more people over to see what was happening, and Carlos helped Thomas keep bystanders away. The first responders had formed a barrier around the dragon. When Carlos had removed the headpiece from the costume, I hadn't recognized the man, but then again, everything had happened so fast.

"Don't you think that lends more credibility to the possibility?" I tried not to watch as the paramedics loaded the dragon onto a gurney.

"Why?"

"Well, let's say whoever that is in the costume was at the hospice shop. Maybe they knew they were in trouble. Maybe they were running from danger and tucked the note into the mahjong set."

Mom nodded, loosening her grasp slightly. "I follow what you're getting at, but why put a note in a game set that may or may not have even been sold? For all the man knew, the mahjong set could have sat on the shelves for months. It doesn't seem like a very effective way to reach out for help."

She had a point.

"Why not alert the authorities?" she continued, looking at the Professor.

"True, but what if there was a reason he couldn't go to the police? Maybe he stuffed the note into the box in a moment of panic. Maybe he was followed into the store, and he planned to go back for it, and then when he did, the set had been sold."

Even as I said it out loud, I knew it was a far-fetched theory.

Mom basically said the same thing, only in a kind way. "Listen, Juliet, I know this is upsetting and distressing, but let's see what Doug has to say about the situation before you go too far down a rabbit hole."

She was right. I had a tendency to create stories in my head. I'd done so for as long as I could remember. Sometimes it served me well, like when crafting new recipes, but at times like this, my overactive imagination felt like a curse.

"There's one more thing," I said, making sure to keep my voice low.

"What's that?" Mom responded with a touch of caution, as if she was worried that I was losing my grip on reality.

"I saw Marcia confront Jax and that whole group, including the dragon. You don't think she could be involved, do you?"

"Marcia, no." Mom didn't hesitate. "I know she was upset about a mistake at the groomer's with King George, but she would never hurt anyone."

The first responders continued to work on the dragon inside the ambulance. Kerry, Thomas, and the Professor huddled for a minute before the Professor came over to us. His face was solemn and his tone somber. "I'm afraid it doesn't look good."

"Is he dead?" I clenched my jaw.

"We don't know yet." The Professor exhaled slowly. "Do you know anything about him? A name? He didn't have any identification on his person."

"No." I shook my head and thought back to the start of the parade. "I don't know if it's the same costume, but I did see someone wearing a similar one. They were all part of a dog group. Could the man be Anton, the famous dog trainer?"

"A dog group?" The Professor raised one eyebrow.

Mom explained about Marcia and King George. "According to Marcia, they call themselves the puparazzi."

"I recall you mentioning that." He took his Moleskine notebook from the pocket of his Elizabethan vest. I couldn't believe he kept his notebook on him even at the Halloween parade.

"Can you share the names of anyone you know associated with the puparazzi?" He cleared his throat. "I must say that I do appreciate the pup-ish pun."

"You could certainly talk to Marcia," Mom suggested. "She knows them all from the auditioning process."

"And Lance," I offered. "He'll likely know who else was part of the dog theater community."

"Excellent." The Professor made a note.

"We're supposed to be meeting them for dinner and drinks. Do you want me to go find him and bring him over?" I asked. For the first time since discovering the dragon, my eyes focused on my surroundings. It was clear that everyone in our near vicinity was aware that something was terribly wrong, but those enjoying drinks and dinner along the Calle were none the wiser that a death had occurred.

The Professor tucked his pencil behind his ear. "That would be most helpful."

Carlos was still helping Thomas with crowd control. They stood shoulder to shoulder, keeping onlookers away. Strobe lights from a restaurant across the street darted back and forth, blending in with the flashing lights from the emergency vehicles.

"I'm going to the Green Goblin to find Lance," I said to him. "I'll be back in a few."

"How are you doing, Julieta?" Carlos reached for my hand and clutched it with unusual desperation. His hand was cold and clammy. I could tell from the ashen tone of his skin that he was shaken too. I had a feeling that was why he was standing guard over the scene of the crime. I knew that feeling. After trying to breathe life back into someone—the need to do something—anything.

"I'm okay. Good. Not great. What about you?"

Thomas stepped away from us, to give us some space.

"Same." Carlos kept his body rigid and refused to let go of my hand.

It was surreal to hear the thump of music and to see people dancing on outdoor balconies when we had just witnessed a death.

I leaned into him. The smell of his earthy cologne made me breathe in deep.

He kissed the top of my head. "It is terrible. I can't stop seeing his lifeless face."

I pulled just enough away to meet his eyes. "I understand."

"Sí." His voice cracked a little. "I know you do."

I wasn't sure how long we stood there. Time turned fuzzy. I didn't care. We needed this moment to simply hold each other. That was the thing about marriage, about a partnership, having a safe place to land. Carlos was my safe place, and I wanted to make sure I was always his too.

After a few minutes, or maybe longer—I wasn't counting—he let out a long sigh. "Thank you, Julieta. I needed that."

"Me too," I whispered. "Let me get Lance. The Professor needs to talk to him and then we can regroup, okay?"

He gave me a half nod.

I caught Thomas's eye. He had stayed unusually quiet. He tilted his head, signaling that it was okay for me to go. I knew that Carlos was in good hands, so I hurried down the sidewalk through the throngs of people, toward the Green Goblin, which sat at the far end of the plaza across the street from Lithia Park.

A hostess in a chartreuse green goblin costume greeted me at the front. "We're full for the moment. I can put you on the wait list and offer you a green goblin while you wait." A table with drinks sat to her right.

The Green Goblin's signature drink might have been the most photographed in all of Ashland. Anyone who dined at the restaurant took pics of the avocado daiquiri with muddled lime and fresh mint.

"My friend has a table already," I said to the hostess.

"Go on in, then. Happy haunting."

Inside, it was impossible to tell the staff from the guests. Everyone was in costume, and drinks were flowing. Plus, even on a typical day, the Green Goblin wasn't a typical restaurant. Fake leafy trees with branches snaking up to the ceiling gave the effect of entering a fairy forestland. Tiny painted ceramic statues of elves, witches, and goblins were strung from the branches. A huge iron chandelier draped with fake spiderwebs and stringy skeletons offered the only light source in the open room, aside from the flickering tabletop candles. There was no need for the popular bar to decorate. Every day was themed like Halloween at the Goblin.

I squeezed past the bar and spotted Lance and Arlo at a table near the back.

"Juliet, it's about time." Lance raised his martini. His gnome hat sat askew like it was drooping with sleepiness. "We were just about to order another round. What's your poison tonight?" He stopped midsentence and studied my face. "Is something wrong?"

I clutched the edge of the table. "There's been an accident."

Arlo reached over to console me. "Is it Carlos?"

"No, no. I don't know the person. That's why I'm here." I placed my hand on my throat, forcing my voice to keep going. Then I turned to Lance. "The Professor thinks you might be able to identify the victim."

Lance was already on his feet. "Let's go."

"Yes, go, go." Arlo motioned toward the front. "I'll settle the bill and be there as soon as I can."

"What happened?" Lance asked as he deftly weaved his way through the throng of costumes. It was like the parting of the seas when Lance was around. He didn't need to say a word. The way he threw his shoulders back, jutted out his chin, and walked with innate confidence made people naturally give him space.

I gave him a brief recap.

"The dragon. Hmmm. And you think he's connected to OSF?"

"I'm pretty sure he was with the puparazzi group in the parade. Unless it's a different dragon costume."

Lance scoffed. "That name is the worst, and you know me, I appreciate a good pun."

It didn't take long to return to the scene of the crime.

The Professor ushered Lance closer. Mom was standing near A Rose by Any Other Name.

"Have they had any luck reviving him?" I asked.

She shook her head. "They called the time of death a minute ago. They're getting ready to transport the body."

We both stood in silence. Words weren't necessary. I knew that she, like me, was holding space for the loss of a stranger.

Lance returned a minute later. His angular cheeks sunk inward. He pressed his lips together and shook his head. "He didn't make it. They confirmed that he's dead."

"Did you know him? Was it Anton?" I asked.

He pressed his lips tighter. "I did. It is Anton Dudley. The dog trainer and our in-house animal consultant at OSF."

Anton Dudley was dead. The man that Marcia had claimed she wanted to kill a few days ago. I didn't think that Mom's friend could actually have anything to do with his death, but the facts were adding up to too much of a coincidence.

# Chapter Six

The paramedics took Anton's body away, and the crowd began to disperse, returning to bars and restaurants. It was strange to have the plaza feel so alive and festive as merrymakers continued their celebrations none the wiser that a man had just died.

The Professor pulled me aside. "Did you see anything prior to finding Anton outside of the bakeshop?" His demeanor had shifted. He moved with precision, taking in every detail around us. Gone was his lighthearted Shakespearean acting from earlier. He was in full investigative mode. As Ashland's longtime lead detective, he was no stranger to situations like this.

"No, I wish. I remember seeing him during the parade with Jax—I believe that's her name, but Lance or Marcia will know for sure. Marcia had an argument with Jax, something about King George. There was a whole group of dog actors, who call themselves the puparazzi, hanging out together. Newell from OSF was there and the owner of Wizard of Paws. I'm fairly confident that Anton was there too. I'm one hundred percent sure that someone in a dragon costume was with them. I was hyperaware of that because of the note that Wendy found in her mahjong set, but obviously, I'm not sure if it was Anton, because whoever was in the suit wasn't visible."

The Professor gave me a curt nod as he made notes. "Tell me again about this note."

Did he think there was a possible connection?

I told him my recollection of Wendy finding the note.

"Did you notice anything out of the ordinary when the note was discovered?" He ran a finger along his graying well-trimmed beard.

Was he hinting at something?

I thought back to the lunch at Wendy's house. All of the women had seemed surprised when she'd found the note, but I hadn't paid specific attention to anyone's reaction. I told the Professor as much.

He inhaled deeply. "Many thanks. That's helpful."

"Is there a chance that the note and Anton's death are related?" I asked.

"Doubtful, but it's my duty to explore any and every possibility."

"Have you been able to determine if his death was natural or if foul play was involved?" I didn't want details, but I did want to know if Anton had been murdered.

"It's too soon to say for sure. I'll be awaiting the coroner's report, but Anton's injuries do not appear to be self-inflicted."

"Injuries?" I winced.

"Yes. He has multiple stab wounds to his abdomen. Again, the coroner will need to confirm the angle of the wounds and make an official determination, but at this moment in time, we are treating this as a suspicious death."

I sighed. "It's so sad, especially in the middle of Halloween celebrations."

"I fear that more than masks pervade the night." He rubbed his arms. "As the Bard says, 'The air bites shrewdly; it is very cold.'"

Goosebumps rose on my arms at his words. It was true the temperature had continued to drop as the night wore on, but I had a feeling his sentiment had more to do with the investigation. "What do you mean?"

"Deception is here." His intelligent eyes drifted toward a crowd waiting to get into Puck's. "Stay vigilant tonight."

He got called away by another police officer, but his warning repeated in my head. It wasn't like the Professor to raise unnecessary alarm. I hoped we weren't in danger, but then again, I knew that if there was an imminent threat, the Professor would say so. He would never intentionally put me or anyone in harm's way.

I went to look for Carlos. Perhaps it was time to go home and call it a night. He was in a conversation with Lance and the two men I'd seen with Anton earlier.

"Juliet, do you know Trey and Newell?" Lance made introductions. "Trey, Newell, I give you Juliet Capshaw, my personal pastry muse and owner of Torte."

While I'd never met Trey, he was easily identifiable in his bathtub costume and psychedelic hair. He extended a hand and gave me a business card. "Dog groomer and stylist to the stars. Do you have any pets? I can make you a special deal. Twenty percent off your first visit."

"Nope. Not unless you count pets crafted from buttercream." I took his card, which read TREY KELLY, OWNER—WIZARD OF PAWS.

"Don't give him any ideas," Newell said, also shaking

my hand. His velvet suit jacket looked so soft that I had to resist the urge to pet it. "He'll probably commission you to immortalize one of his clients in chocolate."

"Dog sculptures are on trend these days, Newell." Trey looked to Lance to back him up.

Lance shrugged. "Don't look at me. I pay Newell so that I don't have to deal with the four-legged talent."

"You cast the animals in shows?" I asked. I already knew the answer, but I was curious to hear more about Newell's role at OSF and whether his interactions with Anton might have led to more than frustration.

"I do, among other things. I also coordinate rehearsal schedules and all of the busywork that comes with having animals onstage." Newell smoothed his velvet suit jacket. "People assume that it's an easy role, but I assure you there is more drama with our furry cast members than there ever is with humans."

"Easy. Easy." Lance scowled. "I don't know if I would go that far."

Newell shot his index finger in the direction of the line in front of Puck's. "Shall we talk about King George?"

There was no sign of the pug or Marcia waiting with the rest of the crowd for a table.

"Are you trying to pick a fight?" Trey retorted, chewing on the stem of a maraschino cherry. "You want to tell them how much you *love* those animals you manage, Newell?"

Newell removed his top hat as if buying time before responding. The smile he attempted didn't reach his eyes as he stared down Trey. "I wouldn't go there. You're the one who botched that dye job. If you're not careful, you're going to have a lawsuit on your hands."

"What is a dye job?" Carlos sounded confused.

Trey flicked the air as if a bug was flying in his face. "It was a simple misunderstanding. I've explained this to you and to Anton at least a dozen times." He addressed Newell. "I was told that George was supposed to have a full blow-out and pampering session for his role in the parade. Marcia wanted him to look regal for his photoshoot after the parade. Someone tampered with my products. It's not my fault that George's tail was purple. If it hadn't been for my quick reaction when I realized that someone put purple dye in the conditioner, George's entire coat would have been purple." He touched the spiky tip of his hair. "It's not like I'm afraid of color, but I'm not going to give one of my clients a style they don't want."

"A purple pug. Did you see how furious Marcia was? I thought she was going to kill you and Anton on the spot." Newell stifled a laugh and then realized what he had said. "Oh, no, I didn't mean that. Many apologies. May Anton rest in peace." He clasped his hands in a prayer pose. I didn't buy Newell's forced sincerity. He looked like a kid who had been caught sneaking a cookie from the cookie jar before dinner.

"You should be very, very careful with what you say." Trey shot Newell a glare that made the hairs on my arm stand at attention.

Newell bristled but didn't say more. He picked one of Pippa's hairs from his velvet jacket and dropped it on the floor like it was contaminated.

"Look at the time!" Lance glanced at his wrist, though he wasn't wearing a watch. "We are late for dinner. Must run. Let's regroup tomorrow." He dragged Carlos and me away.

"What was that about?" I asked once we were out of earshot.

Lance was never one to run from drama. Quite the opposite—he ran toward it.

"Sorry, I had to put an end to that conversation, and I thought it might be helpful for you two to have some context about what happened," Lance explained. "You missed it, but there was big fallout before the parade. Apparently, human actors aren't the only ones who can end up with a bad hair day. George—a.k.a. King George—showed up for his debut with an eye-piercing purple tail. I'm talking electric, neon purple. Marcia was furious, rightly so. He was supposed to go into Wizard of Paws for a bath and a blowout, and came out looking like he was supposed to be in a Madonna video from the eighties instead of a royal court."

"I can't believe dogs get blowouts." Carlos sounded as incredulous as I felt.

"That's showbiz." Lance threw his hands in the air. "I digress; Marcia claimed that Jax and Trey did it on purpose."

"Why?" I wished my jelly costume had pockets. My fingers were turning into Popsicles. But Marcia's confrontation with Jax and the puparazzi made much more sense now.

"Jax has been pushing hard for Pippa, her poodle, to take over the lead role. Ever since George beat her out, the two dog owners have been at odds." Lance sounded disgusted.

"How does Newell work into this, and do you think any of it could be connected to Anton's death?" I asked.

"Well, Newell was casting for the role, and Anton

trained both dogs, so obviously, there's some inherent competition there."

I thought of Marcia's tone at mahjong the other day. She hadn't minced words about her frustration with Anton. But again, I couldn't imagine Mom's sweet friend killing anyone. Mom had been so adamant as well. There had to be another explanation.

We bumped into Arlo, who was heading in our direction. "There you are. Sorry, it took forever to get up to the bar to pay our tab."

"That probably means we won't be able to get a table again," I said.

"Doubtful. It's a madhouse in there," Arlo replied.

"Leave it to me." Lance twirled in a half circle and swept past the line at Puck's. We watched as he sashayed to the front and chatted with the hostess for a minute. Then he waved for us to join him.

I felt bad cutting the line, but Lance had managed to snag us extra seats at a table already occupied by a few OSF actors, which made me feel better.

The punk band the Rolling Bones was warming up on Puck's small stage. Dozens of customers crammed the bar waiting for frothy pints of ale and mead.

"This way." Lance weaved past the wooden keg barrel tables and Shakespearean artwork to the very back, where two large ornately carved tables had been pushed together to make one long shared space. "Perry, exquisite work in the parade this afternoon." Lance greeted our new tablemate by blowing him a kiss. "You know Arlo, of course, and this is Juliet and Carlos."

"Hey, nice to meet you." Perry stood. He towered over the table; I had to crane my neck to make eye contact, and

I wasn't exactly short. He was dressed in the same style of robe and king's crown that George had been wearing at mahjong. His classic features and strong jawline, paired with his imposing presence, made me understand why Lance had cast him in the role of royalty.

George and Perry must have had matching costumes made for the parade. He shook Carlos's and my hands and then sat down next to a young woman I recognized immediately as Jax. "This is Jax."

Jax was dressed in her *Legally Blonde* costume, and her poodle, Pippa, was in an expensive baby jogger next to the table. "I'm so glad you spotted us. Pippa is thrilled to get to have drinks with the artistic director. Maybe she'll have to put on a little show for you later." She batted her eyelashes at Lance.

"I'd love nothing more—literally, nothing more." He kicked me under the table.

"You were in the parade, right? I heard you and George rode in the royal float," I asked Perry, as Carlos moved over an extra chair for me.

"Yes, technically, *I* was the grand marshal. King George was on the carriage with me. It's a promo for the new season at OSF. I'm the lead in *A Play About a Dragon*," Perry answered, fluffing out his robes as if expecting his loyal subjects to appear at any minute with fruit and wine. "Unless you were near the front, you might have missed me, because we were right behind the drum line. I felt like true royalty, though, because we were riding on the only float."

"Was that the royal float?" Carlos asked. "I wondered about that."

"Yep." Perry repositioned his crown.

I got the sense that he took his role as king seriously.

"Pippa should have been riding on it with him," Jax interjected. "She would have looked so adorable in her pink and you in your royal cape. It's a real shame." She paused and focused her attention on Lance. "I don't know if the casting is final, final, but really I am so glad that we're hanging out tonight, because I think after you spend more time with Pippa, you're going to see that she was made for the stage. She's a star. She isn't meant to be an understudy. She's destined to shine."

"I'm sure she is, and there are always other roles," Lance said with an uncharacteristic graciousness. "And while we can't guarantee any performances, she will be called upon for any performances if the principal dog is unable to perform."

Jax's face flamed with color. "This role was made for Pippa. George is so ordinary, and he's not well trained. Tell them, Perry." She nudged Perry.

I wasn't sure what the relationship was between the two of them. Were they a couple? Friends? Colleagues?

Perry hesitated.

"Tell them, Perry." She punched Perry in the shoulder. "Lance needs to know how terrible his star is. It's not too late to make a change."

Lance leaned closer. "Was there a problem with George?"

"First of all, let's be clear that *I'm* the star, right? Not the pug, okay? Canines are fine as bit entertainment for the audience, but they're not real actors. I'm so tired of everyone making such a big deal about a pug that will be onstage for all of ten minutes at most." Perry's lip curled in disgust.

Jax covered Pippa's ears. "Do not say something so rude in front of the talent," Jax scolded, giving Perry a look to make it clear she was not happy with his response.

It looked like it was taking every ounce of self-control for Perry not to roll his eyes. He sucked in his cheeks and nodded at Jax. "But Jax is right. George howled the whole way down Main Street."

"Howled?" Lance repeated.

"Barked, howled, moaned. It's terrible training, if you ask me," Jax scoffed. "Anton told me outright that he didn't think George was ready for a leading role. His recommendation to your casting director was for Pippa to take over. You can't have a lead dog performing like that. If George was that unhinged in the parade, just imagine what he'll be like onstage."

"Noted," Lance replied, careful not to make any promises.

"Who does animal casting?" Arlo asked, studying the menu and handing me one too.

"Newell," Lance responded.

"According to what I've heard, Newell wanted to cast Pippa in the role, too." Jax fluffed the plush pink blanket in Pippa's jogger. She didn't seem like she was going to let it go. I tried to connect the dots while she launched into more reasons why her prized poodle was destined for stardom. "Look, I don't want to gossip or spread rumors, but I think the police should probably have a long chat with Marcia."

"Marcia?" I was sure my face probably reflected my shock.

"Because I'm convinced that she killed Anton," Jax replied with a smug grin. "That woman is a murderer."

# Chapter Seven

After Jax dropped that bombshell, Lance asked her dozens of questions. I tried to get a read on her as waitstaff ran between the kitchen and bar, delivering plates of pub fare and overflowing pints. The windows began to sweat with condensation from the bevy of warm bodies inside. It was hard to hear over the noise of happy customers and the band.

Jax seemed flippant as she spoke about Anton's death, and when I mentioned that the police didn't even know if it was murder yet, she blew me off and kept spouting out all the reasons why Marcia had to be a killer.

Perry squirmed while she rattled on.

I caught his eye across the table at one point, and he shrugged as if to say he had no idea how she had come up with her theory.

"None of you look like you believe me, but they had a bunch of run-ins," Jax said with authority. "Anton was quite the collector. Did you know he had the largest collection of dog art on the West Coast?"

"What exactly does dog art consist of?" Arlo asked.

I was curious too.

"Everything. His collection was legendary. Figurines,

canvases, tons of original pieces. It's even rumored that he had a Jeff Koons balloon dog. I haven't seen it personally, but I guess he had a couple of spaces around town that housed his collection."

"What is a balloon dog?" Carlos voiced what the rest of us were thinking.

"Jeff Koons. You haven't heard of him?" Jax scoffed. "His pieces are like giant balloon dogs. They look like toys, you know, like you'd get at a restaurant. One of them sold for over sixty million dollars recently."

Jax was obviously well-versed in a niche segment of the art world that I knew nothing about. One thing I did know was that if Jax was right and Anton had an extremely valuable collection of rare pieces, that could give someone a motive for murder.

Our dinner and drinks arrived. Carlos seized the opportunity to shift the conversation to OSF and next year's season. Perry lit up while he talked about his role and how excited he was for rehearsals and costume fittings. "Being king is going to take some getting used to. People are already treating me like royalty. You should have seen the line at the meet-and-greet after the parade. I thought I was never going to get out of there, but duty calls. It's good method for the role, anyway."

"I thought there was a break for the season," Carlos said, swirling his chocolate blood orange martini, one of Puck's many Halloween drink specials for the night.

"Yes, we are officially dark," Lance answered for Perry. "The company gets the next few weeks off, but then it's back to rehearsals and prep for next season. The show always must go on in showbiz."

"That's why you should really reconsider and give

Pippa another chance to audition," Jax said, chugging her beer. Once she had taken a few big swigs, she dipped her pinkie in and held it out for Pippa to lick.

I wasn't aware that dogs were fans of beer.

Lance brushed off her comment and proceeded to give us a rundown of every production slotted for next year. I had already seen the new posters around town, so I figured it was his way of diverting the conversation.

We didn't linger long after we'd finished our meal. It had been an intense day and was made even more so by Anton's tragic death.

"I see that Julieta cannot keep her eyes open," Carlos said after the waiter had taken our dishes. "I think this is our cue to head home. A happy Halloween to all of you. Thank you for including me in the fun."

Arlo and Lance left with us.

"Well, that was something." Lance let out a low whistle. "Did anyone else pick up on the fact that Jax is completely obsessed?"

"Dog obsessed," Arlo agreed. "I think Pippa has a better wardrobe than me."

"Did you see her give Pippa licks of beer?"

"And half her dinner." Arlo shook his head. "I couldn't take my eyes off them. For every bite she took, she gave at least two to Pippa. I'm surprised that dog isn't two hundred pounds."

"She was also quick to point the blame at Marcia," I added.

"Exactly." Lance snapped his fingers. "Her theory doesn't even make sense. King George has the role. What would Marcia's motive be for killing Anton if he helped her pampered pooch land the lead?"

It was still weird for me to associate dogs with leading roles. "Honestly, the entire time she was ranting, I kept wondering if she did it."

"She would kill for that dog, I'm sure of it." Arlo shook his head and shuddered.

"I did not like the wild look in her eyes." Carlos put his arm around me.

"I know. I've heard of people living vicariously through their children, but never their dogs." My teeth began to chatter, not just because of the cool breeze.

"You look like you should be dressed as a Popsicle. Go home and let's plan to have a little tête-à-tête tomorrow morning." Lance kissed my cheeks and clapped Carlos's shoulder.

"Are you guys staying out?" It didn't look like things were anywhere near slowing down. Large, costumed groups were hopping from bar to bar.

Arlo pointed to another group of actors near the pizzeria. "I promised some of the company that we would at least have one more drink."

Lance scoffed. "One? It's Halloween. Let's go. Ta-ta, you two."

They strolled across the plaza arm in arm.

Suddenly the weight of the night came over me. All I wanted was my bed and a cup of hot tea. I had to fight to keep my eyes open as Carlos went to get the car. The police had reopened Main Street to traffic but had roped off the area in front of Torte where we'd found Anton. I wondered if they would be done with their external investigation by morning. Yellow caution tape blocking access to the crime scene might look like part of the Halloween display, but I knew better, and I wasn't sure I could face the day tomorrow knowing that Anton had died here.

Carlos pulled up to the curb. I gave the scene one last glance before getting in. We were quiet on the short drive home, watching college kids traipsing through neighborhoods in search of any houses with lights still left on. When we passed campus, what appeared to be a huge game of flashlight tag had students hiding behind redwoods and sprinting through the quad.

At home, I had about three sips of tea before my head fell onto the pillow and sleep took hold. I tossed and turned all night, dreaming about dragons and dogs.

# Chapter Eight

When I woke the next day, my head was throbbing. I hoped caffeine would help. I got out of bed as quietly as I could, grabbed my clothes, and tiptoed downstairs. I wondered how late Ramiro had stayed out. I hadn't heard him come home.

After a cup of strong French press, my headache eased a bit. I knew that there was no need to rush to open early as the odds were good that Ashland would be off to a slow start the day after Halloween.

I took my time getting ready and even made myself some egg toast before heading to the bakeshop. The simple breakfast delicacy had originated as a way to use day-old bread by liberally buttering both sides of a slice of sourdough, frying it until crisp, and then placing a poached egg over the top of the slightly charred toast. Once I had polished off my meal and wiped down the kitchen, I grabbed my coat and snuck out the front door.

Outside, wispy clouds shrouded the moonlight. A breeze that threatened rain fanned branches on the trees and sent leaves spiraling like mini tornados. I zipped up my jacket and stuffed my hands in my pockets.

The remnants of last night's parade were evident on the sidewalk. There were forgotten candy buckets and glow sticks, blankets and camp chairs still out on front lawns. At Torte, the police tape and evidence markers were gone. That was a relief. And I took it as a good sign that the Professor and his team had completed their investigation into the crime scene.

The memory of Anton's lifeless face put a damper to my morning opening routine. The Professor had mentioned that Anton had been stabbed multiple times. How? Could it have been a random act of violence? Could one of the parade goers have stabbed him in passing? But why?

The more likely possibility was that if Anton had been killed, it was intentional and done by someone he knew. Could that someone be Jax? She certainly had a motive. I was in agreement with Arlo's statement that she would do whatever it took to get Pippa the lead role on the stage. Did "whatever" include murder?

Even with her complete adoration of Pippa, murdering Anton still seemed like a stretch.

I sighed as I turned on the bread ovens and sorted through the list of custom orders. We had Day of the Dead cakes and cookies to bake, along with three birthday cakes and pastries for a corporate lunch. It was a manageable amount for what I was sure was going to be a slow day for both my team and our customers.

I started with the Day of the Dead cakes. The first was our spicy chocolate cake. For that, I assembled butter, oil, eggs, sugar, and vanilla. I whipped them together in our industrial mixers and then sifted in cocoa and espresso powder, flour, baking powder, salt, cinnamon, and just a touch of chili powder and black pepper into a separate bowl. I alternated adding a half cup of coffee with the dry ingredients. Once the batter was thick and creamy, I spread it into greased eight-inch round pans and put them in the ovens to bake.

The second order was for gluten-free spiced apple and honey cake. It was one of our most popular gluten-free cakes. The base was oil and buttermilk with vanilla bean paste, locally sourced honey, and apples. This was a single-layer cake that we would frost with our honey and salted buttercream, and Steph or Bethany would pipe a colorful sugar skull on the top. While Torte wasn't a gluten-free bakery, we tried to accommodate special dietary requests. One of the things that our customers appreciated was that we didn't simply offer a basic vanilla or chocolate gluten-free alternative. We infused our gluten-free cakes with flavor and decorated them with the same artistic care given to anything that graced our pastry cases.

Once those cakes were in the oven, too, I focused my attention on the pastry order. The customer had asked for an assortment of our baked goods, which gave me complete creative license and meant that whatever we baked for the luncheon could also be featured in the pastry case upstairs.

I pulled up a barstool and grabbed my sketchbook. As I doodled drawings of what I wanted the display to look like, my thoughts returned to Anton's murder. I needed to find a way to talk to Marcia today. I wasn't sure that I shared Jax's perspective that Marcia was a killer, but she was connected to Anton and had made it clear at Wendy's game group that they'd had a falling-out. If nothing else, maybe Marcia could give me more insight into Anton's personality and if he had enemies or if she knew of anyone who might have wanted to hurt him. If she had worked with him closely, maybe she could shed some light on his financial situation and his extensive art collection.

I also wanted to talk to the Professor or Thomas or Kerry and see if they had determined Anton's cause of death and confirm that he had actually been murdered.

For the next hour, I concentrated on layering warm spiced apples between puffed pastry dough and hand-rolling sugar horns that I would fill with vanilla and pumpkin custard.

Andy was the first to arrive, as usual, but to my surprise, Mom was with him.

"What are you doing here?" I was coating tin cylinders with baking spray. To make the sugar horns we would wrap the dough around the outside of the tins and bake them for ten to twelve minutes until they were golden brown. The key was making sure to be very generous with the baking spray so that once the tins had cooled, the horns would slide right off, leaving us with perfect horns to fill with fruit, custard, and pastry cream.

Mom frowned and scrunched her forehead. "I'm happy to see you, too, honey."

"I didn't mean it like that."

"I know you didn't." She waited for Andy to take off his ski parka and then she hung her knee-length puffy jacket on the coatrack. "Doug needed to get a head start on the investigation this morning, so I grabbed a ride with him and decided to come in early to hopefully be of use. Idle hands, as they say."

"I'm glad you're here." I finished spraying the horns and began wrapping pastry dough around the first one.

"Mrs. The Professor was telling me about what

happened last night on the way in," Andy said, coming into the kitchen. Prior to Mom marrying the Professor, he had called her Mrs. C. Immediately after the wedding, he had dubbed her Mrs. The Professor. A mouthful, to say the least, but nicknames were his love language.

His eyes were puffy like he hadn't had enough sleep. "You found the guy?" he asked.

"Unfortunately, yes."

He reached for a scrap of spiced chocolate cake. "That's rough, boss. Are you doing okay?"

I appreciated his empathy. "Thanks, I'm holding up."

"I can't believe he was killed right in the middle of the plaza. There were so many people around last night." Andy chomped on the scraps.

"One of Doug's theories is exactly that." Mom tied on an apron. "He's considering the possibility that the killer used the crowd, noise, all the activity as their alibi."

"It makes sense." I set the horns on a baking sheet.

"Yeah." Andy reached for another chunk of cake. "It would be almost impossible to get caught with thousands of people walking around last night and everyone in costumes too. I feel bad for the Professor. This might be a hard case to crack."

Mom piled applewood in the pizza oven. "Me too, but I'm confident in Doug's abilities, and as he said on the car ride into town this morning, physical evidence doesn't lie. He's hopeful that there's a chance that the killer left their fingerprints or DNA behind."

"I just realized that you keep saying killer. Does Doug think it was murder?"

Mom put her hand over her chest. "That's my fault. I shouldn't be saying killer because they haven't received the official report yet. Doug is going on instinct, though, and as you know, his instinct rarely misguides him."

"That's for sure."

"How can I help?" Mom lit the bundle of wood. There was nothing like the woodsy aroma of our wood-fired pizza oven and nothing like the taste of a crisp tomato, basil, and mozzarella slice pulled bubbling from the oven.

"I can help by brewing up some nectar of the Gods," Andy said, moving toward the stairs. "I don't know about you two, but I was up *way* past my bedtime last night, and coffee is calling me."

"Did you have fun, though?" I asked.

A brief look of embarrassment flashed on his face. Then color spread from the base of his neck up to his forehead. "Yeah, yeah. It was cool. It was chill."

"Cool, chill," I repeated, raising my brow. "Really? Do tell. Was there anything specific that was cool or chill?"

Andy practically sprinted upstairs. "Can't talk. Gotta brew the beans."

"Did you catch that?" I asked Mom.

"Andy is one of my favorite people on the planet, but I think we can agree that he has no poker face." Mom chuckled.

"I wonder who he was chilling with last night."

"I don't think we need Doug's deducing skills to say that it might have been with someone he has a crush on. His cheeks were a dead giveaway." Mom leafed through the order sheets. "Pretty light day, huh? That's nice."

"You won't get any complaints from me." I finished wrapping the last pastry horn and put the next tray in the oven.

"Seriously, what can I do? I need to do something."

Mom set the order forms on the island. "Shall I start muffins and cookies for the pastry case?"

"That would be great. If you can do a few extra batches of both, I'll add those to this corporate order." I closed the oven doors. "How long have you known Marcia? It's been years now, right?"

Mom tucked her bobbed hair behind her ears and gave me a knowing smile. "I have a feeling why you're asking that—her comments about Anton at mahjong. But trust me, honey, Marcia wouldn't hurt a fly. There's no way she killed him. She couldn't have physically, anyway."

"Why?"

"She and George were signing *paw-tographs* in the lobby of Ashland Springs Hotel until long after you and Carlos found Anton. There were hundreds of people who saw her there."

"Wait, wait, wait. What is a paw-tograph?"

Mom cracked up. "This town does love a good pun. A paw-tograph is exactly what you think it is. Marcia had glossy headshots of George printed. Anyone who wanted an autograph after the parade got in line, and then Marcia would dip his paw into washable paint and press it onto the photos. They also had a backdrop set up with photos of George in multiple Halloween costumes for people to pose with him."

"That is next level." I scooped buttercream into a piping bag. My cakes had cooled, so now I could layer and put a crumb coat on them. I had learned the terminology in culinary school. A crumb coat is basically the first layer of frosting. We coated single-layer and tiered cakes with buttercream to catch any stray crumbs. Then we chilled the cakes to allow time for the crumb coating to set. Typically this only took about thirty minutes in the walk-in. The second layer of buttercream would give our cake artists pristine canvases to create their masterpieces.

She gathered butter and sugar. "Marcia is committed to George's success, but she's not a killer, and she has more alibis than anyone in town. There were hundreds of people who stopped to take selfies with George last night."

"I wonder if she would tell me more about Anton." I placed the first cake on a turntable so I could spin it gently as I used a wide-angled tip to pipe on the buttercream.

"I'm sure she'll tell you anything you want to know." Mom rolled up the sleeves on her sweater. "She and Wendy are stopping in later this morning. You can talk to her then."

"Even better." I filled the first layer with dark chocolate ganache and raspberries and then stacked the second layer.

The team trickled in slowly over the next hour. Everyone looked like they had been out late. Andy offered up shots of espresso, and Mom encouraged our staff to nourish themselves with sausage and egg scrambles and flatbread breakfast paninis with peanut butter and bananas.

In contrast with the energy of Halloween, the day after felt as slow as molasses, and I was completely fine with that. About an hour after opening, I went upstairs with a fresh tray of pastries. The chalkboard menu had already been updated with a quote that had been attributed to Paulo Coelho, but its origin wasn't known. It read IF YOU'RE BRAVE ENOUGH TO SAY GOODBYE, LIFE WILL REWARD YOU WITH A NEW HELLO.

I had a feeling Rosa had picked the quote, which felt fitting for this new day.

Marcia and Wendy were seated at one of the window booths. After refilling the pastry case, I grabbed a carafe of coffee and walked over to see if they needed a top-off.

"Morning. Can I refresh your drinks?" I offered.

"That would be lovely. Thanks, Juliet." Wendy handed me her cup.

"I won't turn down a refill either," Marcia agreed. "Do you want to sit for a minute?"

She had given me the perfect opening. "Sure." I sat down across from her and set the coffeepot in the center of the table. "I'm guessing you heard about Anton?"

"That's what we were talking about," Marcia whispered, and glanced around to see if anyone was listening. "I was at the station this morning giving Doug any background information I could about Anton. It's so sad . . ." She trailed off.

"How well did you know him?" I asked.

Marcia brushed a tear from her eye. "He has been George's trainer for a year. We saw him at least once a week, even more leading up to auditions."

"You mentioned that you were upset with him for taking Pippa on as a client." I glanced longingly at their coffee. I should have gotten an extra cup for myself.

"That's true." Marcia reached for a napkin to dab a tear away. "I feel terrible about that. I was being unnecessarily petty. Anton deserved to have other clients. I knew that George wasn't the only dog he was working with, but I have to admit that I was jealous when he agreed to train Pippa, mainly because Jax is so obnoxious. I don't trust her. She's too cozy with everyone at OSF, especially Perry and Newell, and I'm sure that she and Trey conspired to dye George's tail for the parade. You've seen Trey. I don't think it's a coincidence that his hair happened to be the exact same shade of purple. None of this changes the fact that Anton was free to take on any client he wanted, Jax included. Now he's dead, and I'm going to have to live with my regret. I should have been more gracious. He did so much for George. Without his guidance and expert training, George wouldn't be starring in an OSF production."

She teared up again.

Wendy reached into her purse and handed her friend a tissue. "Marcia, you couldn't have known, and Anton adored you and George. I'm sure he knew how much he meant to you."

"But one of the last things that I said to him was how he was making a terrible mistake taking on Pippa as a client. I told him I didn't trust Jax and that he should watch his back." Marcia clutched her necklace, which I realized was made from dog charms. She ran a finger along a fire-hydrant charm and looked to Wendy for support.

She was clearly distressed about Anton's death, which lent even more credibility to Mom's insistence that Marcia hadn't killed him.

"Do you really think Jax had something to do with George's purple tail?" I asked.

"I can't prove it. I feel it, though. She was so awful to us after the auditions; and she has all three of those men wrapped around her finger. I can't figure out why. " Her voice had a wobbly quality. She wadded up the tissue. "It's so much more than a silly dye job. She's out to get George. I'm worried for his safety."

I looked to Wendy, who gave me a nod to let me know she thought Marcia was being serious. "Do you actually think that Jax would hurt George?" I wanted to make sure I was understanding her correctly. All of it seemed more fit for a Shakespearean farce.

"I wouldn't put it past her, and I don't understand why she has so much behind-the-scenes access at OSF. She's at the theater all the time, even when no one else is around—" Marcia's tone left no room for doubt. "That's part of what I shared with Doug earlier. I hope he makes an arrest soon, because not only did Jax try to sabotage George, but I'm sure that she killed Anton."

# Chapter Nine

Marcia's eyes narrowed as she continued to expound on her theory that Jax had killed Anton. The odds that Mom's friend had anything to do with Anton's death were slim, but I also wondered how much merit there was to Marcia's perspective. She and Jax were about as close as me and Richard Lord, so I didn't want to assume the worst about Jax without doing my own due diligence. Marcia continued to fiddle with the charms on her dog necklace as she spoke.

"I still find it so unsettling that he was wearing a dragon costume when he was killed," Wendy said when Marcia finally took a minute to drink her coffee. "I'm going back to the shop to see if Camille knows anything."

"Who's Camille?" I asked.

"She owns the hospice store," Wendy answered. "She's the one I bought the mahjong set from. I haven't told her about the note and the missing dragon tile, but I feel like I should. Maybe she knows who brought the set in for consignment. That might give Doug another person to interview. I don't have the foggiest idea how my set could be connected to Anton's death, but I'm not going to be able to sleep until I at least raise the possibility with Camille and the authorities."

"That reminds me, do either of you know anything about Anton being an art collector?"

Wendy shook her head. "Not exactly, although I think I saw him at the shop a while back."

Marcia agreed. "He talked about having some pieces, but he always came to us to train George. I've never been to his house, and I don't know if he has a studio or a separate workspace. Maybe Camille would know."

"When are you going to the hospice shop?" I asked Wendy, and then glanced toward the espresso counter. The line was about half of what it would typically be on a weekday. "I've been wanting to swing by the shop and see if I can find a bedside table for Ramiro's room. Today might be a good time, since things are slow and I have an order to deliver to SOU, which is on the way."

"I can go anytime," Wendy replied. "I have a yoga and movement class later this afternoon, but otherwise my day is wide open."

I checked the clock next to the chalkboard menu. Rosa's new quote made me remember to make a mental note to talk with her and Steph later about brainstorms for a November window display. "What about once you two are done with coffee and breakfast?" I suggested. "Come find me downstairs when you're ready, and we can walk over together."

"Sure." Wendy eyed the coffee carafe. "Could I possibly beg you for another splash before you go?"

"You never have to beg for coffee at Torte." I topped off their coffees and returned to the kitchen.

"Did you have a chance to chat with Marcia?" Mom asked. She was up to her elbows in pie dough.

"I did, and I agree with you. She seemed very sincere and shaken that her last exchange with Anton hadn't been positive."

Mom dug her hands into the dough like she was giving it a deep tissue massage. "Did she have any insight into who else might have had animosity toward Anton?"

I leaned closer and kept my voice low. "You're not going to believe this. She's sure that Jax killed him."

Mom was thoughtful for a minute. "Really?"

"She was unwavering about it, but I'm trying to keep an open mind because it sounds like the two of them didn't get along."

"That's very mature of you, honey." Mom formed the dough into a ball.

I checked in with Steph, who was painting skull sugar cookies with edible watercolor frosting. Dozens of brightly colored cookies lined the counter. "How's everything in the baking zone?"

She took one AirPod out and looked at me. "Fine. I don't want to jinx it, but it's kind of nice to have a slower morning." She returned to concentrating on the intricate pattern on the cookie.

"It's weird," Bethany added. She used her left hand to steady her right while piping the cake that I had crumb-coated earlier. Creating the outline of a skull in black royal icing was meticulous work. "I just said to Steph that I'm used to things being constantly busy, and I was wondering if my time away had me remembering wrong, but nope—it's the morning after Halloween."

"Do either of you need anything? I'm going to walk over to the hospice shop and can make a stop if necessary."

"We're good." Steph dipped her miniature paintbrush into a bright yellow edible paint. "I think the catering box is ready to go. Not sure if that's on your way or not."

"It is." The luncheon was taking place at SOU, which was only a few blocks from the hospice shop. "I can feed two birds with one scone, as they say."

I packed up the pastries in our large Torte boxes with our fleur-de-lis logo stamped on the top right as Wendy peered into the kitchen. "Are you ready?"

"As long as you are. I don't want to interrupt your work."

"Nope. I'm all set." I picked up the first box. "I'm going to drop these off on our way."

Wendy offered to help with the boxes as we took the back stairs up to street level. "Am I the only one who feels spooked by the fact that Anton was dressed as a dragon?"

"Not at all," I assured her. "I feel the same. I mean, it's probably not connected, but I think you're right to try and figure out who donated the mahjong set to the hospice shop."

"That's what your mom told me, too. I guess I feel a bit silly." Wendy sounded sheepish.

"It's fair." We crossed the street toward the police station. The hospice shop was located at the north end of town. "But the harsh reality is that Anton is dead, and even if there's a one percent chance his stabbing and your note are connected, you would want to know that, right?"

"Yes." She nodded in agreement. "You Capshaw women always know the right thing to say."

"I wouldn't go that far," I teased. "I think I stick my feet in my mouth at least a dozen times a day."

"Doubtful." Wendy laughed.

I changed the subject as we passed London Station, where the front of the three-story mercantile had been transformed into a haunted mansion. "Do you know Camille well?"

"I'm one of her repeat customers," Wendy replied. "She moved to Ashland last year after selling a successful antique shop in the Bay Area. Instead of getting back into the business, she decided she wanted to get involved in volunteer work here, which is why she partnered with hospice. She has a real eye for value and what will sell, thanks to her background. I have found some treasures, nothing quite as valuable as the mahjong set, but pottery and art."

Wendy went on to explain that profits from sales at the shop were donated directly to hospice. It was a good business model in that Camille sourced donations, displayed and sold them, and then shared the proceeds with a well-deserving local nonprofit.

"I'm going to go deliver this order," I said to Wendy when we arrived at campus. "I'll meet you at the shop in a few."

"Do you need help setting up?"

"Thank you for the offer, but it will be quick. I just need to drop these boxes off, and they'll take it from there." I went inside and made sure the pastries were delivered to the right person. The university staff would finish arranging them on platters. As I had said to Wendy, it was a breeze, and I wasn't far behind her.

The hospice shop sat on the corner across the street from a quad of dorms at SOU. Nothing about the exterior matched the Elizabethan esthetic on the plaza. Buildings on this end of town were nondescript, and the hospice shop was no exception. Its white awning needed some sprucing up, but Camille had done a nice job of featuring a fall display of hats from the 1940s, umbrellas, and gently used rain boots in the front of the shop. The door jingled as I stepped inside.

Wendy and a woman about her age, who I assumed must be Camille, were chatting near the register. There were two levels to the store. The first floor primarily housed furniture. Walnut bookcases, wingback chairs, dining sets, and mid-century modern couches had been arranged in groupings to allow customers to easily visualize what the pieces might look like in their own homes. The second level had sections for clothing, jewelry, pottery, art, and collectibles. There were coatracks filled with selections of raincoats, winter jackets, and even heavy cloaks. Another sign that the season was shifting.

I took a minute to wander through the furniture to see if there was anything that might work for Ramiro's room before going up the short flight of stairs to join Wendy at the register.

"Juliet, that was so fast. I was telling just Camille about you." Wendy introduced us.

"You've done a great job remodeling the store," I said. It was true. The previous resale shop had felt dark and dingy. Camille had lightened up the space by adding skylights, tearing down the old, thick curtains that had blocked light from the front windows, and made the shop feel like a showroom.

"Thank you." She pressed her lips together in a tight smile. Camille was dressed in an elegant silk wrap. The material had patterns of songbirds on it, and the way the fabric flowed as she moved gave the illusion that the birds were taking flight. She had accessorized with turquoise bracelets and earrings.

"And for such a good cause," I added. "Hospice is near and dear to my heart."

"Mmm-hmm," Camille replied with a forced smile. "It's an important service."

The subject must have been painful for her. She didn't appear to want to expand on the topic.

"As I was saying before Juliet arrived, I have a question about the mahjong set," Wendy continued.

Camille continued pricing a set of porcelain teacups as Wendy spoke. "Go ahead. What do you want to know?"

"Who donated it?" Wendy leaned over the counter like she was trying to get a better look at the register. "You must keep records. Many of the people who donate get a percentage of the sale if they consign, right? You must track that."

"That's correct." Camille held one of the dainty cups up to the light to examine it for any cracks or imperfections. "I would say it's about a forty/sixty split in terms of customers who donate items and don't want a cut of the sale versus customers who do consignment with us."

"Do you remember if the person who donated the set did so on consignment?" Wendy strummed her fingers on the counter.

"Not off the top of my head. Why?" Camille gently placed one of the teacups she had been examining on the counter and reached for another one. "Is there something wrong with the set?"

"I wouldn't say wrong, but I did find something inside that I think might belong to the original owner."

The teacup in Camille's hand slipped. She caught it at the last second, saving it from being shattered on the counter. "What did you find?"

Was it my imagination, or had Camille's passive smile evaporated?

"Nothing major, but I want to find the owner if I can so I can return the item." Wendy was being noncommittal, which raised my suspicions. Was there a reason she wasn't telling Camille about the note?

Camille wrapped the teacup in bubble packaging.

"Would you mind checking?" Wendy asked again.

"Uh, let me finish this." She wrapped one of the tea-cups before putting it back in the box. "When did you buy the game? Not very long ago."

"No, a few days before Halloween." Wendy nudged me.

"That's what I thought. I think it came in the same day you bought it." Camille searched through a stack of pa-perwork and then checked the computer. "Here it is." She read her notes. "One of my volunteers accepted the dona-tion four days ago. The person did not sign up for our consignment program or leave a name. I'm sorry. That's not much help to you, is it?"

Wendy frowned. "Do you remember what the person looked like?"

Camille shook her head. "I'm afraid I didn't see them. I can ask the volunteer who took the donation."

Wendy looked at me. "What do you think? Is it worth a shot?"

"Sure. If it's not too much trouble for you," I said to Camille.

"Not at all." She put away the consignment paperwork

and went back to work examining the tea set. "Can I ask what you found in the set? Was it valuable?"

"No, not in a material sense." Wendy shook her head. "As I said, it might be of value to the owner and even the police. I found a note that could be connected to a criminal investigation."

Camille's hand slipped again. This time the teacup hit the countertop and shattered into dozens of tiny pieces.

"Klutzy fingers," she scolded herself, and began scooping up the fragments.

Was it klutzy fingers, or something more?

Her face had turned red as she cleaned up the mess. What if she was lying? What if she knew exactly who had donated the mahjong set and her reaction had more to do with Anton's murder?

# Chapter Ten

"Sorry about that," Camille said tossing the pieces of the broken cup in the garbage. "What kind of criminal investigation?"

"Did you know Anton?" Wendy asked.

"The name isn't familiar, but since I'm relatively new to town, I can't claim to know all of my customers by name yet." Camille brushed her hands on her shirt. "Faces, yes."

"I'm sure he's come in before. He was quite a collector, but I don't have a picture of him," Wendy responded. "Sadly, he died last night."

"Oh, that's terrible." Camille sighed and put her hand on her heart. "But how is that connected to the mahjong set?"

There was something different about her demeanor that made me take notice. Gone was any trace of the skittishness. Camille appeared composed and professional. Had our earlier questions rattled her and now she'd had enough time to collect herself?

"It might not be," Wendy admitted. "The police will follow up. We simply wondered if you happened to know who donated the set."

Camille promised that she would ask the volunteer who had accepted the mahjong set and get back to Wendy. It was time for me to return Torte, and Wendy had other errands to do so, we parted ways.

"I'll let you know what I hear from Camille," Wendy said, giving me a hug.

"Thanks. I'll fill the Professor in on what we learned. The police station is on my way."

"Did you find anything odd about her reaction to being asked about the set?" Wendy stole a glance inside the steamy windows.

"She seemed hesitant, but I wondered if maybe she's being protective of her customer's privacy." Charcoal clouds rolled over Grizzly Peak and the east hills. My prediction of rain earlier was feeling truer. Hopefully, I could get back to Torte before the sky unleashed.

Wendy cinched her black polka-dot raincoat. "That could be. We'll see what she says. I do believe that if we can find the set's original owner, some of our questions will be answered."

"Agreed."

She pointed to the bank of clouds headed our way. "We should get moving."

I took Wendy's advice and picked up the pace on my return walk. Our conversation with Camille hadn't revealed much. Short of selling the mahjong set, she didn't have any apparent connection to the investigation into Anton's death. I kicked myself for not asking her more about Anton. Ashland was a small town, but Camille was relatively new, and I doubted their paths would have crossed much unless Anton had been a customer at the shop.

*Or maybe Camille has a dog,* I thought. I should have asked her that, too.

*Oh well. I can always come up with another excuse to pop into the shop and make casual conversation.*

As fate would have it, Thomas was refilling the water dish outside of the police station. The team kept water for dogs who passed by. They also made sure that the exterior of the small building was welcoming, with seasonal flowers planted in window boxes and posters with resources for the unhoused, trail maps, restaurant guides, and OSF brochures for tourists to pick up while exploring downtown.

"This is synchronistic," I said to him. "I was hoping that someone would be here."

"What's up?" He set the water dish next to the door and wiped his hands on his blue shorts. Thomas wore shorts no matter the season. It could be dumping snow, and he would be walking his beat in a pair of shorts and hiking boots. "Kerry's teasing me about watering the flowers, because it's obviously going to rain, but the awning acts as a shield."

"I know, I practically ran here from the other side of town, trying to beat the rain."

"It's good. The storm will wash away all of the sidewalk chalk from the parade." He gestured to the sidewalk where squares had marked spectators' spaces.

As much as I enjoyed Thomas, I didn't want to stand around and talk about the weather, so I got to the point. "Have you heard any more about the cause of death?"

"You don't waste a minute, do you, Jules?" He shook his head in mock disappointment.

"How long have you known me?" I joked.

"Fair point." He plucked a faded leaf from one of the golden geraniums in the flower boxes. "Well, I won't keep you in suspense. Word came in about an hour ago that the cause of death was not natural."

"So, Anton was murdered?" I sucked in a breath.

He nodded.

I took a minute to let the news seep in. Wind sent leaves scattering up Main Street. Shop owners were battening down the hatches, putting away sandwich boards, and picking up any loose pieces of their Halloween displays.

"You okay, Jules?" Thomas stepped closer.

"Yeah." I sighed. "It seemed like that was going to be the case, but I guess the reality of it is still shocking somehow. He was killed in front of Torte. On Halloween. Here in Ashland."

Thomas didn't say anything, but his expression told me that he completely agreed.

"Why would someone want him dead? It doesn't make sense."

He let me process. I appreciated that he didn't try to fix it or offer me a platitude about death. The horror of the reality sink in.

I massaged my temples. "Sorry. I didn't mean to unload on you."

"Unload anytime. That's what I'm here for."

I leaned in and gave him a half hug. "You're the best."

"Right back at you, Capshaw."

"What I have to share might be even more important now," I said. I told him about my conversation with Camille.

Thomas made a quick note on his phone. "Got it. It's

probably nothing, but I'll let the Professor decide if it's a lead worth pursuing. I know he spoke with Wendy and Marcia earlier. I'm sure he'll want to follow up with Camille. Honestly, right now any lead is a good lead."

"Do you think there's a chance the note can be connected?" My ponytail blew with the wind.

He shrugged. "Stranger things have happened. There's not an obvious line that can be drawn between the two, but as the Professor has told me again and again, detective work is rarely linear."

"And you don't have any other leads?"

"Nothing that I'm at liberty to share." Thomas gave me an apologetic smile.

"That's fair. A better question would be, is there anything I can do to help?"

He thought for a minute. "You don't happen to have a dog you could borrow, do you?"

"A dog? Why?"

"Do you remember Trey from Wizard of Paws?"

"Remember him? I mean, I met him after the parade, but should I remember him from something else?"

"He was, like, five or six years younger than us in school. I knew his older brother. Trey was kind of a mess back then. He got in trouble for tagging around town. His brother told me that it was an art teacher who helped him channel his art into grooming. He got his dog grooming certification and went to work for a few different shops before branching out on his own last year. It sounds like Wizard of Paws is doing well." The watering can Thomas had been using caught a gust of air and went rolling down the sidewalk. He ran to grab it.

"Is Trey a suspect?" I asked.

"Everyone is a suspect at the moment," he said, setting the watering can near the door. "I thought if you knew him, it might be a good chance to go reconnect. Get him talking about old times. See if you could get a feel for him."

I searched my memory, but Trey didn't seem familiar. "I don't remember him from school, but I'm happy to swing by and chat. I could bring him some pastries. The store hasn't been open for long. Maybe it could be a gift to welcome him to the Ashland community."

Thomas twisted his face in thought. "That sounds pretty obvious."

"Wait, I've got another idea. What if I tell him that Carlos and I are thinking about getting a dog and ask him a bunch of questions about breeds and stuff?"

"Breeds and stuff?" Thomas wrinkled his brow.

"I don't know—dog stuff."

He laughed. "Dog stuff. You have been spending way too much time with Lance. I might have to ban that friendship."

"I mean, it's not completely untrue. We have discussed the possibility of adopting a dog."

"Really? Cool." Thomas sounded surprised. "No pressure, but if you happen to bump into him, I wouldn't mind getting your opinion on the guy. We've had a hard time pairing up what we're hearing about him. Having unbiased insight always helps, but just promise you and Lance won't show up at his shop dressed as dog groomers in training or something."

"Me? Never." I gave him a thumbs-up. "I'll let you know if I have a chance to talk to him." I waved and headed toward the street. Thomas wasn't off base. If Lance caught word of what I was doing, I could rest assured that a costume or some scheme would be in my future.

Back at Torte, Mom and Bethany were going over ideas for a wedding consultation in the kitchen. Sterling stirred a vat of red sauce at the stove while Marty kept watch over bread baking in the pizza oven.

Wedding consultations were some of my favorite meetings to have at the bakeshop. We invite the bride, groom, and whomever they want to bring as guests, to a special tasting. Typically we bake miniature cakes in a variety of flavors for them to sample and then go over previous examples of our work, along with getting their input and vision for what they want their cake to look like on their special day.

"How's it going?" I leaned over Mom's shoulder to take a peek at the sketches.

"Aren't these designs sweet?" Mom replied, beaming at Bethany with pride. "I love a fall wedding, and I think the couple is going to have a hard time choosing between these."

Bethany tucked a colored pencil behind one ear. She handed me her sketchbook, which had multitiered cakes in a variety of shapes. There was a square cake draped in aubergine fondant with dainty pipework in off-white buttercream. Another oval cake with rich chocolate buttercream had a dark chocolate ganache drip and fall fruits and vegetables made from sparkling-sugar-coated marzipan as toppers. The last cake was a three-tiered stacked wedding cake with an ombre painting technique that created the illusion of jewel-toned colors blending together in buttercream.

"These are absolutely gorgeous," I said to Bethany.

"You think? I feel kind of out of it. Three weeks off from the daily decorating grind has me wondering if I remember how to pipe at all." She sucked in her cheeks and surveyed her work.

"I highly doubt that." My gaze drifted to a tray of toasted almond sugar cookies cut out in the shape of leaves, acorns, apples, and pumpkins. "If I didn't know better, I would think those are real. I don't think you've lost even an ounce of your artistic talent."

Bethany's cheeks were spotted with color. Her dimples became more pronounced when she smiled. "Thanks, I appreciate the vote of confidence."

"We have complete confidence in you, my dear." Mom patted her shoulder.

I reached for a sugar cookie and took a bite. The buttery cookie base had strong notes of almond and melted in my mouth. "How does it feel being back in Ashland? I want to hear so much more about your experience with Pass DeSalt."

"That's what I said, too," Mom agreed.

Bethany got out her phone and showed us photos of her food truck travels. "I have so many ideas, but I don't want to bombard you right away."

"Bring them on." I waved toward myself. "I'm fairly confident I can speak for Mom when I say that we are open to any and all of your ideas."

Mom bobbed her head in agreement. "Absolutely. You obviously had an immersive food experience these past few weeks, and Torte will be better for any of your suggestions."

If possible, the redness in Bethany's cheeks deepened. "Thanks. I was thinking I might put a little proposal together. I was talking to Andy about it last night, and he's got some new coffee concepts brewing that could be really on trend for what's hot in the industry at the moment."

"Oh, does *Andy*."

Bethany tried to hide a smile. "We hung out after the parade to talk shop, that's all."

Mom pressed her hand on Bethany's arm. "I was hoping that young man might finally come to his senses."

"As they say, absence makes the heart grow fonder," I said. "And I'm speaking from experience."

"It's not a big deal. We just hung out." Bethany changed the subject by showing us examples of a new technique for painting buttercream flowers she had learned from a chef in Portland while on the road. Mom and I took that as our cue to follow her lead and look through her photos.

While they continued to go over the tasting menu for the bride and groom, I did a walk-through of the basement and upstairs dining area, gathering empty dishes and making sure the pastry cases were stocked and that things were running smoothly.

I was about to return to the kitchen when I noticed Jax across the street. She was standing near the Lithia bubblers talking to Newell, the special casting director at OSF. I decided to seize the moment and went outside. It must have rained, since the pavement and sidewalks were wet and soggy bundles of leaves collected near the storm drain. The storm clouds had moved on, giving way for bits of blue sky to break through.

For a second, I wondered if Jax had a baby. She had one hand on a baby jogger that she was pushing back and forth as if trying to lull an infant to sleep. As I came closer, I realized that her poodle, Pippa, was tucked inside the jogger. Newell had his back to me, so he didn't notice me come up behind them.

"I know what happened," he said to Jax in a threatening tone. "And I'm not going to stay quiet about it." He broke into a fit of sneezes. "Can you please push that dog farther away from me?"

Her glittery pink eyeshadow glinted in the sunlight as she narrowed her eyes at Newell and rolled the dog stroller closer to him. "Oh, like this? I hope Pippa isn't bothering you."

I was directly in her line of sight, but she was locked in on Newell. "You do whatever you think you need to do, because Pippa and I know your secret. If you so much as say a single word about me, then I will spill everything—and I mean *everything*—I know about you."

Newell let out another violent sneeze, nearly bumping into me as he recoiled from Jax and Pippa.

They both realized I was there.

Jax squeezed her hot pink lips together in a tight, fake smile. "Oh, hi, Jules. I didn't see you."

"Sorry. I didn't mean to startle you," I lied. "I was on my way up to OSF."

"You didn't startle me," Jax said, continuing to rock Pippa in the stroller. "We are late for a grooming session, anyway. Good talking to you, Newell. Don't forget what I said."

With that, she steered the baby jogger in the opposite direction and took off.

Newell brushed imaginary dog hair from his shirt and watched her go.

"Is everything okay?" I asked once she was out of ear-shot.

He fought back a sneeze and held a finger in front of his nose. "Yeah, yeah. It's fine. Fall allergies. Tree pollen. I should go. I have auditions in an hour." His movements were jerky as he started toward the Shakespeare stairs. Then he paused as if considering what to do next before changing directions and running after Jax.

What was going on with the two of them? I didn't know if it had anything to do with Anton's murder, but whatever it was put me on edge and high alert.

# Chapter Eleven

A familiar voice called to me as I was about to return to Torte. "Darling, over here!" I looked to see Lance exiting the Merry Windsor Hotel. Lance was at the Windsor? Why?

I wasn't about to risk a run-in with Richard Lord, so I waited for Lance to come to me.

"What were you doing at the Windsor?" I stuck out my tongue.

"Nothing of interest. Don't give it a thought." He tucked a black umbrella under his arm and moved toward the fountains. "Any news? Any developments?"

Why was he being cagey?

I could tell there was more he wasn't sharing, but I also knew that Lance could be a vault on the rare occasion that he wanted to keep something secret. "I did have a strange interaction with Camille at the hospice shop, and I just overheard Jax and Newell threatening to reveal each other's secrets. Otherwise, in terms of things at Torte, it's pretty sleepy at the moment."

"Ah, yes, the post-Halloween candy hangover is real.

So much sugar." Lance rubbed his temples. "What sort of secrets?"

"No idea." I shrugged. "They didn't stick around long when I showed up."

"Tell me more about Camille." He gave a two-fingered wave to a couple I didn't recognize who passed by us. As the public face of OSF Lance was used to getting recognized around town—a tendency that didn't seem to bother him. "I can see you're much too considerate to ask for a photo, but please allow me to oblige. It would be my utmost pleasure to pose with you."

The delighted couple hurried over to grab a snap. I offered to take the picture on their phone. Lance struck a model-like pose, jutting out his chin and angling one hip forward. I made sure to get the charming backdrop of the plaza in focus while Lance peppered the couple with questions about which shows they had seen during their visit and gave them a teaser for what was to come next year.

As much as Lance played up his stardom in Ashland, it was heartwarming to witness the joy he brought by simply taking a minute to pose for a picture.

Once the photo shoot was over, I gave Lance a brief recap of my conversation and Camille's reaction when she heard about the warning note Wendy had found in the mahjong set.

"The plot thickens." Lance tapped his chin with his index finger. "The question is, what's our next move?"

"I'm going to talk to Trey later." I didn't tell him that Thomas had asked me to speak with the graffiti-artist-turned-dog-groomer.

"Excellent. We have a few auditions this afternoon, so

I'll see what I can get out of Newell. I wonder what sort of information he has on Jax. I'll have to pour it on thick to see if I can convince him to spill the tea." He wiggled his eyebrows. "Let's reconvene later and see what we both come up with."

"Sounds good."

We parted ways near the Lithia bubblers. The aroma of sulfur was overpowering by the healing waters. Soon the city would turn them off for the winter to keep the historic fountain safe from the deep freeze that was coming.

Since I was already out, I decided now was as good a time as any to swing by Wizard of Paws. The pet shop was located on the north end of town, not far from the hospital. I enjoyed stretching my legs and taking in the autumn air. The flaxen rolling hills to the east were illuminated by the afternoon sun. Visitors often commented on Ashland's un-Oregon-like rain. Sure, during the rainy season we would get a good downpour, like earlier today. But the rain rarely stuck around for long. Cloudbursts would pass by, unleashing water into our high mountain lakes and streams, and then give way for the sun to return. Unlike our neighbors to the north in Portland, known for endless soggy gray days, Ashland's climate was much more Mediterranean, with cold winters, hot summers, and year-round sun.

Soon Grizzly Peak would be covered in a blanket of snow. One of the many gifts of life in the Rogue Valley was embracing the ever-changing seasons. Carlos had commented on how different it was to physically see the mountainsides transform from a symphony of fall colors to bright white snow. During our years on the ship, it had been endless summer—turquoise waters and the constant heat of the sun. That was wonderful for vacationers, but the permanent warmth made it difficult to differentiate the days, which bled into each other. I appreciated having to break out my snow boots once a year, and like Carlos, I felt it was impossible not to be captivated by Mother Nature's changing beauty.

At Wizard of Paws, Trey was in the front of the shop, placing sale stickers on the costumes that hadn't sold for Halloween. The shop was housed in a converted auto garage in the Railroad District. Half of the storefront was retail space where Trey featured organic pet treats and accessories. The back part of the store was the grooming station with giant tubs, trimmers, and industrial hair dryers. Even though the grooming area catered to dogs, it could have passed as a spa with its galvanized tubs, gleaming hardwood floors, and overhead chandeliers.

"Welcome, what can I do for you?" Trey greeted me at the door.

"Actually, I'm here to see you," I replied.

"Me? I'm flattered." He tossed a yellow tennis ball as big as my head into a large wicker basket. His hair drooped to the left side of his head.

There were baskets filled with a variety of balls, chew toys, stuffed animals, and plush blankets. A smorgasbord of treats took up the far wall.

I picked up a plush blanket and nearly gasped out loud at the price. Did people pay this much for their pets?

"I was hoping to get some insight into dog breeds from you," I said, putting the blanket back in its spot.

"What do you want to know?" Trey continued to adhere sale stickers to the costumes.

"You work with Jax and Marcia, right?" I took in the hand-painted pet portrait gallery behind him.

Was it just my imagination, or did his body tense at the question?

He kept his attention focused on the costumes and flipped his hair out of his eyes. "Define 'work.' They're both frequent customers. Between the two of them, they keep me in business. It's cool. I need the clients, and the special grooming is fun."

"How often do the dogs have grooming appointments?"

"It depends. Both dogs have standing appointments for monthly grooming sessions and sometimes more frequently if they're auditioning or taking a role." He laid a silky princess costume on the counter next to a vampire catnip toy. Then he pointed to his hair. "I like the clients who are game to play around with color and changing styles. Hair should be about expression. It's an art form, you know? Jax is great about letting me do whatever I want with Pippa. Marcia's more buttoned up, but that's cool. I get it."

"I heard that a grooming session gone wrong caused George's tail to be dyed by mistake." My eyes drifted to the spa.

"That wasn't my fault." Now I knew I wasn't imagining the way Trey's entire body went rigid. "What does that have to do with dog breeds?"

I tried to keep my tone casual. "Oh, I just wondered how that happened. I'm guessing it's not typical for pugs to get their fur dyed. Anyway, my husband and I have been considering adopting a dog, but with our busy schedules, we want to have a very clear idea about the kind of time commitment required. Does every breed need to be groomed that often? Are there better breeds for busy small business owners like us?" I was slathering it on thicker than buttercream.

My questions seemed to put Trey at ease. He stopped down-pricing costumes and unclenched his jaw. "No. Not at all. Not every breed requires grooming. Most dog owners don't bother getting their pets professionally groomed. They should. Dogs love being pampered as much as we do. Are you interested in a small breed like a pug or poodle?"

"I don't know. Mainly, we wouldn't want to be irresponsible pet owners. My husband and I are gone a lot. I definitely couldn't bring a dog to the bakeshop. That would go against every health code. Carlos, my husband, might be able to take a dog to the vineyard, but if he did, then we would want a bigger breed, is that right?"

"Would he use the dog for hunting on the vineyard?"

"Hunting?" The question surprised me.

"Do you have a rat infestation?"

"I hope not." I winced. "None that I know of."

"Okay, so you're not thinking of a working breed for the vineyard, more for companionship?"

"Yes." It was hard not to experience sensory overload in the shop. Nearly every inch of wall, floor, and shelving space was filled with every pet accessory imaginable. A stack of flannel beds looked so cozy, I could almost curl up and take a nap in one of them myself.

Trey motioned for me to follow him to the cash register. He proceeded to hand me a three-ring binder. "Take a look through this. It's a style sheet for grooming different breeds and should give you a good feel. I've always been an animal lover, so it's pretty cool that now I get to put my creative spin on grooming. You gotta think out of the box and not be afraid of funky."

I flipped through the binder. There were dozens of before and after photos of Trey's work. Like a Maltipoo with a tail dyed to resemble a unicorn and a Yorkie with black and yellow leopard spots. Trey wasn't kidding about his unique artistic style.

"Off the top of my head, you seem like you could be a good match for a golden retriever or Lab," Trey said, trying unsuccessfully to push his floppy hair back up to standing. "They're both friendly, chill breeds. They'd love running through the vineyard, but they're bigger dogs. If you go with a big breed, you have to get them out for daily walks or runs or say goodbye to your furniture. Do you have any allergies? If so, a Labradoodle is another good option. They are bred not to shed."

"Bred not to shed, I like it." I chuckled. How was I going to bring the conversation back to Jax and Marcia? "Do you train dogs, too?"

"No. That was Anton's role. We sent a lot of business each other's way. He was smart that way. Good with money. He wasn't an artist, but he appreciated art. He had a huge collection, and I think he saw potential in me. He knew that this is my art form."

None of this sounded like a motive for wanting to kill him. Why would Trey want to give up a reciprocal business partnership? How lucrative was the pet business? Trey's inventory alone must have been worth hundreds of thousands of dollars.

"Anton approached me when I opened the store and said that he would exclusively recommend Wizard of Paws to his training clients if in exchange I would give anyone looking for private dog training his information," Trey continued. He kept moving as he spoke. I wasn't sure if it was his personality or if I was making him nervous.

"That sounds like a good deal for both of you."

"It was, until recently."

Was he going to open up? I held my breath for a second, hoping that he would say more. He didn't.

"Did something happen with you and Anton?"

Trey busied himself with organizing receipts. "We had a falling-out."

A falling-out? Now things were getting interesting, as Lance would say.

"Anton was furious about the mix-up with George. He freaked out on me at the parade." Trey shifted his weight from foot to foot as he leafed through the receipts. "He wouldn't believe me when I told him it wasn't my fault. He noticed that my hair was the same purple and accused me of playing a prank. Don't let the hair fool you. I take my business seriously."

"I believe you." I wasn't sure yet whether that was true, but I wanted to keep him talking.

He yanked a ballpoint pen from a container and scribbled a note on one of the receipts. "I would never do that to a client, and I'm not an idiot. I was in the middle of a shampoo and condition when I realized that there was dye in the bottle." He stuffed the receipts in the cash register and then began to rip open packages of Pup-Peroni to fill a dog dish on the counter. "Marcia was furious with me when she picked him up. She was convinced that I did it on purpose. She had Anton threaten to sue me at the parade. Like, how was he going to sue me? It wasn't his dog. George was just another one of his clients."

The smell of the dog treats was overpowering. "Why did she think you did it on purpose?"

"She claimed that I was working with Jax and that Jax and I were trying to sabotage George together."

"And were you?"

Trey's nostrils flared. "No. Why would I do that? It's terrible for my business. Anton told me that he was never going to refer a single customer my way again. Marcia demanded her money back and told me she was going to the press. It's been awful. It's the worst week of my life."

For a minute I thought he might break down.

"Do you have any idea how hard I've worked to build this?" He gestured to the custom shelves lining the store. "Those gemstone collars you see behind that display case—a few of them are worth over five figures. I've got the largest collection of high-end pet supplies and accessories in southern Oregon. Do you know the immense amount of trust it takes for clients to allow anyone to so much as lay hands on their furry friends? Why would I possibly risk that? This is my passion and my only source of income. I worked hard to get here, and I'm not about to let a stupid dye job kill my dream."

I started to respond, but he ripped another piece of the dog treat into pieces and kept talking. "The answer is that I wouldn't. I would never deliberately mistreat an animal."

"I wasn't accusing you of mistreating George," I clarified.

"But George was mistreated," Trey insisted. "Put

yourself in his shoes. How mortifying it must have been for him."

We were talking about a dog, weren't we?

"Does George wear shoes?" I tried to lighten the mood by making a joke.

Trey rolled his eyes and let out an annoyed exhale. "I'm speaking metaphorically. What people don't understand about dogs is that they are innately attuned to stress. There isn't a shred of doubt in my mind that George picked up on Marcia's reaction and the reaction of everyone who saw him with a purple tail."

I would at least give Trey credit for picking the right line of work. He was clearly an animal lover.

"I believe that I was set up." He craned his neck toward the grooming station. "A crime occurred here. A crime that will not go unpunished."

I shrank back. What did he mean by that?

His eyes drifted to me again. "You don't have to look at me like that. All that I'm saying is that George's accident wasn't an accident, and the person responsible is going to pay."

"Do you have any idea who would have done it and how?"

He tossed the chunks of dog treats into the bowl. "Oh, I know exactly who did it, and I have a pretty good idea how they did it."

I waited for him to continue.

He brushed his hands together. I wasn't sure if he was trying to get rid of debris from the Pup-peroni or if the gesture was for shock value. "Perry Shaw."

"The actor?" I hadn't had Perry on my suspect list.

"Yeah." Trey walked to the grooming area and

motioned for me to follow him. "Perry came in that morning. I thought it was weird. He told me that since he and George were going to be acting together, he wanted to see every part of the process that George went through to prepare for a role."

"Okay." My face must have matched the skepticism in my tone.

"I thought maybe he was a method actor. I'm sure you've heard of actors who refuse to break character for the duration of a show."

I nodded. Lance had had a few actors over the years who had become so immersed in the characters they were portraying on the stages that the lines between fiction and reality were completely blurred. It wasn't common for an actor to go that deep into a role, but it was certainly possible.

"I let him stay for the grooming session. The guy is intimidating. He acts like he's really a king, you know. He took notes and photos, watched the whole thing, took, like, a zillion selfies, and talked to George like he was a person the entire time."

Quirky, but again not impossible to believe, especially in Ashland.

"I should have been paying more attention. I don't ever let customers participate in the grooming process. I made an exception for Perry because I thought he was a professional. Now I realize that I made a fatal mistake."

Trey and Lance would get along well. He was equally dramatic and obviously took his work very seriously. Perhaps too seriously.

"While I was in the middle of shampooing George, a customer came in. Usually, I have an SOU student who helps in the afternoon, but she had a midterm. Perry offered to stay with George while I went to let the customer know they were welcome to browse but it was going to be a few minutes before I could help them." Trey shook his head in disgust as he told me the story, like he couldn't believe he had been duped. "I don't know, but maybe that's when it happened. Maybe Perry did it."

"You think Perry dyed George's tail?"

"No, but he could have swapped the bottles on me. When I came back again, I finished the rinse and applied what I thought was a conditioner that would give George's coat a nice shine for the parade. Thankfully, I started on his tail. I realized right away that the bottle contained semipermanent dye. There's no possible way I could have made a mistake." He paused to point at the wall of high-end grooming products in the back. "The dye comes in those colorful tubes. Conditioner is in those bottles. I have been doing this for years. I'm not a total screwup like some people have tried to claim. I wouldn't have squeezed the dye onto George's tail. No, someone tampered with George's conditioner. Perry squeezed a tube of purple dye into the bottle when I wasn't looking. The minute I saw purple, I scrubbed it off right away, but it was too late. I can't even imagine what would have happened if I had applied the conditioner to his fur first. His entire coat would have been purple. I think Marcia would have probably sued me, and I wouldn't blame her."

I took a minute to let everything that he had shared sink in.

"Why would Perry have wanted to sabotage George if they were acting partners?" It still felt weird to call a dog an acting partner, but I supposed that was what they were.

Trey's eyes bulged like he couldn't believe I hadn't connected the dots. "Because he didn't want to act with George. He hates that dog. He's been campaigning to replace George for weeks."

"What?"

"I learned this after the fact. If I had known that when he asked to watch the grooming process, I never would have allowed it." Trey shrugged. "He outsmarted me, but this isn't the end. Like I said, I've worked too hard to let an actor ruin Wizard of Paws' reputation. He's going to pay for what he did."

# Chapter Twelve

I chatted with Trey a bit longer, keeping up the ruse that I was curious about finding the perfect pet. On my way back to Torte, I couldn't stop thinking about Perry. If what Trey had said was true, it meant that Perry was so determined not to work with George that he went out of his way to alter the dog's appearance in an attempt to hopefully get his four-legged castmate kicked off the show. The theory was so outrageous that it almost made me believe Trey more.

Still, though I didn't know Perry well aside from our post-parade hangout last night, he hadn't said or done anything to make me think that he wasn't a fan of George. Although, come to think of it, he had emphasized the fact that he was the star of *A Play About a Dragon* more than once. Could he be jealous of a pug? Was he upset about sharing a stage with a dog? But how would that connect to Anton's murder?

There was one more thing to consider. Perry had also appeared to be cozy with Jax. Or at least indebted to her in some way. Could the two of them have been working together to get George off the cast list and create an open-ing for Pippa? That would not shock me.

Jax was obsessed with her poodle. She and Perry were definitely friends, maybe more. When I connected with Lance later, I would have to ask him what he knew about Perry.

At Torte the afternoon was winding down. Bethany had finished the individual cakes for the wedding tasting. The lunch rush was over, and the pastry cases had been cleaned out. By the time the last of my team headed out for the evening, I found myself in an empty kitchen again. It was interesting how the rhythm of my days shifted. I started and closed out each day in a quiet, peaceful kitchen. I liked it that way. Working alone all day would have felt isolating, but I enjoyed the balance of a bustling kitchen and then the calm of having Torte all to myself.

Carlos had texted to let me know he would swing by and pick me up on his way home from Uva. I checked the clock. The winery was closing now, which meant I had at least an hour before he would be here.

I decided to use the time to make dinner, and nothing sounded better after consuming one too many bite-size candy bars yesterday than a soup. I decided on creamy chicken soup. For the base, I chopped onions, carrots, and celery. I added a couple of healthy glugs of olive oil to my favorite soup pan and then sautéed the veggies over medium heat until they were tender. Next, I added diced garlic and let that cook for another minute before adding our house-made organic chicken stock; dried ba-sil, oregano, and thyme; salt and pepper; and chopped chicken breasts. I brought the soup to a low rolling boil, covered it, and turned the heat to low. That would simmer for thirty to forty minutes. Once the chicken had cooked through and the veggies were soft, I would add a cup of stelline, a tiny star-shaped pasta that would give the soup an almost nutty flavor. Right before serving, I would stir in light sour cream to finish it with a creamy tang.

While my soup was simmering, I thought about what to serve it with. There was a baguette left over from our daily bread baking. Since my chicken and stars soup felt like a nostalgic meal, I opted to slice the baguette in half and build fancy grilled cheese sandwiches to pair with it. I spread a thin layer of herbed butter on both sides of the crusty bread. Then I piled on prosciutto, Taleggio cheese, and caramelized onions. The soft cheese would melt well and had a fruity savoriness.

Once I had assembled the sandwich, I put it in a Tupperware to bring home and bake. Ramiro had soccer practice until seven, so I would have soup and hot sandwiches waiting for him. With dinner done, I looked through the pantry in hopes of finding inspiration for a quick dessert. Nothing was striking my fancy. I hoped that I wasn't losing my muse when it came to baking. It was probably just exhaustion setting in after the frenzy of preparing for Halloween and then the shock of discovering Anton's body. My thoughts drifted to his murder. There were so many possible suspects—Perry, Jax, Trey, Camille, and even Marcia. I didn't want to believe that Mom's good friend was a killer, but I still couldn't rule it out.

Jax had the most obvious motive, and from what I had learned from Trey earlier, she and Perry could have been working together to get Pippa a starring role. If Anton had really told Newell that Pippa wasn't ready for the stage, could Jax have resorted to murder? With him out of the way and George sporting a bad dye job, that opened a huge door for Pippa.

But had one of them murdered Anton because of a dog? *That's ludicrous, Jules.*

Then there was the warning note in Wendy's mahjong set. Odds were good that the hidden message was a coincidence, but then again, Camille's reaction when Wendy had asked her about the set had been strange at best. What if there was a connection between her and Anton that I was missing? And how did Newell and Trey fit into everything?

I sighed and massaged my temples. I needed to talk to Lance and see what he had learned and then try to have another conversation with Camille, this time alone. I wondered if there could be anything else to glean from the mahjong set. Had Wendy checked it thoroughly? Could there be another clue tucked in one of the drawers?

Tomorrow I would try and swing by Wendy's and see if I could take another look.

I shut the pantry and glanced at a bowl of Halloween candy on the island. Suddenly inspiration struck. I knew what to bake—leftover Halloween candy cookie bars. I grabbed butter and eggs from the walk-in fridge and scooped up the bowl of candy. The butter went into the mixer along with brown and white sugars, which I creamed together for a good long time. That was a tip I always shared with new staff. When a recipe called for creaming butter and sugar, it didn't mean to simply mix them together for a minute or two. Creaming required whipping air into the butter to give it a light and fluffy quality. It was a process we took seriously at Torte. First

I slowly incorporated the butter and sugar into our industrial mixer, then I turned the speed up higher and higher and let it whip for at least five minutes before moving on to the next step. Once I had achieved that, I added creamy peanut butter, vanilla, and eggs. Then I sifted in the dry ingredients—flour, oats, salt, and baking soda. Soon I had delicious cookie dough. I chopped an assortment of leftover candy bars and stirred them, along with some orange and black M&M's, into the dough by hand. I greased a large glass baking dish and spread the dough evenly.

The bars would only take about fifteen minutes to bake. I slid them into the oven and made myself a cup of decaf while I waited for everything to finish and for Carlos to arrive. He showed up as I savored the last sip of coffee. Typically, I prefer my coffee fully leaded, but I wanted to sleep tonight, and consuming a cup of strong roast before dinner would probably keep me humming for hours.

"Perfect timing," I said to Carlos, depositing my empty cup in the sink. When he had decided to stay in Ashland, a tiny part of me worried that we would get bored with each other. There had never been a dull moment on the *Amour of the Seas*. We stole away moments between shifts or soaked up a brief sunrise. That nagging voice in my head cautioned that too much time together might make our spark go dim. However, the way he greeted me with instant tenderness sent quivers through my stomach and made my mouth go dry. If anything, being together in Ashland had made me fall for him harder.

"Something smells delicious." He kissed me and then followed me to the stove and lifted the lid to take a whiff. "You made soup?"

"For us."

His dark eyes locked on me. "How did I get so lucky to deserve you?"

I leaned into him. "Trust me, the feeling is mutual."

"You seem sad, mi querida." Carlos massaged my arm and pulled back to study my face. "Did something else happen?"

"No. It's just Anton. The whole thing. I haven't been able to stop thinking about it all day. Not even while baking."

"Sí, I understand." He rubbed my arm with his thumb. "I feel the same. When I was talking with customers in the tasting room, I could take my mind off of it for a moment, but as soon as I had any time to myself, I could not stop seeing Anton slumped right out the window upstairs. Have the police learned more?"

"They know it's murder." I removed my cookie bars from the oven. "Can you reach one of the large to-go soup containers?" I asked, motioning to the cupboard next to the stove.

Carlos got the container and began ladling soup into it without me asking. "He was killed for sure?"

"According to Thomas, the coroner's report stated that he was stabbed multiple times."

"This is terrible."

"I know, especially because it happened here. I feel connected somehow."

"I agree." He finished portioning out soup. "What should I do with the rest?"

"Can you divide it up into smaller to-go sizes? We can sell it tomorrow."

Carlos got to work, while I sliced a few bars to bring

home and got my grown-up grilled cheese from the walk-in. My creamy chicken and stars soup would make for a cozy dinner tonight and save me a step in the morning. We sold a variety of premade items like soup, chicken potpies, and quiches for customers to grab and go. They were especially popular on cold fall and winter nights when a quick stop at Torte on the way home from work meant that the only dinner preparation needed was to warm it in the oven or on the stove.

"Are you ready?" Carlos asked when he was done packaging the soup and storing it in the fridge.

"Yes. I cannot wait to put on my PJs and slippers and curl up on the couch with a hot bowl of soup."

"I will make a fire. You can rest while Ramiro takes a shower after practice. I can heat dinner up."

"That would be a dream." I gave him a kiss as we tucked Torte in for the night. As it turned out, I wasn't far behind the bakeshop in my need for slumber. As promised, Carlos lit a fire, and the second my head hit the plush throw pillow on the couch, I dozed off in a restful nap. I woke long enough to enjoy dinner with Carlos and Ramiro, expecting that I would have trouble falling back asleep later. Only I didn't. Not long after our meal, I headed for bed and drifted into a dreamless sleep for the remainder of the night.

# Chapter Thirteen

The next day was a swirl of activity. Between our wedding tasting client, a rush of wholesale orders, and daily walk-ins, Torte was busy from the moment we opened until long after lunch. The leftover Halloween candy cookie bars were gone by midmorning. We made three more batches. Each sold out within an hour of restocking the pastry case.

"These need to be an annual tradition," Rosa said while she and I went over the lineup for Thanksgiving specials. Halloween was barely behind us, and we had to shift our attention to the next holiday. We would announce our holiday items next week to give customers time to put in their orders. Our pumpkin pies and cranberry lemon bread were so popular that we usually had to put an end to orders the week before Thanksgiving because my team would be baking from dawn to dusk to handle the rush. I never took being part of people's family celebrations for granted. It was a gift to serve this community with love. Love in the form of pumpkin cheesecake and bread pudding tarts. Though prepping for Thanksgiving would mean some long hours ahead, I wouldn't have had it any other way.

"I'm glad they've been selling well," I replied. "It's a good way to get rid of the Halloween candy quickly."

"And I think adults like getting to sneak some candy in, too." Rosa smiled. She wore her long dark brown hair in a braid and little makeup. From the moment I met her, she had felt like a kindred spirit. We were about the same age and shared a love of family and baking. Over the last year, she had taken on more responsibility, managing the front of the house and mentoring some of our younger bakers. With Mom scaling back, we had offered Rosa a raise and a new title, which she had accepted, cementing how invaluable she had become to the team.

"I have to admit that I had two after dinner last night," I said. "I think the oats and peanut butter help offset the sweetness of the candy. At least that's the story I'm telling myself."

Rosa chuckled. "Hey, whatever works."

We finalized the Thanksgiving specials so that Rosa could have Steph design a flyer and Bethany could post them on our social media accounts. Then we went over staff schedules, vendor orders, and all of the less-than-glamorous work that goes into running a family-owned bakeshop. In culinary school, my instructors hadn't sugar-coated the cons of operating a small bakery business—like long hours and lower profit margins on buying ingredients like organic butter and locally sourced produce. For me, the pros far outweighed them, but over the years, a few of my classmates had abandoned the idea of working for themselves in favor of a steady paycheck and stable hours in commercial kitchens.

By late afternoon there was finally a lull in activity. I used the chance to hand-deliver a pastry order to OSF.

They had called and asked for an assortment of cookies and cupcakes for the team running auditions.

"I'll take these up to campus," I said to Bethany, who had boxed cupcakes decorated with plum, forest green, and red-currant-colored buttercream flowers. "They turned out beautifully."

"You're just saying that to make me feel better." Bethany wiped purple food gel from her fingertip with a wet dish towel.

"Do I need to call a team meeting?" I pursed my lips and scrunched my forehead. "Do we need an intervention?"

"I guess not." Bethany made a face. "Are you sure they're good? I feel like my fingers forgot how to hold a piping bag."

"She's in her head," Steph interjected.

"Tell me about it." I agreed. "The question is what do we do?"

"I vote decorate-off." Sterling tossed a towel over his shoulder and came over to inspect Bethany's work. "You know, like a dance-off, only with buttercream."

"I like the way you think, young man." Marty clapped twice.

Bethany's cheeks matched the red currant color on the cupcakes. "I take it back. I take it back. I'm happy with my work. Don't make me do a pipe-off with Steph."

"I don't know." I bit my bottom lip, pretending like I was giving the idea real consideration. "A decorate-off does sound right up your alley and like it could go viral on social, yeah?"

Bethany's mouth hung open. "You're using my own favorite thing against me? How could you, Jules? And I thought we were friends."

"All's fair in love and pastry." I grinned.

"Decorate-off! Decorate-off! Decorate-off!" Marty and Sterling chanted.

"That doesn't exactly roll off the tongue, does it?" Marty said.

"Nope, not at all, but we can keep going, Bethany." Sterling tossed a dish towel over his shoulder and gave her a little smirk.

She threw her hands up in surrender. "I give in. I'll stop whining about my skills, and maybe we'll have to put together a decorating competition with you two."

"Oh, she got us." Marty gave Bethany an air high five.

I left them to their teasing. We had promised OSF to deliver the order by four. They wanted a late afternoon pick-me-up to get the company through auditions. But the truth was that I also wanted to see if I could get a minute alone with Lance. I needed to know if he had learned anything from Newell or Perry.

The bricks, where throughout the spring and summer locals and theatergoers gathered each night to take in outdoor preshow performances, had been transformed into a staging area for breaking down sets. Crew members carted sections of flooring, couches, lights, and carts loaded with props. It never ceased to amaze me how much work went on behind the scenes. The Bowmer Theater had full set changes every day during the season, and now that the season had come to an end, the interior and exterior sets needed to be dismantled in order to clear the stages to make room for entirely new set designs to take their place. It was a process that occurred year after year.

I was careful not to get in anyone's way as I rapped on

the doors to the Bowmer. A member of the company I recognized by face only came to let me in.

"I'm delivering an order for auditions."

They pointed me in the right direction, even though I knew the way. I breathed in a faint hint of popcorn lingering at concessions. The Bowmer's deep red carpets and arched windows brought back so many happy memories of my youth. This was the place where I had grown up. I knew every inch of the corridors that led downstairs to the costume and props department.

I waited outside the auditorium doors, listening for a break in the dialogue on the stage before entering the theater. Even though I was only on-site to deliver pastries, my stomach knotted as I approached the first row of seats where Lance, Newell, and three other people were seated with clipboards. It had to be so intimidating to stand alone on the historic stage and audition for a part.

Lance noticed me and jumped to his feet. "Ah, Juliet. Best news, everyone—our afternoon delights have arrived."

I handed him the box, which he proceeded to offload to one of his colleagues. "Help yourselves. Take a stretch break. Grab a cup of coffee or tea, and we'll reconvene in fifteen."

He took my arm and led me away from everyone. "You are here right on cue. I simply could not sit through another second of *Gatsby*. Do tell me, why is it that every actor on the planet seems to decide to perform the same passage?"

"Are you doing *The Great Gatsby* next year?"

"No. But everyone on my stage is. I swear the universe

conspires with creative minds. It only takes one actor, and then suddenly everyone and their brother is auditioning with the same piece."

We walked through the lobby and outside onto the bricks. Lance's catlike eyes darted in every direction, making sure no one was near enough to eavesdrop on our conversation. "Hit me with it. What have you learned? We don't have much time."

I told him about my conversations with Camille and Trey.

"Trey thinks that Perry doesn't like King George?" Lance scoffed. "I beg to differ. He fawns over that dog. They've been inseparable since the cast list was announced. They are starting to look alike, embodying their roles as kings. Every time I've bumped into Perry, he's either snapping a selfie with or posing with George."

"Really?" Crews were dismantling the outdoor stage where preshow acts had performed every night through the season.

"Cross my heart and hope to die." Lance made an X across his chest. "Something is not right about that story."

"What about Newell? Did you learn anything from him?"

Lance started to speak but stopped when a crew member passed by carrying a huge section of what had once been the diner for the musical *Waitress*. "Keep up the great work," Lance called out. "Pizza later!" After they were out of earshot, Lance dropped his voice. "This is where the plot really begins to thicken, darling. I have it on good authority that Newell is not whom he claims to be." He paused and waited for my reaction.

"How so?"

"He was hired as a special casting director and co-ordinator—focusing on our furry cast members—a few months ago, but apparently, he's ruffled more than a few feathers in the short time he's been here, and I'm not talking about birds, although there was talk of opening a role for a parakeet, as it so happens."

"What kind of feathers has he ruffled?" I tried to keep him on topic.

Lance's dark brows arched like two bridges. "It didn't take any prying to get my company talking about their impressions of our newest hire, and let's just say that no one, and I mean not a single soul, had anything kind to say about Newell."

"The cast doesn't like him?" I had to speak over the sound of drills.

"The cast and crew loathe him. Absolutely *loathe* him." Lance watched with unabashed skepticism as two staffers climbed ladders on either side of the stage to begin the process of removing twenty-foot-tall Green Show banners.

"Did they say why?"

Lance held up his index finger. "Oh, I thought that might be your next question, and the answer is yes." He paused for dramatic effect.

"Are you going to tell me what it is?"

"What's it worth to you? Free pastries for life?"

"You already get free pastries, and you hardly need a discount," I bantered back. The truth was that Lance was one of our best and most loyal customers. He always paid for his orders and gave my team generous tips.

"Fine. I'll have to think of something else." He strummed his fingers on his chin.

I punched him softly in the arm. "Get to the good stuff. We're going to run out of time. You gave your crew a fifteen-minute break, and I need to get back to the bake-shop."

"So pushy." Lance curled his lip. Then he rubbed his hands together. "Okay, listen to this. Every single person I spoke with this afternoon about Newell said the same thing, verbatim. I mean without fail."

Lance was a master storyteller, but in moments like this, he made me crazy. He knew how to spin a tale and keep listeners on the edges of their seats. It was a great tactic and an important skill for running a national theater company, but not so much when it came to getting to the point.

"Those crinkly lines on your forehead almost make me wonder if I'm irritating you." Lance gave me a devilish grin and tapped the side of my head.

I glared at him.

"Okay, okay. Don't ruin that fine face. I'll cut to the chase." He twisted his wrist with a flourish. "As I was saying, I casually mentioned Newell's name to my staff this afternoon and quickly learned that he has not amassed a single fan. We might assume that his personality didn't mesh or perhaps that he comes across as controlling or condescending, but no." He paused and narrowed his left eye. "Oh, no. Do not be mistaken. The reason for so much distrust amongst the company? Newell hates animals."

"Yeah, that makes sense." I thought back to Newell picking dog fur from his coat and sneezing every time he was around Pippa. "But he's the animal casting director."

Lance gave me a knowing smile. "It's a shocker, isn't it?"

"I don't know if I would say it was a shocker, but I

would bet money that he's allergic too." I told him about the sneezing fits.

"You're ruining my moment, Juliet. I thought I had a big reveal for you." Lance let out a little growl and contorted his face before continuing. "I suppose I shouldn't be surprised. According to everyone I spoke with, Newell barely tolerates our four-legged friends. I'm quite glad that this has come to light because he's on a temporary contract, which will not be extended."

"Why would he take a job as an animal casting director if he doesn't like animals?"

"The better question is who doesn't like animals? That's what has me worried. Now, don't get me wrong, no harm has come to any of our furry cast, but it was made clear that Newell goes out of his way to avoid having any unnecessary interaction with the pets on set. He keeps hand wipes and sanitizer on him at all times. I heard one anecdote about him storming offstage when a dog licked his pant leg."

"Do you think this could be connected to Anton's death?"

Lance's grin vanished. His face turned serious. "I have no doubt about it. For starters, I don't trust anyone who doesn't like animals. That's a glaring red flag, and I have a new theory."

"What?"

A few of his colleagues were returning from their breaks. Lance motioned to them that he'd be right in. "What if Anton was going to spill the beans? What if he realized that Newell was not a champion of our pampered pooches? That would give Newell a clear motive for murder, wouldn't it?"

I thought for a second. "Yeah. It's certainly a possibility."

"Oh, it's more than a possibility. I'm convinced. We are on the trail of the killer. Now we just need to find proof." He glanced at his watch. "I must go. Let's chat in more detail later, but in the meantime, keep one eye out for Newell. I'm sure that he's our killer."

# Chapter Fourteen

How was it possible that three separate people all believed a different person was responsible for Anton's murder? The absurdity wasn't lost on me, but I couldn't tell who might be right.

I thought about what Lance had told me on the walk back to Torte. Newell didn't like dogs. Not just didn't like but loathed them. What could possibly have motivated him to take a position working directly with animals? Money? Was he desperate for a job? Or could it be that he thought landing a role with OSF would be his big break? The theater's reputation was on par with that of the Globe or any other world-renowned repertory company. Maybe Newell had lied about his credentials to get the job, hoping that he could use OSF as a stepping stone. Plenty of actors had gotten their start in Ashland and gone on to land roles in TV and major movies. I supposed that it wasn't much different for staff. If Newell could list OSF on his résumé, he could probably land a position as a casting director at any movie studio in LA. But would experience with animals translate to casting people?

Lance was right; something didn't add up.

I wasn't sure what it meant yet, but if Newell had lied about being a dog lover to land the gig at OSF, what else could he be lying about?

I was about to cross the street in front of the Merry Windsor when I saw Perry and Jax deep in conversation at the Glamper, a new pub at the far end of the plaza catty-corner from Lithia Park. The Glamper's owners had completely remodeled the space with roll-up garage doors, ample outdoor seating, and fire pits that were packed, no matter the weather. Barnwood walls, long picnic tables, lanterns, and even a converted retro RV had made the bar a popular hangout spot for locals and tourists from the day it opened.

I decided I couldn't pass up a chance to talk to Jax and Perry, so instead of continuing toward the bakeshop, I headed for the Glamper. They were seated at one of the picnic tables on the corner with a view of the park, where a herd of deer nibbled on the grass.

Before I had come up with an excuse to interrupt them, Jax caught my eye and waved me over. "Jules, how's it going?" Even though Halloween was over, her pink theme continued. She looked like an advertisement for Pepto Bismol with her pink joggers, sweatshirt, and matching tennis shoes.

"Good. I just finished a delivery and had to take the long way back because it's so gorgeous right now." My gaze drifted to the entrance to the park, where Japanese maples and leafy oaks guarded the grassy area. "I heard rain is in the forecast."

"Do you want to join us?" Jax pointed to the seat next to her. "We'd love some company, wouldn't we, Per?"

*Per?* Was that her pet name for him?

Perry barely looked up from his drink, but I caught him rolling his eyes.

"Maybe for a minute." I squeezed onto the bench. One of the cons of having long legs is fitting into narrow spaces. "Where's Pippa?" This was the first time I'd seen Jax without her beloved poodle. And why was she being so inviting? Our previous interactions had been filled with tension and consumed with discussions about how Pippa had been wronged. I hated feeling cynical, but I didn't trust her motives for welcoming me to join them.

"She's with Trey at Wizard of Paws. She's been getting the works recently—massage, shampoo, blow-dry. The kind of concentration and focus that's required with her training is so taxing, so I've made sure to treat her to some extra spa days. Doesn't everyone need some bonus pampering now and then?" Jax finished the last sips of her drink and stood. "I need a refill. Can I get you guys anything?"

"I'll take another hard cider," Perry replied, handing Jax his glass.

She looked at me.

"Oh, no thanks. I have to be back at work soon."

Jax went inside. Perry shook his head as he watched her approach the bar. "I don't know what to do about her. Jax spends more money on that dog than most people spend on their children. She's out of control."

I was surprised that he was opening up to me, but I wasn't about to stop him. "I read a statistic about the exorbitant amount of money Americans spend on their pets each year, and it's astronomical, like, in the billions." Jax's description of Pippa's spa treatments was a perfect example.

"Jax is certainly adding to that." Perry sounded disgusted. He paused briefly to check his appearance on his phone. "As an actor, I understand the importance of caring for your body. We have to keep our vessels in shape. I get paid to make sure my face looks like this, but Pippa has more spa treatments than me. This is the third time in a week that she's been at Wizard of Paws, and I have to tell you that it's not cheap."

"And Jax takes Pippa there that often?" I asked him, while internally spinning on the idea that a dog would have three grooming sessions a week. What could the poodle possibly need to have done that would require that many trips to the spa?

"Yeah. You heard her. The dog gets the full works every time. I'm telling you, it's like a freakin' spa, but for dogs. She gets a bath, a blow-dry, fur grooming, her toenails 'touched up,' as Jax likes to call it. Apparently, Pippa needed a full day of styling for new headshots. Jax is going to go broke with how much she's spending on that dog." He clicked a selfie. Then he set his phone on the table and flicked a pine needle off the edge of the picnic table. "If you ask me, it's animal abuse to paint a dog's toenails, but don't get into the topic with Jax. She'll kill you."

I flinched at his words. He was probably being flippant, but then again, Anton was dead, and Jax had been furious with him. Could there be another reason he was uptight about the topic of Wizard of Paws? Trey had mentioned that he thought Perry had swapped the purple dye while he was grooming King George for the parade. Perhaps Perry was worried that his secret would get out.

"I take it she got angry at you about that?"

Perry flicked another pine needle from the table. It was

the time of year when pine needles rained from the evergreen trees and transformed sidewalks and hiking trails into a blanket of aromatic green. "That's an understatement. She lectured me for three hours about how much Pippa loves getting her toenails painted." He rolled his eyes. "Did you know that they have to use special toenail polish for dogs?"

"No, I guess I've never been in the market."

"I made the mistake of using the argument that toenail polish could be toxic if a dog were to scratch it off and eat it, because, you know, they're *dogs*."

I chuckled. "And that didn't win you points in the argument?"

"Not even." He put up a hand. "Jax made sure to school me on the fact that Trey at Wizard of Paws has a special polish just for dogs that isn't toxic or full of chemicals. The fact that there are companies that make a product like that blows my mind. I don't even want to know how much that costs."

"Hence, the billion-dollar pet industry." Could there be a financial connection with Anton's murder? I knew that money was always a motive. Was there a chance that Anton and Trey's symbiotic business arrangement had gone sour, like old milk?

Perry shrugged. "Yeah. I just wish Jax could get a little perspective, you know?"

I didn't know, and again I was surprised that he was sharing this with me. I stole a quick glance at the bar where Jax was still waiting in line. "It sounds like you two are close."

Perry pulled his entire body backward like he was worried I was going to reach across the table and grab him. "Who? Me and Jax? Why would you say that?"

It was an odd reaction to what I thought was a benign question. "Sorry. I didn't mean to offend you. I only mentioned it because I wondered if maybe you could offer her some of that perspective if you were close. I've found that a well-intended message from a good friend can often provide much-needed insight."

"No. Nope. No," he insisted. "We're not close. We met through OSF when she had Pippa audition, but I'm not about to say a single word to her about that dog. No way. I value my life too much."

His response was strange for two reasons. The first was his utter insistence that he and Jax weren't close. Every time I'd seen them as of late, they were together. It was midweek, and they were hanging out at the Glamper having drinks. They'd been together at Puck's on Halloween. Why would he be so adamant that they weren't close?

The second thing that put me on edge was his choice of words. He sounded like he was seriously concerned for his safety and well-being when it came to Jax and her adoration for Pippa. Just how threatened did he feel?

I didn't have a chance to follow up, because Jax returned with their drinks.

"I got you an apple cider this time. The bartender says it's amazing and made from Pink Lady apples here in the valley." She held a fluted glass to her sweatshirt. "Isn't the pink so cute? It matches my look."

"Cool." Perry took the pint from her.

"So have you heard the news?" Jax rested her head between her hands and stared at me with a look that said she was bursting at the seams to share whatever she had heard.

"I don't think so, but—"

She cut me off before I could finish my sentence. "The police have asked Marcia to come to the station. I knew it. I knew it was her all along. That woman is a pathological liar, and she did whatever it took to get George that role. I mean *whatever* it took." She shot Perry a triumphant grin.

Perry looked as confused as I felt.

"Where did you hear that?" I hadn't gotten the impression from either Thomas or the Professor that they considered Marcia a top suspect.

"News in the dog community travels fast." Jax reached for her cider and took a long, deliberate sip.

"Why are the police talking to Marcia?" I tried to keep my tone innocent.

"Because she killed Anton. It's obvious, and it's about time that the police finally catch up with what the rest of us know."

"What do we know?" Perry asked the question that I was thinking.

Jax's shoulders folded over as she twisted her lips into a tight frown. "Why are you being so difficult? We just talked about this before Jules got here. The police are going to arrest Marcia. We all know that she was furious with Anton because he was going to make sure that Pippa was recast in George's role."

"He was?" Now I was even more confused. "But isn't Newell in charge of the animal cast? How would Anton have been able to change the parts?"

"Anton ran the show. Newell might be casting director in title, but it was Anton who called the shots."

This was a revelation.

"Newell followed Anton's orders," Jax continued. "Now that Anton is dead, I've got my work cut out for me if I want to get Pippa in the show."

"There is no chance that Newell is going to cast Pippa." Perry finally added to the conversation. "I'd give it up if I were you."

Every muscle in Jax's face tightened. She glared at him with such negativity that it made me want to disappear into the park. "Oh, he's going to do exactly as I say."

"Given that King George and I already have call times for rehearsals, I wouldn't count on it."

Jax chugged the rest of her cider. She slammed her empty glass down on the table. "Pippa is getting in that show, okay? My advice to you is not to get too comfy with King George, because he's going to be back chasing mutts in the dog park soon. The police are going to arrest Marcia for Anton's murder, and King George is out. Trust me." She stood up. "It's time for me to pick up Pippa. I'll see you guys later."

Perry took slow sips of his cider. "I should get back to the theater. Lance has me reading lines for auditions."

"I'll walk that way with you."

I waited for him to bus their table. Then we fell in stride as we headed toward the plaza.

"So, you're right that Jax is pretty intense about Pippa," I said, choosing my words carefully.

"Yeah, I told you." He kicked a pinecone. "She's intense about everything. That's her thing. If she's not careful, I have a bad feeling that things aren't going to work out well for her."

The Merry Windsor came into view. One of Richard Lord's employees, dressed in pantaloons at least two sizes too big, was repairing a section of faux-wood timbers on the side of the building with duct tape.

Classic.

"What are you worried about?" I asked Perry.

His steps were so long that I had to practically run to keep up with him. "Her mental health. Her stability. Her finances. Everything."

For a minute I thought he was going to say more, but instead, he kicked the pinecone harder, sending it rolling onto the street. "I've got things to do on campus. Catch you later."

He took the Shakespeare stairs three at a time. I watched him for a minute. His nonchalant attitude about his relationship with Jax didn't match his words. If he wasn't close with her, why would he be concerned about her financial and emotional well-being? Not to mention, why were they constantly hanging out? There was no doubt in my mind that they were more than casual acquaintances. What I couldn't figure out was why they both kept insisting otherwise.

I returned to Torte with more questions than answers. The first was whether there could be any truth to Jax's theory that Marcia was about to be arrested. And the second was about Jax herself. Perry hadn't been subtle in his claims that she was obsessed with Pippa. Nothing I had witnessed proved otherwise. What had seemed like a far-fetched theory was suddenly becoming more real. Was it possible that Jax could have committed murder in order to land her poodle a lead role?

# Chapter Fifteen

There was one way to get some answers about Marcia—to go directly to the Professor. I stopped by Torte to box up an assortment of cookies. It never hurt to bring a little buttery bribe.

Was this my way to justify my drop-in?

Absolutely. I knew the Professor had a weakness for cookies in any form. Before he and Mom started dating, I had thought his daily stops into Torte for one of our signature melty chocolate chip cookies or spicy snicker-doodles were an excuse to see her. Which turned out to be true, but his cookie addiction had only become more pronounced since they tied the knot.

Was it also that I was hoping to learn a little inside information? Definitely.

A young cadet was taking down cardboard pumpkins and skeletons when I peered into the reception area.

"Hi, I brought over some treats. Help yourself." I offered the box of pastries. "Is anyone around—the Professor, Thomas, or Kerry?"

The cadet took a chocolate molasses crinkle. "The

Professor and Thomas are out of the office, but Kerry is in the back. Do you want me to call her?"

"That would be great." I kicked myself for not sticking in a couple of our classic jelly-filled donuts—Kerry's favorite.

Kerry emerged from the hallway a minute later with a stack of file folders under one arm. "Hey, Jules, what's going on?"

"I brought over some afternoon treats."

"Out of the goodness of your heart, right?" Her green eyes twinkled.

"Something like that."

"You want to come to my office?" She moved to her right. She and Thomas shared a small office across from the Professor. Otherwise, the station had a temporary holding cell and a reception area, which was more like a glorified welcome center.

Kerry's side of the office was nondescript aside from a few framed photos of her and Thomas from their wedding and honeymoon. Thomas's half of the space was cluttered with stacks of paperwork, books, and at least a dozen coffee cups, each with a varying amount of stale coffee inside. "I would tell you to have a seat at Thomas's desk, but you would have to excavate for days to find his chair."

"You two are proof that the old adage 'opposites attract' is true." I set the box of cookies on her tidy desk.

"Do not get me started on his clutter. Do you have any idea how many collections he has at home?" Kerry lifted the lid and picked a double chocolate chunk cookie.

"Collections?"

"Yep. A Pez collection, comic books, vintage fishing gear. It's so much stuff, but fortunately, I'm a minimalist, so I balance out his stacks of who knows what. The most impressive thing is that he knows exactly where everything is. His piles seem completely random to me, but the system works for him." Kerry brushed a strand of hair from her face and took a bite of the cookie. "I'm guessing you didn't come to talk about Thomas's organizational habits, though."

"I mean, we can commiserate," I said with a sheepish smile. "Carlos has more kitchen gadgets than we had in the *Amour of the Seas* kitchens. I can barely open any drawer or cabinet because they are packed with strawberry slicers and forty different sizes of tongs."

Kerry laughed. "Seeing as how my idea of cooking is opening a can of soup, I didn't even know that there were forty variations of tongs."

"I might be exaggerating a tad." I scrunched my fingers together to make the sign of an inch. "But not much."

She savored another piece of cookie. "Aside from lamenting about pack-rat husbands and dropping off delicious sweets, did you have another reason for stopping by?"

"As a matter of fact, yes. I'm wondering about Marcia."

Kerry's body shifted. It was subtle, but I could tell that she was going into detective mode. "What specifically?"

"I heard that she might have been arrested."

"What?" Kerry didn't hide her emotion as she curled her lip and shook her head. "So that's the rumor going around. You know that I adore Ashland, but sometimes the amount of misinformation that spreads faster than wildfire shocks me."

"So Marcia hasn't been arrested?"

Kerry continued to look incredulous. "No. I can't say that she's not a suspect, because until we make a formal arrest and have concrete evidence, no one is off the list, but I will say that Marcia is not on our radar."

"Good." I felt an unexpected release of tension in my jaw. I hadn't even realized that I had been clenching it in anticipation of Kerry's response. Not that I believed Marcia could be the killer, but hearing confirmation that Mom's dear friend wasn't about to be taken into custody was a glimmer of good news. "That's a relief. I didn't think so. She and Mom have been friends for years. I couldn't imagine her being involved."

Kerry broke the cookie in half. "Unless the Professor or Thomas have uncovered new information or evidence, I would say that Marcia is on the very bottom of our suspect list."

"Do you have any leads?" I knew that she wouldn't—or in fairness couldn't—answer the question, but I had to ask.

"None that I'm in a position to share."

"I understand."

"Thomas mentioned that you were going to speak with Trey." She pulled her coppery hair into a ponytail, being sure to tuck in the strands that fell in front of her eyes.

"I did."

Kerry picked up her yellow legal pad. "Anything you can share?"

I told her about my conversation with Trey and filled her in on what I'd heard from Lance and that Jax had been the source of the rumor about Marcia's impending arrest.

"Interesting. I'll fill Thomas and the Professor in." Kerry made a few notes. "I'll make sure to have a chat with Jax soon."

We talked for a few minutes about holiday plans and how Ramiro was liking school. A call came in for Kerry, which I took as my sign that it was time to leave. On the short walk back to Torte, I felt disappointed that I hadn't learned anything new, but at the same time, it was good to unburden myself of the information I had been carrying around. I didn't know if any of what I had shared with Kerry was connected to the case, but at least the police were looped in and could take it from here.

Mom was waiting by the front door when I crossed the street. "Juliet, you're just in time."

"Where are you heading?" I noted her coat, purse, and cake box.

"Wendy's. She's having a small gathering for some of the cast members who are heading home for the season. Would you like to come?"

"Are you playing mahjong?" I checked my watch. Ramiro had soccer practice and Carlos wasn't due to pick me up for another hour.

"No. She's having light appetizers for happy hour as a goodbye. Janet, Marcia, and Camille will all be there. She told me to invite you."

"Camille? I didn't realize she was part of your group."

"She isn't. Wendy thought it would be nice to extend an invitation since Camille is still relatively new."

I didn't want to pass up a chance to get to know Camille better, especially if there was even the slightest chance that the warning note in Wendy's mahjong set was connected to Anton's murder.

"How is the end of day going?" I motioned to Torte's cheery front windows. "I don't want to leave the team if they need help."

Mom pursed her lips. "As if. They have it under control. Things are running as smooth as a ship through still waters, like usual."

I smiled. "We lucked out with our team, didn't we?"

"Absolutely." Mom looped her arm through mine. "To Wendy's, then?"

"Appetizers sound great."

"I figured you might be hungry, metaphorically speaking," Mom said as we cut through the park.

"You know me too well." I leaned into her shoulder. "I was hoping to get another look at Wendy's mahjong set. Do you know if the Professor took it in as evidence?"

"Not that I know of, but they could have." Mom waved to a couple taking photos of the confetti-like colorful leaves floating in the duck pond. "I will say that Doug does seem to think that it could be more than a coincidence—the note and the dragon costume, but that's a hunch, and as you know, he is by the book when it comes to detective work."

"Do you know Camille?" I was glad that I had opted for a hoodie when I left the house this morning. Cold funneled into the valley from the surrounding Siskiyou Mountains. The pathway along the creek was probably a good five degrees cooler than the plaza.

"Only in passing." Mom turned onto a paved pathway that led underneath a canopy of oak trees. This section of the walk always made me feel like I was stepping into a storybook, with the way the branches twisted together to form an archway. "I've been into the shop a handful of times, and we've made casual conversation. Wendy hinted that Camille might be lonely, which is why I'm glad that she invited Camille to come tonight, but I also wonder if, like us, Wendy has an ulterior motive."

"You mean, Wendy might suspect Camille?"

"Suspect is a strong word. She told me that the two of you stopped in and asked Camille about the set. She was under the impression that Camille's reaction was a bit out of the ordinary."

"I agree." I gave Mom my recollection of our conversation. "She wasn't very talkative to begin with, but the minute Wendy brought up the mahjong set, she got even more closed off and I sensed that she didn't want us asking any more questions."

Mom tucked her hair behind her ears, but it blew in the breeze. "That's what Wendy said, although we both wonder if Camille regrets selling the set to Wendy at such a discounted price. She could have realized that the set is very valuable and worth more money."

"Good point." Although if Camille was skilled at recognizing antiques, that theory didn't hold up. Then again, I still made mistakes when baking, so it could have been that Camille was in a hurry to price the set and get it listed for sale and hadn't done her due diligence.

"It will be nice to get to know her in a social setting," Mom continued.

When we arrived at Wendy's, there were already a dozen people mingling in her cozy cottage. Camille was in the kitchen pouring a glass of wine. Rings with dazzling gems and cut stones adorned her fingers. I wasn't a jewelry expert, but to my untrained eye, they looked expensive.

"Juliet, right?"

"You can call me Jules."

Nice to see you again, Jules," she said, topping off her drink. "Can I pour you a glass?"

"Sure. Thanks." I waited for her to fill one for me. "How are things at the shop?"

"Fine. Why?" Her reply was abrupt, like she was put out that I had asked. She must have realized that she sounded irritated because she twirled a silver tennis bracelet on her wrist and gave me an apologetic smile. "I'm sorry. I guess I'm on edge. I'm sure you were just making casual conversation. This is a party, after all."

"No worries. Is something bothering you? I'm happy to lend a listening ear." That was true, and not only because I was curious if Camille had learned anything about the mysterious original owner of Wendy's mahjong set, but because I had learned the importance of active listening from Mom. Having someone to bounce ideas and worries off without judgment or without them even offering advice had been invaluable to me. If it hadn't been for Mom and other friends who sat with me through breakups and grief and major shifts and changes in my life, I wasn't sure I would have been in Ashland now. I was always happy to reciprocate.

Camille clutched her wineglass with such force that I thought she might shatter it. "It's this whole murder mess. The police have been by the shop asking all kinds of questions. I've told them again and again that I didn't know Anton. He came in the shop a handful of times, but I didn't even know his name until this week."

I wondered if they were following the dragon lead. "Is that because of the mahjong set?"

"Yes." She gulped her wine. "Unfortunately, I haven't been able to trace the owner. I've explained this to the police, but they have gone so far as to ask to see our shop camera footage from the day the set was dropped off through Halloween. It must be a random coincidence, but I will admit that I've been on edge. What if something more nefarious is happening at the shop? I've been scared to open and close on my own. I'm wondering if I need to hire a security guard or at the very least upgrade my surveillance equipment. I moved to Ashland because I thought it was a safe and serene place to slow down as I move into my retirement years, but now I'm wondering if I made a terrible mistake." Her hands trembled as she spoke, sending her wine sloshing from side to side like a tsunami rumbling on shore.

"Ashland is a very safe and serene place to live," I assured her. "Anton's murder was awful, but don't let one isolated event ruin your impression of our little hamlet."

"That's the reason I moved here, but now I'm not convinced. One of the theories the police are exploring is whether Anton's killer could have been using my shop to stash evidence or transport stolen art. I don't have a staff. We are volunteer run, and I learned that one of the volunteers gave him access to our storage area in the back. Who knows what kind of criminal activity could have been going on right under my nose?" Camille tried to lift her glass to her lips, but she was shaking so violently that she ended up spilling the wine down the front of her shirt. "Look at me. I'm a mess. I haven't been sleeping. I haven't been eating." She set her glass on the counter.

I handed her a dish towel and then wet the edge of a sponge for her.

She blotted the wine from her shirt with the sponge and then patted it dry with the towel. "It's unsettling to think that my shop could have a connection to a man's murder. I don't understand what the police are looking for, either. Do they think that someone snuck in and put that note in the mahjong set? Could there be other hidden notes in items throughout the shop? Or worse? Drugs? Guns? They're not telling me anything. I've had half a mind to close the store for the weekend and go item by item to see if there are any other secret notes lying around. It gives me anxiety to think that a killer could have gone through my inventory. And why? The proceeds of the store go to charity. Why would anyone involve us in this?"

"All fair questions." I reached for the wine bottle to refill her glass. "I'm sure the police have their reasons. The one thing I can say with certainty is that the Professor—Doug—is one of the wisest and kindest men I've ever known. I understand that it must be unsettling, but the police have your best interest at heart."

Camille took the wine with shaky hands. She chugged it. "I hope you're right, because at this point, I'm ready to close up shop for good."

"What about the security cameras? Maybe the police can review the footage?"

She unlatched the clasp on her bracelet. "I'm afraid that's a dead end. I did install cameras when I took over the lease, but when the police reviewed the files, there was some kind of a glitch, and all of the footage for the past two weeks is gone."

That was an unfortunate coincidence, to say the least.

Or was it?

Could the killer have intentionally sabotaged the video files in order to remove tangible evidence?

I didn't have a chance to probe further, because a couple of women came into the kitchen, and we became wrapped up in a new conversation. I half listened, trying to keep my attention focused on Camille. Maybe she was overreacting, but she seemed spooked. It made me wonder if she could actually be in danger.

# Chapter Sixteen

After listening to Camille's perspective, I wanted to see the mahjong set more than ever. If there was even the slightest chance that Camille's theory was true and that the killer could have used the hospice shop as their go-to spot for stashing evidence and who knew what else, then maybe Wendy's set did hold the answers to the many questions swirling in my head. The problem was timing. I couldn't interrupt Wendy in the middle of her party and ask to examine her game.

I stole a quick glance at the dining and living room, where guests huddled in front of the fireplace and mingled with festive drinks in hand. Every inch of Wendy's mission-style furniture from the buffet to the coffee table had bowls and platters filled with nuts and crackers and cheeses. Bookcases flanked either side of the fireplace. In between collections of Sherlock Holmes and playbills from nearly every production at OSF in the last two decades, there appeared to be a few game sets. But I couldn't exactly squeeze by and start going through her things.

Mom gave me the perfect excuse a few minutes later

when she swept into the kitchen carrying a tray of appetizers. "Juliet, can you do me a favor and get another tray like this? Wendy said she has two or three more like this in her guest room. Everyone brought appetizers to share, and we're running out of space."

"No problem." I moved through the crowd grazing the gorgeous spread at the dining room table. As I took the two short steps that led down a narrow hallway toward the bedrooms, I noticed the first door on the left swing open and someone race toward the next room. Not just someone, but someone wearing a thick chocolate brown velvet cloak with gold trimming.

It reminded me of the costumes from OSF's production of *The Lord of the Rings* a few years ago.

What was a cloaked stranger doing sneaking around Wendy's private rooms?

Was I imagining things?

I exhaled slowly and tried to rationalize with the irrational side of my brain.

I approached the bedroom. Whoever had run away had left the door partially open. I peered inside to see a ceramic vase shattered on the floor.

This wasn't my imagination.

Someone had been snooping in Wendy's spare room and had broken a vase in the process. What had they been looking for?

I had one guess—the mahjong set.

I looked around the room. There was a four-poster bed with two bedside tables and a matching dresser. A desk in front of a large bay window had the trays that Mom had sent me to find, but no mahjong set.

The guest bed was piled with coats and purses. This must have been the place Wendy had told people to store their belongings. Maybe that was why the person had been in the room. But that didn't explain the broken vase or why they had raced away.

I checked the dresser and bedside tables for the mahjong set. It was nowhere to be seen. Wendy could have hidden it away for the party. Or maybe she stored it in another room for safekeeping. But I couldn't shake the feeling that something else was going on here. My senses were on high alert. Goosebumps spread up my arms and a tingly sensation reached my toes.

Could the mysterious person have taken the set?

What if they grabbed it, broke a vase in the process, and then made a quick getaway?

Was there a chance I had just seen Anton's killer?

*Or are you spinning wild theories, Jules?*

*Probably.*

There was one way to find out. I would have to follow them. They had gone into the next room. Odds were good that a killer wasn't here at Wendy's happy hour party, but that didn't stop my throat from tightening as I closed the door to the guest room and moved to the next room. The door was unlocked. I knew I wasn't in real danger. There were dozens of people just a few feet away in the living room. Of course, between the music playing and the sound of friends chatting happily, if I came face-to-face with a killer, I was going to have to scream.

The room was dark.

I swallowed hard, attempting to silence the tiny voice inside warning me not to go in any farther.

I ran my hand along the wall to find the light switch. When the lights came on, I had to blink for a minute to let my eyes adjust. The room was empty.

Wendy must use this space for crafting. There were bundles of yarn, knitting needles, and a half-finished shawl on a large table in the center of the room. The walls were lined with bookcases that contained collections of books, puzzles, and games. Maybe this was the room where she kept the mahjong set.

I wanted to look through the shelves to see if I could find it, but also to know where the cloaked person had gone. They weren't in the craft room. There was no other place for them to hide. The room didn't have a closet or a bed, or anything large enough for a body.

Was I the one overreacting?

Was I jumping to conclusions?

Thomas was likely right. I had been spending too much time with Lance.

Maybe the person I had seen had simply gone into Wendy's guest room to grab their coat and then had hurried to try and find a bathroom. Maybe they were late for a dinner date. But what about the broken vase?

I was going to have to ask Wendy about that, but first I took a minute to look through the bookshelves for the mahjong set. There were four or five other sets. There were sets with bright red, yellow, and blue plastic tiles and one that had hand-painted tiles and a long and narrow wooden box, but her newest, most valuable set wasn't on any of the shelves.

I sighed and returned to the guest room to get a tray. When I took it to Mom, who was organizing mini quiches and chips and dip in the kitchen, I asked, "Hey, did you see anyone race out of here?"

"Race out?" Mom repeated, looking around the galley kitchen like she expected to see the person.

"Yeah, when I went to grab a tray, I saw a cloaked person in the guest room. They took off like they were running from something or someone. Then I noticed that there was a broken vase in the room. That's why it took me a minute to get this." I offered her the tray.

Mom's walnut eyes narrowed. "That's odd, but I didn't notice anyone making a break for it. However, I've been in here with the food, so they could have left through the front door, and I might not have noticed."

"There's no back exit, either," I said aloud, already knowing the answer.

"There's a door in her garage, but that's on this side of the house." Mom motioned behind her. "You know this house as well as I do."

"I know. Wishful thinking." I sighed. "Let me take that. I want to let Wendy know about the broken vase." I took a tray of cheese, veggies, and bread from Mom.

Wendy and Marcia were chatting in front of the fireplace. I placed the tray on the food table and went to join them.

"I'm so thrilled you could join us tonight, Jules," Wendy said, holding her martini in a toast.

"Me too. Thanks for inviting me." I scanned the bookshelves in hopes that the imported mahjong set might be on display. That would prove that I was leaping to conclusions. But it wasn't here.

"We've been graced by your presence twice. You know

what that means—you're officially part of our game group now." Marcia winked and clinked her martini glass to Wendy's.

"I would love that," I replied, pulling my gaze away from a set of hand-painted floral bookends. I'll try to make room in my schedule for it. Although I can't promise to come every week."

"That's fine. We'll take you anytime you are free." Wendy patted my arm.

"Not to change the subject, but Mom sent me to get a tray from your guest room, and I noticed that a vase had been broken."

Wendy gasped. "A vase? What vase?"

"I'm not sure. I can show you." I motioned to the hallway.

"I hope it's not my Royal Copenhagen vase. I bought that on a cruise decades ago."

Wendy and Carlos had an instant connection when they first met because Wendy had been sailing on boutique ships like the *Amour of the Seas* for as long as I could remember. She documented her oceanic travels for Mom and me, taking pictures of Italian pastries and honey-glazed baklava for inspiration for future Torte menus. She had also amassed a collection of pottery and art on her adventures.

We went to the guest room together.

Wendy placed her hand on her mouth and set her martini on the bedside table. "Oh no. It *is* my Royal Copenhagen." She fell to her knees and begin picking up chunks of the broken porcelain.

"Should I get a broom?"

"It's hanging in the closet at the end of the hallway."

Wendy didn't look up as she tried to piece two large sections of the vase together like a puzzle. "I want to see if I can salvage some of these bigger pieces."

I went to get the broom. I couldn't resist taking a quick peek into her bedroom and the main bathroom. But the cloaked guest who had been in the room before me was long gone. I returned shortly with the broom.

Wendy had managed to collect the largest sections of the vase, but the rest of it had scattered on her hardwood floors in chunks. "It's a lost cause." She got to her feet and stared at the remnants of the vase. "I can't believe that someone broke it and didn't have the decency to come tell me. I wouldn't have been angry, but it's rude, don't you think?"

I nodded and took the dustpan off the broom. "Definitely. I would say it's common courtesy if you break something to let the host know. I can't imagine any of your friends not telling you. Accidents happen."

She tossed the large pieces into the garbage can. "Here, I can sweep up. You don't need to do that."

"No, it's fine. I'm happy to help. I just didn't want to start sweeping if you were going to try and glue it back together."

Wendy shook her head. "I don't think there's enough glue for that."

I swept under the desk. "Hey, is the mahjong set in here?"

"Yes, it's on the dresser. Right next to where the vase was." She turned in that direction. Then she turned back to me and gasped, "Juliet, it's gone. Someone has stolen it."

# Chapter Seventeen

Wendy's wide eyes reminded me of our Halloween ghost macarons. "It's gone. The mahjong set is gone. Someone must have stolen it. I had it right here." She tapped an empty spot on the dresser. "I was going to bring it out later and show everyone."

"You're sure you didn't move it when you were preparing for the party?"

"No. It was right here. I'm positive I didn't touch it," she insisted.

"What about one of the guests? Maybe someone moved it when they came in to drop off their coat or their purse?"

Wendy opened the dresser drawers and began riffling through linens. There was no chance the antique set would fit in any of the drawers, but she searched through each of them anyway. "I suppose one of the guests could have moved it, but why?"

"That I don't know."

"Let's go find out. This party is going to be short-lived. First my vase, now the mahjong set."

I finished sweeping the broken porcelain and then followed her to the living room. She turned down the music and picked up an empty wineglass which she proceeded to ding with a spoon. "Can I have your attention, please?"

Conversations came to a halt. Everyone turned to Wendy as if expecting her to make a speech.

"Did any of you happen to move my mahjong set in the guest room?"

Guests glanced at each other in confusion.

"It's fine if you moved it," Wendy continued. "It's a very valuable set, and I want to make sure it doesn't get damaged."

A few heads shook.

The front door swung open as Wendy was about to speak again. Jax breezed in carrying Pippa in an expensive baby carrier. "Whoa, what's with the somber mood? I thought this was a party."

"You invited Jax?" Marcia asked. She was only a few feet from Wendy, but she said it loud enough for everyone to hear.

"Sorry, uh, I invited her," Perry responded to Marcia's comment. "I was told I could bring a friend."

Jax plastered on a fake smile and moved next to Perry. He and Newell had been talking near the fireplace before Wendy had called for everyone's attention. This was getting weirder by the minute. Why would Perry invite Jax? Given their interaction at the Glamper earlier, I had gotten the impression that things weren't great between them. Plus, Perry had to know that Wendy and Marcia were friends.

Wendy was undeterred. "Listen, I don't have time for this. I need to know if anyone moved the mahjong set in my guest room. It was sitting on top of the dresser."

"What's mahjong?" Jax asked.

Marcia shot her a nasty look. She had scooted closer to me.

"Sorry, Wendy. We'll help you look," someone said.

Mom jumped in to console her friend. "It will turn up. Let's go look through the other rooms." People spread out to search for the missing set.

As the search began, Trey sauntered in the front door. A basket of dog treats tucked under his arm made him instant friends with Wendy's dog, Cooper, and King George, who greeted him with licks and yappy requests for snacks. Trey bent down to greet the pups. "Hey, everyone."

He must have sensed that the party vibe had shifted, because he stood and came over to me and Marcia. "Is everything cool? Why does it look like people are playing some kind of version of hide-and-seek?"

King George trotted after him and sat at Trey's feet, waiting patiently for another treat.

"It's nothing of your concern," Marcia said. She scooped up her dog. "I didn't realize you had been invited."

"What a welcome." Trey's attention drifted to Jax, Perry, and Newell. "I'll go say hi to the puparazzi for a minute."

Marcia lowered her voice, keeping her gaze focused on Jax. "I have a pretty good idea who took it."

"Jax? But she just came in," I said. It was hard to miss an entrance by Jax. Tonight she was dressed in a lemon-yellow-and-black-striped ensemble, as Lance would say. Pippa was strapped to her chest in a baby carrier. I could only see the top of the poodle's head, but in true Jax fashion, her dog wore a matching bumblebee yellow visor.

"Or did she?" Marcia tilted her head toward the front

door. "I swear I saw her earlier and I heard Pippa's high-pitched bark. It's a very distinct sound."

"You think she was at the party earlier, snuck in, stole the mahjong set, and then came casually strolling in through the front door?" Come to think of it, Trey had also fortuitously appeared right after the set had gone missing.

"That is exactly what I think." Marcia turned to tuck George into his basket near the fireplace. "She's studied staging with all of Pippa's auditions and training. I think this is an elaborate ruse that she and Perry are in on together. They're a couple, you know?"

"They are?" I tried to be discreet when I looked in their direction. Perry was pouring glasses of wine at the dining table and chatting with Trey. Jax was standing near the entrance to the kitchen next to Newell. If she and Perry were together, they certainly weren't into any public displays of affection.

"Please, they think they're so secretive, but everyone knows. *Everyone*." Marcia reached for a piece of cheese. Instead of eating it, she broke off a bite for George. "I'm convinced that the two of them killed Anton together."

"How does the mahjong set factor in?" I asked.

Marcia popped the rest of the cheese into her mouth, then cracked her knuckles. "I haven't figured that out yet, but no one can convince me that those two aren't conspiring together. Poor Wendy. I should go see if I can help look for it. Maybe Jax stashed it outside in the bushes."

I knew that Marcia wasn't a fan of Jax, but could she be onto something? Had it been Jax that I'd seen sneaking out of the guest room? If she had been in a hurry to grab the set, she could have broken the vase in the process, and then hidden out in Wendy's craft room until it was clear for her to make a break outside.

But she would have had to go through the living room. There were nearly twenty people gathered. Could she have used the tight quarters and cozy space for her getaway? People had been chatting, eating, and drinking. It was possible, though unlikely, that she could have passed by unseen, especially wearing a heavy cloak. But could she have done so carrying a large antique game box?

I moved in the direction of the kitchen.

Jax was laughing at something Perry said, which must have been incredibly funny, or she was intentionally trying to make a scene.

"What's so funny?" I asked.

"Nothing. Inside joke," Jax said, turning off the laughter as quickly as it had begun. She had removed Pippa from the baby carrier. The dog was now swaddled in a large yellow tote bag at Jax's feet.

I bent down to get a closer look at Pippa's yellow sun visor. Jax yanked the dog away. "Don't touch."

"Sorry."

Jax clutched the tote toward her chest. "She can't be petted right now. She's just been groomed, and you'll ruin her blowout if you pet her. Isn't that right, Newell?"

Newell blended in with the background. He leaned against the door frame and raised his hands in surrender. "I'm not getting any closer to pet her if that's what you're asking."

I pulled my hand away. Was Jax telling the truth? Pippa's black fur did appear to be fluffy, but it was the oversized tote and the way Jax was holding it with a death grip that had me curious. Pippa would fit in most purses. The tote Jax was clinging on to was large enough to pack a Torte picnic feast for six people. Was there another reason Jax had opted for the big bag?

Could Wendy's mahjong set be hiding beneath Pippa's feet?

That would explain why Jax didn't want me to pet the toy poodle.

As Jax spoke, I tried to gauge how heavy the tote was and whether it could hold something the size of Wendy's set.

"What is everyone freaking out about?" Jax stood on her toes to try and see behind me.

"A very valuable game set is missing, and whoever moved it broke an expensive vase." I didn't use the word "steal" on purpose. I wanted to see how the three of them reacted.

"So mahjong is a game?" Jax asked.

I knew she was young, but mahjong was part of popular culture. It seemed strange that she had never heard of it before.

"It's a game," Newell answered in a condescending tone. I wondered how he had convinced anyone at OSF that he was animal lover to begin with. The way he kept his spine glued to the wall and as far away from Pippa as possible would have made it evident to a stranger that he didn't want to be anywhere near the dog.

Jax stuck out her tongue. "What *kind* of a game?"

"It's a bit like Rummikub or cards but played with beautiful tiles that are sort of like dominos," I added.

"I don't know any of those either. The only games I play are on my phone." Jax sounded uninterested. "Are there drinks?"

"In the kitchen." I pointed her in that direction.

Perry went with her.

Newell stayed behind. "It's a shame that Wendy's set is missing. I can't imagine why anyone at the party would want to take it."

"Neither can I. Hopefully it was misplaced and will turn up." I glanced around us. "Have you been here most of the evening?"

"At the party?" Newell wrinkled his brow.

"I mean here in the living room."

"Yeah. Perry and I came together. He and I have been talking shop, which I know you're not supposed to do at a party, but we've got a lot going on at the theater, and I don't know that many other people here." He reached into his pocket and removed a black handkerchief. Then he dabbed his nose. "My allergies won't let up. I had no idea the Rogue Valley had such a robust fall pollen season."

"Neither did I." Why was Newell still pretending that his allergies were from trees rather than Pippa?

"Did you happen to see anyone go in or out of the front door?"

He thought about my question for a minute before answering. "I don't think so, why?"

I wasn't sure how much information I wanted to share, particularly if Wendy's set didn't show up and was in any way connected to Anton's murder. "I thought I saw someone leaving right before Jax showed up. I've been waiting for a friend and had been helping in the kitchen so was hoping I didn't miss her."

"You know, come to think of it, there was someone." He stifled a sneeze with his handkerchief.

"Do you remember who?"

Newell shook his head. "I didn't recognize them."

"Was it a woman?"

"No, I don't know. I'm not sure. That's what triggered the memory. Someone did come past us. They had a heavy hood up over their head, though, so I couldn't see them. I thought it was strange, but like I said, Perry and I were in the middle of a conversation about auditions. I figured maybe they were heading outside and put their hood up in anticipation of rain." He stuffed the handkerchief back into his pocket.

*The cloak.*

*It had to be the cloaked stranger I saw.*

"That's probably it," I said to Newell.

Perry, Jax, and Trey returned with glasses of wine. If Trey thought that Perry and Jax had anything to do with trying to sabotage his business with King George's bad dye job, why was he hanging out with them?

Mom waved at me from the dining table. "I should go see if I can help," I said to the three of them, and made my exit.

"Any luck finding the set?" I asked Mom.

She shook her head. "We've looked in every closet, nook, cranny, even the bathtub. It's not here."

"Suddenly, the coincidence of the note and Anton's death isn't feeling very coincidental, is it?"

"That's why I tried to get your attention. I promised Wendy I would help her look through the garage. Would you mind letting Doug know what's going on? My phone is buried under a dozen purses, and Wendy is pretty upset, so I want to be with her."

"Of course. I should head back to Torte, anyway. Carlos is picking me up soon. I'll call on my way, and if I don't get through, I'll swing into headquarters before we go home."

"Thanks, honey." Mom kissed my cheek. "Be careful out there. It's already dark, and I have a bad feeling about this."

"I'll stay on high alert and have my phone at the ready." I took my phone out of my pocket as proof that I was taking her warning to heart.

"Will you ask Doug to come by when he can? I'll see you tomorrow."

I left the party with more questions than answers. There was one thing I was sure of now: I hadn't been imagining things or jumping to conclusions. Someone had stolen the valuable mahjong set, and I had a feeling that was because they knew it linked them to Anton's murder.

# Chapter Eighteen

It was getting dark earlier, another sign that winter would soon be upon us. I didn't linger in the park. I couldn't imagine the killer coming after me, but then again, I never would have imagined that Anton would turn up dead in front of Torte amidst all of the Halloween activity on the plaza. No way. I wasn't taking any chances. Instead of following the trail through the park, I opted for the longer route, which kept me on sidewalks the entire way.

Unfortunately, the police office was closed and dark. I called the Professor instead. He didn't answer, so I left him a message explaining that Wendy's mahjong set had been stolen and that Mom could tell him the rest.

Carlos texted to tell me he was on his way, so I waited in front of the bakeshop. It was nice to have a moment to reflect on what I had learned thus far. I wished I had asked Newell directly about the rumors that he didn't like dogs. His sneezing fit had been the perfect opportunity. It was obvious that he was allergic. I should have taken the chance at Wendy's, but I'd been so intent on finding out who the mysterious person sneaking around her house had been that it completely slipped my mind. I would have to try and track him down tomorrow and see if I could determine whether the rumors were true.

Then there was Perry. While he didn't have a clear motive, he was always around and yet seemed checked out, somehow. He gave the impression of being aloof and uninterested in anything except for his appearance, but I didn't think that was true. He was trying too hard to pretend he wasn't listening to conversations. When he did speak up or interject, it was obvious that he heard every word. I wasn't sure if that was simply his personality or if it was an act. He was a professionally trained actor, after all.

Jax was my current top suspect, but that didn't mean she was the killer. It was equally possible that she was simply obsessed with Pippa's future stardom. The concept was foreign to me, but clearly, there was an entire dog culture that I didn't understand. Yet why had she yanked Pippa away? Could she have been hiding the mahjong set in plain sight? Usually she was begging people to fawn over her poodle. Why the sudden shift?

I couldn't rule out Camille either. She was the most connected to the mahjong set. Although I still had no proof that the warning note and Anton's murder were tied together. The fact that the set had gone missing made me more convinced that they were.

The last person on my list was Trey. He was immersed in the drama with Jax. He had been responsible for King George's purple tail. Was he telling the truth that someone (perhaps Perry) had swapped the dye? Or was that lie to take me off the scent? It was an odd coincidence that he had shown up when he had, and why would he be casually sipping wine with the two people he claimed had tried to ruin his business?

There was an outside possibility that he had been who I had seen in the cloak. Perhaps he had grabbed the set, made his exit unseen, and then strolled back inside as if nothing had happened. It was a clever trick and gave him an automatic alibi. But why? Unless he was lying, he seemed genuinely distraught that King George's purple tail would ruin his reputation. I had to be missing something.

I sighed as Carlos pulled up to the curb. I needed to give it a rest.

"Mi querida, I hope you were not waiting too long."

"Not at all." I buckled my seat belt.

"Good. I have a surprise for you."

"A surprise? What is it?"

"It would not be a surprise if I told you." Carlos's eyes twinkled with mischievous delight. "We need to swing by the house to change first."

Now I was really intrigued. "What should I wear to this surprise?"

"Something nice, but not formal, and warm. Very warm."

He refused to give me any more details while we changed out of our work clothes. I opted for a pair of black leggings, knee-high boots, and a long soft gray sweater.

"You look perfect." He had swapped the jeans he wore to prepare the vineyard for winter with another pair of deep blue denim jeans and a cream cable knit sweater that made his eyes look even more deliciously dark, like rich chocolate.

"Are you going to give me a clue as to where we're going? And what about Ramiro?"

"He is staying with a friend tonight, and no. If you are a good sleuth, then you will figure it out yourself."

I nudged him in the waist. "That's not fair."

"Nothing is fair in love and war, as they say, or don't say." He winked.

"Are we at war?"

He kissed the top of my head. "Never." Then he offered his hand. "Let's go. We don't want to be late."

I tried to guess the surprise as Carlos steered the car past SOU and turned onto Siskiyou Boulevard heading south, away from the plaza. Were we going to Mom and the Professor's house? They lived out by Emigrant Lake. After we had passed the handful of restaurants and the small shopping complex on the south side of town, I had a feeling we must be heading for the lake or else Carlos had plans to take me up to the lodge at Mount A, but I didn't think the lodge was open yet. Ski season was still a few weeks away.

"Are we going to Mom's?" I asked, but as I did, I realized while we were at Wendy's, she hadn't mentioned anything about dinner or getting together.

"Nope."

"But we're going toward the lake."

"Sí." Carlos's impish grin told me he wasn't going to give me any hints.

We drove past the golf course and along the dark highway that was surrounded by small family farms on one side and sweeping hillsides to the other. There wasn't much to see at this hour. Streetlights every few hundred feet were the only lights around, other than the expanse of stars overhead. The moon was full, giving the illusion that it was double its normal size.

Carlos pulled into the gravel lot at Emigrant Lake.

"I was right. We are going to the lake. Why?"

"You'll see." He got out of the car and then went around to the back to get blankets, a flashlight, a thermos, and a reusable grocery bag.

There was a strong smell of woodsmoke in the air. One of the farms nearby must have been burning a fire. I loved the ashy aroma.

"Do you need a hand with all of that?" I asked.

He gave me one of the blankets. "Take this. I'll get the rest."

I waited for him to balance everything.

"This way." He pointed his flashlight to illuminate a pathway worn through the gravel. It led uphill to the top of the reservoir above Emigrant Lake. A town had once sat where the still lake waters rested today. In the 1920s a small lake was created to help irrigate the fertile farmland of the Rogue Valley. Decades later, in the 1960s, the Army Corps of Engineers constructed dams on the higher lakes, flooding the town completely and burying any evidence of its existence under hundreds of feet of water.

I'd always found Emigrant Lake to be both serene and slightly creepy. There was something eerie about swimming in the lake on a hot summer day, knowing that somewhere deep below your feet lay long-abandoned houses and gas stations.

"What are we doing at the lake?" I asked Carlos as we crested the trail.

"We are going to a bonfire." He stopped and nodded toward the lake. "Lance calls it the Birnam Wood bonfire."

That's where the smell of fire was coming from. On the banks of the lake, someone had started a bonfire. There were chairs circling the crackling flames and music playing. I had completely forgotten about the Birnam Wood post-Halloween bonfires of my youth. My parents used to take me to celebrate the end of the season. Dad, the Professor, and a bunch of their friends from the Midnight Club had started the tradition. In *Macbeth,* Macduff's army conceals themselves with branches in Birnam Wood, creating the illusion that the wood is alive and moving. The witches warn Macbeth that he will be defeated when Birnam Wood arrives in Dunsinane, and indeed he is.

To symbolize turning the theater dark, actors, playwrights, technicians, directors, and anyone in the company, along with family and friends were invited to the lake to burn branches of wood beneath a swath of stars. It was a great excuse to continue the Halloween celebrations. There was always food and drink, and usually a reading from *Macbeth.*

"It's been years since I came to a Birnam Wood bonfire."

"I was told this is what you would say. Lance wants to revive the tradition." Carlos positioned the flashlight so I could see. "Be careful. Watch your step going down."

We inched our way down the rocky shoreline. A trio of actors strummed guitars. There were card tables loaded with food, wine, beer, and jugs of apple cider. Aside from the bonfire, which had to be at least six feet tall, the only light was from candles and the stars overhead.

"Finally, the soirée can begin. Our guest of honor has arrived." Lance bowed as if he were being introduced to the queen when he came to greet us.

"Why am I the guest of honor?" I asked, looking around the fire to see many familiar faces from OSF, including Newell.

"Darling, you're always the guest of honor."

"I don't understand." I turned to Carlos. "It's not my birthday or anything."

"Details, details," Lance replied with a dismissive wave. "We are reviving the tradition, and since you are a Capshaw, you are our honored guest this lovely evening."

"Thanks. What does that mean?" I tried not to sound too distrusting, but this was Lance.

"Uh, what kind of an ungrateful response is this?" He rolled his eyes and stared at Carlos, hoping to loop my husband into his antics. "We simply intend to pamper you all evening." He paused for a brief second and then smashed his words together so I could barely decipher what he was saying. "Perhaps have you perform a quick skit or passage from *Macbeth*."

"I'm sorry, what did you say? Perform a skit?"

"Think of the bonfire as our Hasty Pudding, and you are being recognized as woman of the year, as you should be. I've decided to level up the event. Adding some new special touches while reviving the *Burn 'Em* Woods tradition, get it?" He waited for us to laugh at his play on words.

"Hasty Puddings, what is this?" Carlos asked.

"It's Harvard's annual master class in theatrics," Lance promptly replied, not giving me an opportunity to protest. "We have a bit of a roast planned for our dearest Juliet and maybe a wig or two."

"Wait, what?" I didn't like the sound of this.

Lance proceeded to offer up a coifed white wig straight from the royal court. It stood at least two feet tall on its own.

"You want me to wear that for a bonfire?" A troupe of ghosts in flowing white sheets twirled around the giant flames, tossing new logs onto the ever-growing fire.

"Only if you want to, darling," Lance cooed.

I gave him the pleasure of taking a few pictures of me posing in front of the fire with the ridiculous wig before abandoning it in favor of a hot toddy and a ham and ched-dar hand pie. Logs were constantly added to the bonfire, keeping the heat radiating in every direction and smoke circling up to the stars.

Arlo finally stepped in and saved me from Lance. "Give her a break, dearest." He shooed Lance over to refill their drinks. "How are you, Jules?"

"I'm okay, thanks for asking. How are you?"

"Okay is a good description. Not only the recent turn of events, but as you know, Lance is committed to continu-ing to revolutionize the theater. That's why he has pushed the board to hire me permanently. I don't have to tell you that OSF has been ahead of its time. We've produced groundbreaking works and given voice to playwrights, actors, and directors from all backgrounds. Our focus on equity is unmatched. The next phase of our vision is exciting and . . ." He paused to blow out a breath. "Well, daunting. Digital theater, pushing boundaries even more, expanding and centering BIPOC stories. Obviously, as a Black man in this industry, it's a mission that I have helped spearhead and something that deeply resonates with me. Pardon the pun, but as much as I embrace the di-rection we're taking the company, I'm responsible for the theater's fiscal well-being, and I'm concerned that Lance could be biting off more than he can chew."

"Lance has never been one to take the easy route or shy away from doing hard things," I replied, watching Lance join in a group sing-along of "Ophelia."

Arlo massaged his bald head. "True. That's what I love about him, but reining him in, that's another issue entirely, especially when I'm responsible for things like OSF's annual budget."

"Right." I winced. "I don't know how to help you there."

"You don't need to. I appreciate you listening and being such a good friend to Lance. He might brush it off, but he would be lost without you."

I leaned in to hug him. "He's so lucky to have *you*." Arlo arriving in Ashland had been the best thing for Lance. He might have been worried about not being able to temper Lance's expectations, but I knew without a doubt that Lance would listen to Arlo's guidance and wisdom. He had a natural ability to balance Lance's grandiose plans without shattering his dreams.

Carlos pulled Arlo into a conversation about the upcoming soccer playoffs, so I moved over to Newell. "Hey, long time no see. How are the allergies?"

"Fine. Dry air out here by the lake helps." He cleared his throat as if remembering that he had been sneezing when I saw him at Wendy's. "Yeah, it's from one party to the next right now, but it's not going to last long."

"Why is that?"

"It's the end of the season. From what I've heard, Ashland turns into a theater ghost town starting next week. Half the cast are already boarding planes for New York and LA."

He wasn't wrong about that. Members of the company had been performing the same shows since March. The fact that actors could tap into energy that kept a show fresh and the audience cheering after a hundred matinee and evening performances of *Macbeth* or *King Lear* never failed to amaze me. When the lights went dark in the Bowmer and Elizabethan, many of the cast and crew seized the chance to travel for a few months. During the season they rarely had more than a day or two off. Just enough time for a quick trip to the beach but not enough for a true getaway. There was a mass exodus that occurred after Halloween. It was like a great migration. Actors packed up their belongings and headed out in search of bright lights and big cities or to their hometowns in the off season. The vast majority of the company wasn't from the Rogue Valley, a fact that often surprised theatergoers.

"That's true," I said to Newell. "Ashland will be fairly quiet for the next couple of months."

"Fine by me. I'm done with this place."

He had given me an in, and I took it. "You're not returning for next season?"

"Nope. I can't take any more of the unprofessionalism and backstabbing. I'm out of here." He wasn't mincing his words.

"It has seemed like there's been some angst about casting, for sure."

"Angst? That's putting it nicely." He kicked a chunk of bark into the bonfire. "If I had known what this job was before signing my contract, I never would have taken it."

"Is it that bad?"

"Worse." The flames reflected in Newell's eyes, making him look like a cartoon villain. "It's a good thing I'm on a temporary contract. I've been applying for jobs every-where. I've got to get out of this town. It's way too small, and everyone is way too connected to the theater."

"Where will you go?"

"Hopefully LA. Maybe New York. I'm putting feel-ers out."

"Are jobs like yours hard to come by?"

"You mean casting directors?"

"For pets," I pushed.

Newell scoffed. "No. I'm not working with dogs ever again." He must have realized that he had revealed more than he wanted, because he backpedaled. "I—I—I mean, I am hoping to take a step up in my career."

"It must be challenging to work with animals," I said, willing him to keep talking.

"You have no idea." He kicked the ground again. "It's the pet owners as much as it is the animals. I can deal with cleaning up dog poop more than I can deal with the poop that gets hurled at me by some of their owners."

I caught Carlos's gaze across the fire and gave a slight shake of my head to warn him not to interrupt. I was so close to learning the truth about Newell. I didn't want the moment to disappear.

"I could tell you stories for days, but you wouldn't be-lieve them."

"Try me." I wrapped my arms around my chest, not to give the impression that I was trying to close off from him but because my fingers were cold and turning into Pop-sicles.

Newell looked like he was about to say more, but then he stopped himself. "Uh, I should get going. I'm late for another party."

He took off without another word. I glanced in the direction he had been looking when he cut himself off. Lance and Arlo were chatting with Jax and Perry. Was that why Newell hadn't finished what he was going to tell me? If he was interviewing with other theaters, he probably needed a recommendation from Lance. He probably couldn't risk letting his secret, which wasn't so secret, out yet.

He didn't bother to say goodbye to anyone. Instead, he jogged up the steep bank and vanished into the darkness.

I wished I had gotten official confirmation from him about his pet allergies and his apparent loathing of working with furry cast members. He hadn't admitted it, but he had come pretty close. And he hadn't been shy about wanting to get out of Ashland as fast as possible. Could there be another reason behind him intending to make a quick escape?

"Penny for your thoughts, darling." Lance's smooth voice interrupted the swirl of questions running in my head.

"A penny doesn't go very far these days."

"True. True. A gold coin, perhaps?" He pretended to press an imaginary coin into my palm. "I saw you attempting to pry valuable information out of Newell. Do tell, were you successful?"

"Not exactly." I told him what I had learned.

"Ah, so he's jumping ship. He has yet to inform yours truly of his impending departure."

"Maybe he's waiting until he's been officially hired with another theater."

"Perhaps. Word could have gotten around that he was about to get the boot." Lance tapped his chin with his finger. "Or perhaps your last theory is correct. If I'd had a hand in Anton's death, I'd be racing for the hills too."

"Except in this case, the hills are major metropolitan areas."

He flicked the air with his finger. "Details, darling, details. Stick with me. We're narrowing in on the killer. I can feel it in my bones."

"I think what you're feeling is the cold."

"Always the pragmatist, aren't we?"

"I can barely feel my fingers." I rubbed my hands together to prove my point.

Lance stepped closer to the fire. "It's much warmer here. Come join me. I have one bit of *news* to share."

We were inches away from the four-foot flames, which gave off more heat. I held out my hands and waited for Lance to continue.

He gave a subtle nod to Jax and Perry. "I caught those two in a passionate embrace earlier."

"Jax and Perry?"

"They are most definitely getting cozy. I came upon them by complete happenstance. Quite fortuitous, don't you think? They broke apart and went red in the cheeks. As if I care."

"So they're a couple for sure?" I watched orange flames devour the branches. Crackling sparks shot into the darkness like tiny fireflies, lighting up the night sky. Were Jax and Perry a couple? It made sense, but what I couldn't wrap my head around was why Perry was so insistent that they were just friends.

"Yes, but the question becomes, why the secrecy?" Lance sounded as perplexed as I felt. "It's hardly as if there's a policy at OSF about dating. Well, there is when it comes to dating within the cast or company at large, but Jax isn't attached to the theater."

"She wants to be, though." I picked up my hot toddy and cradled it in my hands.

"Nailed it." He pressed his finger to the tip of his nose. "As I said, I think we're closing in on a killer—or killers."

# Chapter Nineteen

I sucked down my drink wrong. "You think Perry and Jax killed Anton together?"

Lance patted my back as I choked.

"Not so loud, darling, you never know who might be listening." He pressed his index finger to his lips. "Jax reeks of desperation. We've established that she'll do anything to get Pippa onstage. Now that we've confirmed that she and Perry are an item, it seems very plausible that she could have roped him in on taking out the one person who stood in the way of her ultimate goal."

"Anton." I blinked, not only because I was mesmerized by the fire, but also because Lance might be onto something with his theory.

Lance nodded. "Anton was blunt in his feedback about Pippa. I got ahold of his casting notes, and let me tell you, he didn't hold back."

"You saw his notes?"

"He eviscerated Pippa. It was brutal. I mean, don't get me wrong, I thoroughly enjoyed every minute of reading his notes, but he said—in writing—that the dog isn't fit for any stage. Not just the OSF stages. He went on to say that he didn't believe Pippa to be purebred and that, without hours and hours of consistent training, he saw no future for Jax's beloved pooch when it came to acting."

"Really?" I watched a group of our fellow bonfire goers tear off their shirts and shoes and sprint toward the lake. Even during the heat of summer, the lake ran cold. It was fed from high alpine waters. I couldn't imagine taking the plunge tonight.

Lance grimaced. "It was so biting that it almost made me feel sorry for Jax. I mean, if I had read the same notes about my pampered pup, I might have murdered him."

"That does give her motive. Why do you think Perry is involved, though? Do you think she talked him into helping her? Or do you think he's a silent witness, like he knows that she did it but he's protecting her?"

"Either option doesn't put him in good light, does it?"

"No." I sighed and held my hands closer to the flames. They had warmed some. "The problem is that we need proof. From what I understood, Perry was on the float with King George and then they were signing autographs and meeting fans at the hotel at the end of the parade. When could he have done it?"

"That is the question. Unless Jax did the deed on her own and Perry is covering for her." Lance reached into his coat pocket and pulled out a bag of dark chocolate mints. "Contraband leftover from Halloween. Want one? Don't let Arlo see."

"You're hiding candy from Arlo?"

"He thinks I have a chocolate problem. The nerve." Lance crammed a handful of chocolates into his mouth. "Do we know the time of death? If Anton was killed later, then Perry could have done it after he finished signing photos."

"True." I hadn't asked the Professor, Thomas, or Kerry about the time of death. I thought back to Halloween night. "How long was Perry at the hotel? Carlos and I discovered Anton's body on our way to meet you and Arlo for dinner, but that had to be at least an hour and a half or two hours after the parade."

"I'll have to check with the publicity department tomorrow. I don't know off the cuff, but cast appearances don't tend to last more than a half hour. Maybe an hour at the most. All the more reason to suspect Perry. Unless he got caught up in a conversation with a superfan. I've had my fair share of issues getting away from my rabid fan base."

"I'm sure you have." I shook my head and suppressed a laugh.

"What, darling? You have to give the people what they want."

"And they want you?"

He ran his hand from his shoulder down his torso. "Need I say more?"

I rolled my eyes. "Okay, this gives us a direction. You check with publicity on how long Perry was slotted for the signing. I'll see if I can get a firm timeline on when Anton was killed."

"That's my Watson." Lance patted my shoulder.

"Wait a minute, I'm Watson? *You're* Watson."

He sucked in a breath as if I had just punched him in the gut. "I beg to differ. I'm most certainly Sherlock."

Carlos and Arlo came over to us. Carlos offered to refill our drinks. "What are you two bickering about?" He untwisted the lid on the thermos.

"Your dearest wife is disillusioned."

"I am not. Lance is under the impression that I'm his sidekick, and I want you two to correct him immediately."

Arlo held his cup for Carlos to top off. "I'm not touching this with a ten-foot pole. Why don't you call a truce and shake hands like real partners?"

Lance scrunched his face and stared at me like we were in an Old West battle and he was waiting to see who would draw their weapon first.

"Fine. Partners." I extended my hand.

"Partners." Lance shook my hand, then he yanked me into a half hug and whispered, "Watson."

"Did you hear that?"

"Break it up, break it up." Arlo stepped between us and wrapped his arm around Lance. "That's our cue to go mingle more. This is your bonfire."

"You two are best friends," Carlos said as Lance and Arlo moved away.

"Or mortal enemies." I glared at Lance's back.

Carlos tightened the thermos lid and motioned to two empty chairs. "We should sit and finish our drinks. Have you eaten anything?"

"I had a little bite when we first got here, but suddenly I'm famished again, and I'm guessing a handful of Lance's candy stash doesn't count as dinner, does it?"

"No, mi querida." He unpacked savory hand pies and another thermos with soup.

"You brought perfect food for a bonfire."

"Lance told me what would be best." He poured the soup into a camp mug.

"Does it bother you?"

"What?"

"My friendship with Lance?"

"No. Why would it bother me? I love that he loves you the way he does."

"You're a good guy, you know? Some men would be threatened." When Carlos had made the decision to leave the *Amour of the Seas* and live in Ashland permanently with me, I had been worried that he might be intimidated by my relationship with Lance. Nothing had been further from the truth. Carlos had embraced the family I had created here in Ashland, Lance included. It made me happy to know that he wasn't interested in keeping me small. That he understood that our capacity to love grows with each person we let into our lives.

Carlos caressed my hand when he gave me a spoon for my soup. "I would never want you to take away from your other friendships for me."

"I know. That's one of the many reasons I love you." I practically inhaled the soup and a second hand pie. I couldn't believe how hungry I was. Between the cold wind kicking up from the lake and the long day, I fell into an almost dreamlike state, watching the bonfire crackle and people dance and sing.

We were so lucky to be a part of this community. Of course, I regretted that thought shortly because Lance demanded that I don the wig and join in the dance. How could I refuse? Carlos and I bounced to the beat of the music, dancing and singing along with everyone until the last log burned out. We left long past the witching hour. I knew that I might pay for our late night the next day, but I didn't care. It was worth it.

# Chapter Twenty

The next few days passed without any new developments in the case. I was able to confirm with Kerry that Anton had been killed sometime between six and eight the night of the murder, but otherwise between my duties at Torte, Ramiro's last home soccer match, and closing the outdoor tasting room at Uva for the season, I didn't have extra time to dig any further into Anton's murder. Fortunately, by the end of the week, things had slowed down.

My team and I gathered around the kitchen island to plan the next Sunday Supper.

"Should we stick with a dark and stormy theme?" Sterling asked. He had a notebook at the ready and a pencil tucked behind his ear. "Rain and wind are in the forecast for next Sunday."

"What if we do magical potions to go along with that theme?" Steph added as she scooped luscious cream cheese frosting into a piping bag.

"Magical potions, tell me more." I appreciated that my staff thought out of the box and constantly came up with new ideas to keep our monthly dinners fresh. Sterling had recently suggested a pasta and poetry night for our Sunday Supper, which had been a huge hit. We had decided to make it an annual tradition.

"You know, like, lean into the dark and stormy night concept. Flickering candles, witchy food, like layered potion puddings, mocktails, punch with dry ice." Steph twisted the piping bag closed. "Maybe a spooky post-Halloween tale."

Marty let out a boisterous laugh. "Ba-ha-ha."

Bethany jumped. "You actually startled me."

"That's the goal." Marty turned a dish towel into the form of a ghost. "It will be a Torte Spooktacular."

"Any menu ideas?" I asked.

"I've been wanting to put my own spin on a recipe I saw for a rustic stew. We could level it up by serving it in a cauldron." Sterling showed us the sketches in his notebook.

"Yum." Bethany smacked her lips together. "We could do dark chocolate desserts along with the potion puddings to bring in the dark part of our stormy night."

"I can do you one better," Marty said with a sinister grin that was clearly for show. It was nearly impossible for his jovial face to be anything but upbeat. "I have a recipe for Russian black bread. It's got rye and cocoa and a touch of fennel seeds, which I think could work with a stew."

"I'll do a kale salad with fall root vegetables." Sterling made a note.

"It sounds like perfection to me." I addressed the team, taking a few notes. "Does anyone know a good ghost story?"

"I know someone who would absolutely die to tell a ghost story." Steph had inserted a star tip. She proceeded to swirl the cream cheese buttercream on the top of black raspberry cupcakes with such ease it didn't even seem like she was paying attention to what she was doing.

"I have a feeling I know who you're going to suggest." I pretended to brace myself for the news.

"It has to be Lance." Steph kept her focus on her work. "He's a fabulous storyteller. The theater is dark. You should ask him if he'll do it."

"Oh, he'll do it," I replied with confidence. Lance would never turn down an opportunity to perform, even if it was for a couple of dozen dinner guests at our Sunday Supper. "I think they're finishing auditions today. I'll head up to campus later and ask him."

Bethany clapped. "Awesome. Steph and I can work on invites, and I'll get posts up on our social. I'm sure we won't have any problem selling out."

Because our suppers were intimate and served family-style around a shared table, we could only accommodate about twenty guests. It made the monthly events popular and highly sought after. When tourists were in town, locals sometimes had trouble securing tickets, so I had a feeling that Bethany was right. Our regulars would probably scramble to snag seats, especially if Lance agreed to tell a ghost story or two.

After we finalized the menu, I decided there was no time like the present to go see if Ashland's most beloved artistic director would lend his talent to our dinner. The weather had shifted. Heavy clouds rumbled over the mountains, threatening rain. I cinched my coat tighter and hurried past the Merry Windsor Hotel. I stopped in midstride when I spotted someone who bore an uncanny resemblance to Lance shaking hands with Richard.

Was that Lance?

He took off for the Shakespeare stairs before I could get a closer look. What would Lance be doing at the Windsor?

I picked up my pace again, but I wasn't fast enough to escape Richard Lord. He caught my eye and bent his index finger to signal me over. We all joked that Richard must seriously believe he was holding court on the rickety porch that led into the hotel. He spent a good chunk of every day outside, watching people pass by and harassing me and anyone he could engage in conversation.

"Capshaw, where are you going?" he bellowed.

"I don't know how that's any of your business, Richard."

"Why? You have something to hide?"

"What would I have to hide?"

"I've seen you sneaking around town. I know that you're meddling in the police's murder investigation and spying on me and my staff."

Richard had been convinced since the day I returned to Ashland that I was secretly obsessed with him. Nothing could have been further from the truth. I could have cared less what happened at the crumbling Merry Windsor Hotel.

"Nope. Not sneaking. Just heading up to campus."

"What do you have going on with Lance?"

"Look, Richard, it's cold." I rubbed my arms. "Did you need something? Because if not, I don't have time to stand around playing the same game we play every time."

"It's not a game, Capshaw. This is business, and in this town, it's either kill or be killed."

"Whoa." I threw my arms up. "That's dark, even for you."

"You know what I mean."

"I really don't."

"You and Lance are up to something again. I've heard murmurings."

Murmurings? That was a new one.

"I'm keeping my eye on you, Capshaw. Be warned."

I gave him a salute. "Got it. Thanks so much for the heads-up." I raced away before he could say more. Why did Richard care what Lance and I were up to? And where had he heard that? Were we being obvious? I hadn't seen Lance since the bonfire, and I had barely left Torte, with the exception of heading to Uva to help Carlos put away the outdoor furniture for the winter. Richard was probably just fishing. He had to be in the know about anything and everything that was happening in Ashland.

The only thing that was slightly worrying was if Richard was aware that Lance and I were looking into Anton's murder, the killer could be too. That might put us in danger. We needed to make sure we were careful.

Trey was outside on the bricks when I crested the Shakespeare stairs. I was surprised to see him.

"Are you doing on-site grooming?" I asked as I approached him.

He had a Wizard of Paws hoodie on and a fanny pack secured around his waist. The pack was unzipped, revealing a pair of shears and nail clippers. "Yeah, something like that." He didn't seem pleased to see me.

Jax came down Pioneer Street at the same time. She froze, her eyes darting from Trey to me and then back again. "Oh, I didn't know you were with someone."

Trey fiddled with his fanny pack. "I'm waiting for you."

Jax gulped as if she was choking on air. "I . . . uh, I . . .

uh, thought we were meeting at Wizard of Paws." She tapped the top of Pippa's head. Pippa was tucked into a baby carrier on Jax's chest. If I had passed by her quickly, I probably wouldn't have registered that there was a dog in the carrier instead of an infant.

"No. We're meeting here, *remember*?" The way Trey emphasized "remember" made me suspect that he was speaking in some kind of a code.

Jax wasn't breaking the code. She squinted. "Huh?"

"You told me to meet you here for the special grooming session before Pippa's audition, remember?" Trey's fingertips were robin's-egg blue. I recognized the look. It happened to new decorators when they opted not to wear gloves when working with food-safe dyes.

"Oh, the audition. Right, the audition. I guess I'm so excited about Pippa finally getting her big break that I'm a bit of a space cadet." Jax laughed at herself and came over to us.

"Pippa is auditioning?" I asked.

"She is. I'm sure it's simply a formality. Her days as an understudy are numbered. They have to make her jump through hoops—literally and figuratively—in order to be in alignment with equity contracts, but the part is hers. Isn't it, Pips?" She nuzzled Pippa's head and cooed.

"What part is she auditioning for?" I asked.

"The part she was meant to play all along." She didn't take her eyes off Pippa. "You didn't hear? King George had an issue and won't be able to perform. They've asked Pippa to step in in his absence."

They had? This was news to me.

"We should probably get her ready." Trey took out his shears. "How much do you want me to take off?"

"I'll leave you to it," I said, turning toward the Bowmer but trying to keep my steps light in order to eavesdrop. I couldn't be sure, but I thought I heard Trey whisper, "That was close," as I headed into the theater.

Was there another reason for their meetup?

And why had Jax been spooked when she saw me?

Could they be plotting against King George? What if Trey's story about the dye job being a mistake and suspecting that Perry had tampered with George's conditioner was just that—a story? That would explain why he had been hanging out with them. The three of them could have conspired together.

Lance and Newell and Marcia had been so adamant that Pippa wasn't in the running for the part. Had something changed, or was Jax lying? Most importantly, why had King George dropped out? Marcia hadn't given any indication that she was going to turn down the role. Plus, the show didn't premiere for another four months. Why would Marcia pull George from the production now?

It didn't make sense.

A new thought invaded as I headed in the direction of Lance's office. What if something had happened to Marcia's best buddy? Jax had merely said that George had an "issue." What kind of issue?

As soon as I checked in with Lance about the Sunday Supper and anything else he might have heard about Anton's murder the past couple days, I was going to call Marcia and make sure that King George was okay.

I rapped on Lance's door.

"It's open. Come in," he responded in a singsong voice. He sat behind an intimidating desk made for a king, looking through a stack of glossy headshots. "What an un-expected and delightful surprise. Do come in."

I shut the door behind me and took a seat across from him.

"What brings you to my humble abode?"

"Your humble abode? Is anything about you humble, Lance?" His office walls were lined with accolades and awards. His swanky space felt more like a lounge, with its leather furniture; a mini bar with cocktail shakers, fancy glasses, and top-shelf gin; and a wardrobe to house his col-lection of suits and ascots.

"Ouch." He pretended to stab himself. "Why so snippy, darling?"

"You know I'm kidding." I grinned. "Before I get to the reason I'm here, were you just at the Merry Windsor?"

His face remained completely passive, but I noticed the slightest twitch of his shoulders. "Not I. I've been stuck in this cave all day." He removed a pair of thick-framed reading glasses and set the headshot he was holding on the stack. "But, seriously, have you uncovered a new clue?"

"I wish. I'm here to beg a favor."

"Beg away."

I told him about the Sunday Supper theme and Steph's request that he entertain the dinner guests with a ghost story.

"I adore this concept. Count me in. I love everything about it."

"You're the best." I was about to ask him if Arlo would want to come, but he cut me off.

"I know I'm the best. Tell me something new."

"Okay, now you've taken it too far."

He leaned closer and rested his head on his hands. "I'm deadly serious. Have you learned anything juicy? I've been stuck in endless auditions. The auditorium reeks of desperation and stage makeup. I need a distraction, and there's no better distraction than solving a *murder*."

I knew that he was making light of a serious situation as a coping mechanism. When we had first met, it took me a while to peel through his outer layers and discover a squishy, soft interior.

"I've been swamped at the bakeshop and vineyard and haven't had much time to focus on the case. I did confirm that Anton's time of death was in the window of six to eight. What about you?"

"Same, darling. Same." He glared at the stack of headshots with such fire in his eyes I thought they might burst into flames. "If I hear one more *Measure for Measure* monologue, I might have to pen my resignation."

"But you love Shakespeare, and this a Shakespeare company."

"Your point?" He picked up the photo on the top of the stack. "Audition week goes something like this—a monologue of *Measure for Measure* followed by a monologue of *The Tempest*, followed by a monologue of *Twelfth Night*. It's not just me, the Bard would be begging these aspiring actors to do something original. These monologues are so overdone."

"I never considered that actors would audition with the same plays."

"Not simply the play. For *Measure for Measure,* it's Act three, scene one—Claudio's monologue to his sister. I've seen it fifteen thousand times the past week."

"That might be a bit of an exaggeration."

"Barely. First, it was *Gatsby*. Now it's all Will Shakes."

As much as I was interested in the auditioning process,

I steered the conversation back to the reason for my visit. "Like I mentioned, we're still working out the specifics, but my team is thinking a mashup of dark and stormy fall food, maybe with some fun potion mocktails and cocktails and a spooky story to cap off the night. We'll leave the creative concept up to you, unless you want help, but setting a theatric mood is your expertise, right?"

"When you butter me up like that, the answer has to be yes. I'll have to give some thought to a selection, but I can promise you it won't be a Shakespearean monologue."

"Good."

Lance put the date in his calendar. "Now, on to the real fun. You mentioned that Anton was killed sometime between six and eight on Halloween. I was able to sleuth out the time slot for Perry's appearance at Ashland Springs. He and King George were signed up for an hour. The parade ended at five, which means that even if he stuck around to take selfies and pose with adoring fans, he had ample time to meander down Main Street, stab Anton, and go snag a table at Puck's Pub without anyone noticing."

I thought back to that night. Perry and Jax had been at the restaurant for a while before we crashed their party. They were both on their second round of drinks and had clearly settled in for the night.

"You're with me on this, aren't you? I can see your brain cells firing."

"Do you think he and Jax were in on it together?" I asked.

Lance opened his laptop. "Funny you ask. I happened to check the visitor log on a hunch. Jax signed in as Perry's guest three times in the days preceding his murder. They're up to something, that much I'm sure."

"Maybe they were plotting how they were going to do it." I thought out loud.

He turned his laptop screen so that I could see. "She visited twice the day before the murder and once the previous day. Plus, if you go back further, she's been on campus as Perry's 'guest' nearly every other day for weeks."

"The other possibility is that she's been using Perry to try to get Pippa cast," I said, playing devil's advocate.

"It's a valid point, but if that was her only goal, why wouldn't she have been coming to visit Newell? He held the cards. Not Perry."

"Maybe Newell said no?" I suggested.

"Something to take into consideration for sure." He closed the laptop with a flourish. "Or perhaps we have digital proof right here of their nefarious dealings."

"You should tell the Professor."

"Should I, though?" He shot me a formidable look.

"Yes, you should."

"Fine. Always wanting to follow the rule book."

"I should let you get back to the headshots, but before I go, there's one more thing I wanted to ask you about."

"Anything for you, Juliet."

I shifted in my chair. "I bumped into Jax and Trey on the bricks. Jax said that something's happened to King George and Pippa is taking his part."

"You must have misheard her."

"No, that's what she said, verbatim."

"Then she's delusional." Lance peered out the window in the direction of the bricks. "But then again, aren't we all sometimes?"

# Chapter Twenty-One

After my conversation with Lance, I was more confused than ever. Trey and Jax were long gone, so I didn't have an opportunity to ask her more questions about why she was under the impression that Pippa was replacing King George. Lance had been adamant that nothing was wrong with George. In fact, George had been at the Bowmer earlier in the day.

Why had Jax lied?

And what had she and Trey really been doing on the bricks? I had clearly interrupted something. It had been obvious from their body language and Trey's attempt to try to get Jax to go along with his story that he wasn't only there to give Pippa a cut. How many times could a poodle's hair be done, after all?

I swung by Torte to let everyone know that Lance was a go for the Sunday Supper. That would allow Bethany and Steph to proceed with marketing the event. Once I had given the final details, I went to the small office that Mom and I shared to call Marcia. I wanted to hear what she had to say about King George.

She answered on the first ring. "I recognize this number. Torte's calling. Does this mean I'm getting a pastry delivery?"

I laughed. "I can arrange that, but the reason I'm calling is that I heard that King George is dropping out of the show."

"What? Where did you hear that?"

"I heard that Pippa is replacing him."

Marcia screeched. "When?"

"Not long ago. Don't worry, I checked in with Lance, and he assured me that wasn't the case, but Jax seems to think otherwise."

"What is her problem?" Marcia paused like she was trying to compose herself. "Juliet, you've known me for a long time. I'm not prone to hating anyone, but Jax has had my blood boiling for weeks. She won't let it go. King George landed the part, fair and square, but Jax is doing everything in her power to undermine him and me. To be quite frank, it has me on edge. She's not stable. I'm fearful that she's going to do something to harm George. This is why I'm sure that she killed Anton. I just wish that Doug could find proof and put her behind bars before someone else ends up dead."

"I'm sorry to stir things up for you. I wanted to be sure before I looped the police in."

"I appreciate you calling, and yes, please tell Doug and the authorities. Jax needs to be arrested immediately."

When we hung up, I took a few minutes to try to figure out my next step. I didn't have to think long. A knock sounded on my office door.

"Jules, there's someone in the dining room who wants

to see you." Bethany peeked inside. "I can tell her you're busy."

"No, that's fine. Who is it?"

"She said her name is Camille."

"Great. I'll go find her. Thanks for letting me know." I wondered why Camille wanted to see me. Had she discovered the name of the mahjong set's original owner? I found her in the dining room, waiting in front of the espresso bar.

"Camille, welcome to Torte. I heard you were looking for me."

She laced her fingers together again and again, like she was trying to wipe something sticky from her hands.

"Do you need a napkin?"

"No. I'm waiting for my oat milk latte," she said at the same time that Andy set her drink on the bar.

"Would you like to go sit down?" The dining room was sparsely populated at this hour, and the pastry case had nearly been cleaned out.

"I left my things in that booth by the windows." Camille didn't expand on why she wanted to talk to me while we walked to the booth.

She had saved her spot with a stack of coats. I tried to keep my face passive when I realized that one of the coats looked exactly like a familiar cloak.

"You came prepared for the elements," I said, hoping my voice sounded steadier than I felt.

"Oh, these. They didn't sell, so I'm taking them to the winter shelter."

"But isn't the winter fashion season just starting?"

Camille scooted the stack closer to her body. "None of

these are worth anything. Some of our patrons seem to believe that we're the Goodwill, not a curated resale shop. I put a few of them out for Halloween costumes, but since they didn't move, it's to the shelter. At least someone in need will be able to get some use out of them."

It wasn't exactly a heartfelt donation story. Then again, Camille didn't strike me as being heart centered. Could she be getting rid of the cloak for another reason? Say, to rid the shop of evidence?

She stirred her latte with a spoon. "I'm not sure exactly how to say this, so I supposed the best idea is to come out right out with it."

"Sure."

"You and your mother are good friends with Wendy?" She said this like it was a question but didn't give me time to answer. "I think you need to have some kind of an intervention with her."

"An intervention?"

"She won't stop going on and on about the mahjong set. I've had to ask her to please stop coming by the shop. She's disturbing my customers, and I've already explained to her and the police, numerous times, that I don't know who donated the set. That's the nature of a resale shop. Unless our customers bring items in on consignment, we have no reason to keep records on their personal information."

"I understand." Although I didn't understand where she was going with this.

"Wendy won't take no for answer. After the set went missing at her cocktail party, she has come up with a theory that the owner of the set stole it back because they know that there's evidence linking them to the murder in amongst the other tiles. I worry that she might be having a breakdown. This morning at the shop, she begged me to let her search through our storage area where we keep items that haven't been assessed or priced for sale yet. I explained that no one other than me or my volunteers is allowed in that area because we're responsible for our consignment partners' valuable items. When I asked her why she believed the mahjong set's original owner would have returned the game to the store, she didn't have an answer."

That was odd behavior for Wendy. "Wait, so she thinks whoever stole the set at her house hid it in your storage room?"

Camille fanned her latte before taking a careful sip, like she was worried she was going to scald her tongue. "Apparently. It makes no sense to me."

"What are you hoping that I'll do?"

"Talk to her." She drank the latte like a little bird, pressing her lips together and barely letting them touch the rim of her mug. "She's taken this murder personally, and I think it's affecting her more than she's letting on. Out of the kindness of my heart, it feels like my duty to tell the people who really know her and care about her. I don't know her well, and this is above my pay grade, as they say. I can't be responsible for her, and if she continues this erratic behavior, I'm afraid that I'm going to have to ask her to stay away from the shop. I hope it doesn't come to that. I don't want it to, but I'm not willing to put my shop and reputation in jeopardy."

"Is it that bad?" What could Wendy possibly be doing that would put Camille's reputation in jeopardy?

"It's worse. She's scaring my customers. She's accosting people who come into the shop. I'm worried that I'm going to need to ban her from coming inside if you can't reason with her."

"This doesn't sound like Wendy."

Camille swirled her latte like it was a fine wine. "I can't answer that. As I said, we aren't close. She's been lovely up until this point, but I think she's snapped. That's why I'm coming to you. I care about her well-being, but I think hearing this from you will have more impact. Will you talk to her?"

"Of course."

She placed her nearly full coffee cup on the center of the table. "Excellent. I need to be on my way to discard these." She picked up the stack of coats. "Thank you. Please do be careful. I'm concerned that she's not well."

Camille draped the stack over her arm and left without another word.

I watched her cross the plaza. Had Camille come out of the kindness of her heart, as she had said? I wasn't so sure. Unless something had changed drastically, Wendy was one of the most stable people I knew. Could there be another reason that Camille didn't want Wendy hanging around the shop? Camille had been at the party. She could have taken the mahjong set. Was that the real reason she wanted Wendy to stay away? Was she really worried about Wendy, or about herself?

# Chapter Twenty-Two

I didn't hesitate after Camille left. I went straight to the source. I called Wendy, but she didn't answer. After leaving her a detailed message, I considered swinging by her house, but I didn't want to walk there just to discover she was out.

Instead, I focused on finalizing details for our Sunday Supper. Wendy's place wasn't far. If she returned my call, I could take a quick break and go check in with her. In the meantime, I needed to get flowers ordered for the event. Steph had given me a sketch of her magical menu design for our Sunday Supper. It was a whimsical delight, with bubbly potion drinks, wispy outlines of ghosts, and a storm cloud hovering above a candlelit table.

I decided to take the sketch to A Rose by Any Other Name so that Janet could use Steph's artistry as inspiration for flower arrangements. We always added a few extra touches to our Sunday Suppers, like floral bouquets for the table that went along with the theme.

Stepping into A Rose by Any Other Name was a treat for the senses. Gorgeous evergreen garlands adorned with miniature pumpkins, dried leaves, pinecones, and fall flowers draped the entrance. There were buckets of fresh-cut roses, cosmos, and goldenrod waiting to be made into centerpieces or wrapped in kraft paper and tied with twine.

A large cement workstation took up the center of the flower shop with refrigerated cases along the walls that housed ready-to-go bouquets and vases.

Janet was trimming stalks of rosemary.

"That is one of my all-time favorite fragrances," I said as I shut the door behind me.

"Isn't it the best? I love adding herbs to arrangements. They offer a nice contrast, and you're right that the aroma can't be beat." She set her shears on the island, which was littered with stems and cut flowers. "What can I do for you?"

I showed her the menu for the Sunday Supper.

"Ooohhh, so dramatic. Lance must be in his element." Janet wiped her hands on her work apron. "I have some immediate ideas. What are your thoughts on black roses?"

"For a magical potion dinner? Yes."

Janet reached for a binder. She leafed through it until she found the photo she was looking for. "What about something like this?" She handed me the folder so I could get a closer look.

Roses as black as night had been paired with deep eggplant roses, Amaranthus, bear grass, artichokes, and feathers. "This is perfect."

"How fun." Janet took the binder back. "Would you like one centerpiece or a few smaller vases?"

"Let's do one big arrangement for the center of the table because I think Steph and Bethany have some potion candies planned for each of the place settings."

"I'm going to have to see if I can snag a ticket."

"I'll reserve a spot for you if you want to come."

"I would love to, but we're doing a wedding next Sunday and I'll be busy with that."

"Are you sure you have time for this?"

"For Torte? Always." Janet smiled. "I would never pass up the opportunity." She wrote up an order form.

"Have you seen Wendy today?"

"No. It's interesting that you ask. She didn't show up for our Lithia walk."

"Really?" Maybe Camille had been telling the truth. "Was she supposed to walk with you?"

"We have a standing walk date, and she never misses it. She sent a cryptic text saying she had something important to finish and might be late, but then she didn't show."

"Do you think she's in danger?"

"Danger? That thought hadn't crossed my mind." Janet set her pen on the order form. "You think she could be in danger?"

"I don't know. I had an odd conversation with Camille a little while ago." I gave her the condensed version of my exchange with Camille.

"That doesn't sound like Wendy." Janet shook her head with certainty.

"I agree."

"Juliet, I think it's probably a good idea to tell Doug about this." Janet's face was etched with concern. She got out her phone. "I'm going to try Wendy."

I waited to see if she was able to get ahold of her friend.

"She's not answering for me, either." Janet frowned. "Maybe we should have Thomas do a well-check on her. Now I'm worried."

"I can run over there now and see if anyone's in the office," I offered.

"Yeah, why don't you do that. I'm going to text her too. If I don't hear from her before I finish this order, I'll head to her house, but if you don't mind letting Doug or Thomas or Kerry know, I'll feel better."

"Not at all. I'll go right now."

"Let me know if you hear from her, and I'll do the same."

I felt a renewed sense of urgency as I left the flower shop and made a beeline for the police station. Could Wendy be in danger? That thought hadn't occurred to me until now. What if Wendy had managed to track down the original owner of the mahjong set? Could she have put herself in harm's way?

I still couldn't figure out a connection between the antique set and Anton's death, but with Camille and now Janet worried about Wendy, I didn't want to waste any more time. The Professor and his team could take it from here.

Kerry was standing outside the station giving dinner recommendations to a tourist. Once she had sent them off with multiple dining options, she turned to her attention to me. "Everything okay, Jules? You look flushed."

I filled her in on the Wendy situation. She took my report seriously.

"I can head over there right now. If Janet thinks a well-check is necessary, I'm on it."

Kerry didn't say it, but I knew she had developed a deep attachment to Janet, who had become more like a mother than a mother-in-law. Kerry's parents had been in and out of jail throughout her childhood. Her unstable upbringing might have sent her on a similar path, but Kerry was resilient. She had learned to rely on herself from a young age. When her estranged father showed up unexpectedly days before her wedding, she had confided in me about what it was like to hop from couch to couch and never know where her next meal would come from. Kerry had harnessed her trauma for her work as a detective. She had an enviable ability to hold firm boundaries while offering empathy.

"Can I come with you?"

She glanced inside. "Sure. Give me a minute to let dispatch know what I'm doing and then we'll head over there. I'll meet you in the parking lot."

"You think we should drive? It's only a few blocks away."

"If Wendy's had some sort of medical emergency, we'll want to respond quickly."

I hadn't thought of that possibility.

Kerry was quick. She met me by her squad car, directing me to get in the passenger seat and buckle up. The drive to Wendy's took no time.

The minute we arrived, I knew that something was wrong. For starters, her front door was propped halfway open, and her front window had been smashed. The most obvious sign was that Cooper, her yellow lab, barked incessantly, warning us of danger.

Kerry motioned for me to get behind her. "Stay back, Jules." She radioed dispatch and approached the house with caution.

My heart thudded against my chest. I said a silent prayer to the universe, begging Wendy to be okay.

"Wendy, it's Detective Kerry. I'm here for a well-check. Can you give me a sign that you're okay?" Kerry yelled.

There was silence, with the exception of howls from Cooper.

"Wendy, I'm approaching the house. I see potential signs of a break-in or forced entry. Can you let me know that you're okay?"

I was impressed with how calm Kerry appeared. My stomach felt like I was back on the *Amour of the Seas* in the middle of a hurricane.

When we got to the porch, Kerry froze. She tried one more time, knocking on the partially opened door. "Wendy, it's the police. I'm here to make sure you're okay. I'm going to enter the premises." She turned to me. "Wait here. I've called for assistance."

I nodded, not trusting myself to speak.

Kerry kept talking as she stepped inside.

Cooper raced to the door and then to the kitchen, continuing his barking.

I tried to look through the window, but the glass had shattered in a spiderweb pattern, making it impossible to see anything.

"Wendy, it's Kerry," she repeated, venturing further into the living room.

I could hear sirens in the distance. Backup was on the way.

"Jules, Jules, can you come in here?" Kerry called. "I found Wendy."

The queasy feeling sent my stomach swirling more. I clutched the door frame as I stepped inside. That didn't sound good.

Not Wendy.

Not Mom's best friend. My knees went weak, like they might buckle and collapse.

Memories of squirt gun fights, sleepovers, and eating ice cream sandwiches in her backyard came rushing to the front of my mind. Wendy had helped raise me. She had to be okay.

"Please let her be okay," I begged out loud.

From the looks of the living room, I wasn't sure I wanted to go any farther. Wendy's lamps and pottery had been knocked off end tables. Her couch cushions were tossed on the floor. Paperwork was scattered everywhere. Someone had obviously ransacked the place. Did that mean they had harmed Wendy in the process?

"Jules, are you coming?" Kerry called.

I swallowed hard and forced my feet to move.

Kerry was kneeling next to Wendy, who was lying on the kitchen floor. Cooper had planted himself on Wendy's other side. The barking had stopped. It was as if he understood that we were here to help his person, and he wasn't going to leave her.

"Is she okay?"

"She's breathing, and I think she's coming to. Can you get a glass of water? I've already called for an ambulance."

"Who did this?" I went to the cupboard where I knew Wendy kept her glasses and filled one with cold water.

Kerry was right; Wendy's eyes fluttered, and she started murmuring.

That had to be a good sign.

I brought the water over.

"Wendy, how are you feeling?" Kerry asked, keeping her hand positioned on the top of Wendy's head.

Wendy said something unintelligible. Then she tried to sit up.

Kerry stopped her. "Give it a minute. I think you hit your head."

The sirens grew louder. Help would be here soon.

Wendy took a few deep breaths like Kerry was modeling.

"That's right. Just keep breathing. Take it slow." Kerry kept one hand on Wendy's shoulder as she drew in long, easy breaths.

After a minute, Wendy sat up halfway with Kerry's support.

"Do you want some water?" I asked. I realized for the first time that the kitchen, unlike the living room and dining room, was intact. There were no signs of a physical altercation here, no broken dishes, nothing was shattered on the floor or spilled on the countertops. Did that mean that the attack had happened in the other room and Wendy had tried to make an escape here? Or maybe her attacker had dragged her into the kitchen.

"No, thank you." Wendy blinked. "Juliet? You're here."

"Kerry and I came together. We were so worried about you."

"Cooper, you're here too." Wendy reached for the dog and rubbed his head. "What happened?" Cooper gently rested his head on Wendy's legs in a show of protection.

I didn't like that Wendy's skin tone matched the white tile floor, or that her body seemed to sway like she was on choppy waters.

"I was hoping you might be able to tell me that," Kerry said. Her tone was equally calming and directive. "Do you remember how you got in this position?"

Wendy's eyes were glassy. She sighed and massaged

the same spot on her temple. "No. I don't remember. Did someone hit me?"

"I don't know. There are signs that there might have been a forced entry and some kind of a physical altercation. We found your front door open, your window smashed, and the living room torn apart."

"Why?" It sounded like it was painful for Wendy to speak.

"Let's have the paramedics take a look at you, and then we'll talk more," Kerry said, waving the team in.

The emergency response team began assessing Wendy. I stepped aside and put the water glass on the counter. They checked her vitals and ran her through a concussion protocol. Thomas and the Professor showed up shortly after the paramedics. Kerry filled them in.

I felt out of place without anything to do.

Wendy seemed to be doing better. Color had returned to her cheeks, so they didn't have the ashen quality they had when Kerry found her. She appeared a bit dazed, but otherwise, her speech wasn't slurred, and she seemed to be making sense.

"Juliet, how are you?" the Professor asked.

"Stunned. In shock? I don't know. Who would want to hurt Wendy?"

"It's understandable that you're in shock." He looked from Wendy to her living room. "This my responsibility. Please don't attempt to shoulder any of the blame, as it lies solely with me."

"Why are you to blame?"

"I fear I should have seen this coming."

"Does that mean you know who did this?"

He was thoughtful for a moment. I recognized the trancelike gaze that came over him. "Alas, no, but there's a line of inquiry that I've been pursuing that should have clued me in to this outcome."

"Is she going to be okay? She said she doesn't remember what happened."

He gave a curt nod. "They're taking her to the hospital and will likely keep her overnight out of an abundance of caution. I'm hopeful that the amnesia is temporary. It's quite common after a head injury to have short-term memory lapses."

"Do you think she was hit?"

"I have little doubt about that. The question is did whoever broke in discover what they were looking for?"

I glanced at the activity around us. Police were photographing the living room and placing yellow evidence markers near broken lamps and pottery. "Does this confirm that there's a connection between Wendy's missing mahjong set and Anton's murder?"

His tone was solemn. "I believe it might."

# Chapter Twenty-Three

I waited at Wendy's until I had given my statement and answered dozens of questions. I was happy to remain as long as it was helpful to the Professor and his team. When Thomas came over to tell me that they had everything they needed from me, he left me with a word of caution.

"Listen, Jules, the killer is escalating things. This attack on Wendy tells us that they are scared. They must know that we're close. You would think that's good, but this is actually the most dangerous time in an investigation. The killer has likely been observing Wendy and knows that you two are connected. That puts you in danger. I want you to be really, really careful, okay?"

I gave him a solemn nod.

"I'm serious, Jules. Desperation is dangerous. At this point, the killer has nothing to lose. I want you to stay vigilant, and if you see or hear anything that seems out of the ordinary, you call one of us—immediately. Understood?"

I didn't like his intense gaze or how his eyes were filled with fear. Thomas was typically easygoing. He didn't have a propensity toward overreacting. Lance was his polar opposite when it came to dramatics. That meant that if he was this worried, I should probably be on high alert.

"Got it."

"Promise me that you'll go home and let us take it from here. This isn't a time for you and Lance to get involved in any way, shape, or form."

"I promise. I need to finish up at the bakeshop, but then I'll head straight home."

"Good." Thomas sounded slightly relieved. "I can't stomach the thought of someone else getting hurt. Wendy has been like a second mom to me."

"Me too." I squeezed his arm. "I'll be careful, I promise. What about Cooper? Do you think Wendy is going to need to stay the night at the hospital? Should someone take him?"

"We'll make sure he's okay." He got called away. I took that as my cue to leave.

If Thomas was scared, I wasn't about to take any chances. I wondered if there was more he wasn't telling me. Could the police know who had killed Anton and attacked Wendy? Were they waiting for tangible proof? Or had they already found it in Wendy's living room?

Thank goodness Kerry had been so prompt in her response time. Otherwise, who knew how long Wendy might have been unconscious on her kitchen floor.

I shuddered at the thought.

Like Thomas, I considered Wendy an integral part of my childhood. That was one of the gifts of growing up in Ashland. We had truly been raised by a village. Janet, Wendy, Marcia, Mom, friends, neighbors, everyone looked out for each other. There wasn't a day that had gone by when I wouldn't pass by a familiar face when

I was walking to Torte after school. I never felt alone. There was always someone's house to go to for snacks and cartoons if Mom and Dad were busy at the bakeshop. Weekends and holiday breaks were filled with casual get-togethers with an abundance of food and games and laughter. Looking back on my early years in the Rogue Valley, I'd had an idyllic childhood with the perfect balance of freedom to ride bikes with friends or explore the winding trails through Lithia Park, all while knowing we had the safety and support of a community who cared about us.

It was understandable that Wendy's attack had triggered such a visceral response from Thomas. I would take his words to heart and lay off any further investigating on my own.

As I stepped off of Wendy's long porch, I caught a flash of movement out of the side of my eye.

*You're being jumpy, Jules.*

It was only a deer nibbling on an apple still clinging to the branch of Wendy's tree.

I gave the deer a wide berth and turned in the direction of the plaza, but I stopped in midstride when I saw Jax standing in the middle of the sidewalk, looking like a deer in the headlights herself. The whites of her eyes were huge, and her mouth formed the shape of an O as she gasped.

"Uh—uh," she stammered.

"Jax, what are you doing here?"

She swung her head from side to side and took a step backward.

"Hey, wait." I thought for a minute that she was going to make a break for it.

"Uh, what's up?" She didn't run, but she continued to take small steps away from me.

"What are you doing here?" I repeated.

"Just taking Pippa for her evening walk."

"Here? I thought you lived on the other side of town."

"I do, but, uh . . . I, uh, like to give Pippa a chance to explore other neighborhoods. Did you know that walking is the way dogs get their news? Every time a dog stops to sniff, it's like they're reading the newspaper. I like to make sure that Pippa gets a good sense of everything that's going on in town, not just our neighborhood."

Her story made sense, but there were two glaring issues. The first was her body language. She was dancing around like she'd had one too many cups of coffee and needed a bathroom break. The other was that Pippa was nowhere in sight.

"Where is she?" I asked, pointedly.

"Who?"

"Pippa."

Jax sucked in a breath through her nose. "Uh, yeah, I left her over in the cemetery. She likes to sniff around there."

The cemetery she was referring to was a block away. Given the fact that Jax treated her dog with as much tender care as a mother with an infant, I couldn't believe that she would leave Pippa unattended even for a minute.

"You left her at the cemetery?"

"It's safe. It's fenced in." Jax sounded defensive.

"Then why are you here at Wendy's?" After promising Thomas I would drop meddling, I probably should have called one of the police officers and had them come outside to interrogate Jax, but I couldn't help myself. Plus, Thomas, Kerry, and the Professor were all nearby. One scream from me would bring them running. I wasn't in any danger, at least not yet.

Her face blanched. If I'd believed in ghosts, I might have thought she was one from the translucent color of her skin. "What?"

"I asked why you're at Wendy's house if you were taking Pippa for a walk." I wasn't going to back down now. Jax was acting suspiciously. Had she attacked Wendy? What if she was the person who had ransacked Wendy's place? Maybe she had heard Detective Kerry and me coming. She could have snuck out of the garage and hung out in Wendy's side yard until we were inside. Maybe I had caught her trying to get away.

"I wasn't coming here." From the timid quality of her voice, I could tell she didn't even believe her lie.

"Did you hurt Wendy?"

"Hurt Wendy? What are you talking about?" Jax leaned her neck to one side like she was attempting a strange yoga pose.

"Wendy. Did you attack her?"

"Wait, what? Wendy was attacked?" Jax sounded like she was sincere in her disbelief, but I didn't trust her. "That's why the police are here? Oh, okay, that makes so much more sense. Is Wendy okay?"

Was she putting on an act? I knew that she had grand visions for Pippa's stardom. Was that because she wanted to be an actor and couldn't cut it? Was she living vicariously through her poodle?

"They're taking her to the hospital now." I wasn't about to give Jax information without her answering some of my questions first. "The police are inside now. There was a struggle."

Jax covered her mouth with her hand. "No, it wasn't me. I can tell by your face what you're thinking. I swear it wasn't me."

"Then what are you doing here?"

Jax pointed to the graveyard. "I came with Pippa. I wanted to talk to Wendy, that's all. I had some questions for her."

"Like what?" I wasn't buying her innocent act.

"About Pippa and training."

"Then why leave Pippa at the cemetery? I think it's probably a good idea for me to go get the police and have them take it from here. You're obviously not telling the truth."

I don't how it was possible, but Jax went even paler. "Wait, wait, let me explain. I'll talk to the police. I swear I will. I swear on Pippa's life."

Swearing on Pippa's life. Maybe she was serious.

"I get that this looks bad. It is bad. I mean, not in the way you think." Her words sputtered to a halt. She hung her head. "I came here to talk to Wendy. To confess."

My stomach flopped. Confess?

"Confess what? And why to Wendy?"

Jax stared at her feet. "I did something I shouldn't have. I feel bad about it. It was a stupid mistake. I came to Wendy's because she uses Trey too, and I thought she might be willing to facilitate a conversation between me and Marcia, since they're such good friends. I need to apologize formally to Marcia."

"Is this about King George's dye job?"

She nodded. "It's my fault."

I waited for her to say more.

"It's the theater. I got so caught up in making Pippa a star. It started with Anton. He told me that Pippa had potential. He told me that she was special and that he thought she had a real shot at making me some serious money. But now I realize that he said that to everyone. It was his way to get you to keep coming back for more and more training sessions. He didn't think Pippa was special. He made that clear before he died. I love Pippa, and it was so much fun to work through the training protocols with her, and I'm a huge theater fan. It seemed like it was too good to be true. I could get paid to have my dog be a star, and who wouldn't want that?"

I didn't answer.

"I guess I got caught up in it. I was envious of Marcia and King George. He was getting all of the parts and auditions. Pippa didn't have a shot against him. Anton kept telling me that I needed to spend more money on training. I thought that she needed time to improve and get better, but then I realized that Anton was a scam artist. He had no intention of helping Pippa land a role, he wanted my money."

"How does this have anything to do with Marcia?"

"I had heard a rumor that she and Anton were working the scam together. I realize now that the rumor wasn't true. I went to Trey, and with Perry's help, we pulled a prank to get back at them."

"You mean dying George's tail purple."

"Yeah. It was harmless, though. It's not like it hurt him. It's temporary dye. I was hoping that maybe there was an outside chance that Newell would cut him from the show."

I nodded, taking in what she was telling me. "Why did you think Marcia was in on Anton's scam?"

"That's what I'd been told, but it turns out that she and King George were merely innocent bystanders. I feel terrible that I've been so mean to her. I want to make it up to her, which is why I'm here. I thought Wendy would be a good buffer. If Wendy was willing to set up a time for the three of us to meet together, then I was going to apologize and tell Marcia the truth—the whole truth."

"Why not bring Pippa with you?"

"I wasn't sure about Wendy's dog. I know that Cooper doesn't do well with little dogs, and I didn't want Pippa to antagonize him, not in the middle of such an important conversation. I really did leave her at the cemetery, but when I got here, I saw the police cars and I panicked."

"What's the correlation between seeing the police and panicking?" If she was telling the truth, there was no reason for her to be worried about the police.

"I lied about George. I shouldn't have. I get that now, but I'm scared that if I tell them about our silly prank, they'll think that I'm also lying about Anton. I swear I'm not. That's why I wanted Wendy's help. She's reasonable and so nice. I thought if we could talk to Marcia together, then I could explain my side of the story to the police."

"You need to tell them now. Wendy was attacked. Someone else could be next."

Jax nodded slowly. "Okay, I will, but I need to get Pippa first. I can't leave her alone for this long."

"I'll come with you." I didn't trust her not to use the opportunity to make a quick escape.

The graveyard was at the crest of the hill. An ornate black wrought iron gate enclosed the cemetery.

"Pippa, come. Pippa, come here, girl," Jax called, snapping her fingers for her dog.

The sun had sunk behind the mountains, casting a burnt caramel glow on the grass. There was no sign of the dog.

"Pippa, Pippa." Jax's tone was more urgent. "Do you see her? Oh, no. Where is she?"

I called with Jax, but unless Pippa was skilled at hide-and-seek, the poodle wasn't here. "Do you think she got out?"

Jax fiddled with the gate handle. "No, look: it's locked. Someone stole her."

# Chapter Twenty-Four

I tried to console Jax, who had dropped to her knees.

"Pippa, Pippa, my beloved Pippa. Who would do this? Who would kidnap—dognap—Pippa?" she wailed, rocking back and forth on the damp grass.

"We don't know that she's been dognapped," I replied. "Maybe a friendly dog lover could have happened by and noticed that she was here alone. They could have taken her home to watch over her until they could contact you. I'm assuming she has a collar with your contact information on it, right?"

Jax brushed a tear from her cheek. "Yes, but she's not wearing it."

"Why isn't she wearing it?"

"Newell took it when we were at the theater. He said he needed it for her audition records, and I forgot to get it back from him before we left."

"Does she have a chip?"

"Not yet. That surgery is scheduled for next week. We had to wait until she was old enough to be spayed. They do it at the same time."

"Let's go to Wendy's. The police are there. You can

explain everything you told me about George and then we can get their help about what to do next to find Pippa. While you're talking to the Professor, I can call the animal shelter and see if anyone has reported finding a missing poodle."

Jax didn't get up, but she managed to bob her head in agreement.

I helped her to her feet. It was a short walk to Wendy's. I dropped her off with Thomas and followed through on my promise to call the animal shelter. I paced outside on Wendy's front porch, trying to keep an eye on Jax and Thomas's conversation while waiting for the shelter to pick up.

When I finally got through, the staff member told me that there were no reports of poodles found anywhere in Ashland within the last twenty-four hours but took my information and Jax's and said they would call immediately if any information about Pippa's whereabouts turned up.

I waited for Jax to finish telling Thomas what she had done. Her statement about Newell had me on edge. Why would Newell have needed Pippa's collar for audition paperwork? That didn't make sense. Could there be more to the story?

What if Newell was the killer? Maybe he followed Jax to Wendy's. Or maybe he attacked Wendy and then grabbed Pippa from the cemetery.

The question was, why take Pippa? Especially because the rumor was that he didn't like dogs. Could he have taken her to use as leverage? Was he planning to blackmail Jax to keep his secret quiet?

Theories fought for space in my head.

"Juliet, I thought you had left." The Professor interrupted my scattered thoughts.

"I didn't get very far." I gave him the short version of Jax's story. "She's giving her statement to Thomas now."

"As the Bard says, 'No legacy is so rich as honesty.'"

"So you think Jax is telling the truth?"

"I have no reason to doubt her now, although I wish she had been more forthcoming earlier in our investigation. It may have changed our course of inquiry."

"Do you have any sense of who did this?"

He gave the slightest nod of acknowledgment. "I will say this. I feel more hopeful than I did when the day began, but there is still more to be done, and I fear we're in for a long night."

A long night? Did he think they would be able to make an arrest that soon? The thought put me at ease. After Thomas's warning, I'd wondered if I would even be able to sleep tonight, but if the Professor believed they were close to apprehending the killer and Wendy's attacker, that made my breathing slow and the tension I'd been holding in my neck release a little.

"I should return to work." He made eye contact with one of his officers, who was holding a plastic evidence bag. "Do try to go home and get some rest. I know that this has been a difficult time for you, and I must reiterate how much we appreciate everything you've done to assist us, but now it's time for you to take care of *you*." His words were so tender and fatherly that I teared up a bit.

"Thanks." I gave him a hug and went to wait on the porch for Jax. I wanted to tell her what I had learned from the shelter before leaving.

Jax came out shortly. From her puffy, bloodshot eyes, it looked as if she had been crying.

"Did it go okay?" I asked.

She bit her bottom lip. "Yeah, they were really nice. They shouldn't have been that nice to me. I don't deserve it. I feel terrible about everything I've done."

I wished I had a tissue to offer her.

"They're making calls and putting out a notice to the police and fire stations in the valley to be on the lookout for Pippa." Her shoulders heaved as she let out another sob. "I can't believe I was so stupid to leave her in the graveyard. What was I thinking? She's never left my side. She's probably so scared and terrified."

"I'm sure we'll find her." I put my arm on her shoulder in a show of solidarity.

She sniffled. "I hope so. I'm the worst dog mother ever. I shouldn't even be allowed to keep her. She must be so stressed and confused." The thought made her dissolve into another round of tears. Her shoulders crumpled as she tried to suck air through her nose.

"Listen, Jax, do you think there's a chance that Newell could be involved with her disappearance?"

"Newell?" She brushed tears from her cheeks. "Why?"

I told her about my theory.

Realization spread across her face. "Oh my God, yeah. You know, I had a weird feeling about it at the time, and then earlier, before I came here, I saw him near Lithia Park. He was acting super strange. He asked me a bunch of questions about what I was doing and where I was going. I bet he followed me."

"Do you remember what time it was when you bumped into him at the park?"

Jax shook her head and wiped her nose on her sleeve. "I wasn't paying attention. Perry and I were having a beer at the Glamper. Newell passed by and stopped to talk for a few minutes. I felt like he was grilling me. He didn't seem interested in what Perry was up to, but when I said I was going to talk to Wendy, his entire personality changed."

"How long were you and Perry at the Glamper after you saw him?"

"I can't say for sure, but probably at least another half hour, maybe forty-five minutes."

Her phone rang. "It's Perry."

"Go ahead. Take the call. I'm heading to Torte, but I'll be in touch if I hear anything about Pippa."

Jax forced a smile before answering the phone. "Thank you. I don't deserve your kindness."

I wanted to ask her more. Every conversation we'd had involved talk of getting George out of the role to make way for Pippa. Why was she suddenly eager to apologize, and why come to Wendy to mediate?

Marcia had warned me that Jax wasn't trustworthy. The more time I spent around Jax, the truer that seemed. Not to mention, why had she left Pippa unattended? None of it made sense.

I left her to take her call and headed for the bakeshop. I wasn't about to take the shortcut through the park, not with a killer on the prowl and with Thomas's warning ringing in my head.

*Newell.*

*Newell.*

The killer had to be Newell. If he realized that Jax was going to confess to Wendy, he must have gotten spooked. Wendy's house was minutes away from the park. He had plenty of time to get to her house, knock her out, and take whatever evidence he was looking for before Jax arrived. Then he easily could have seized the chance to take Pippa when Jax and I were talking. Had she inadvertently tipped off a killer?

But would Newell do all of this over the fear of his secret being revealed? When I had spoken to him about other jobs, he had made it clear that he was going after traditional casting roles, not pet casting. Would a hiring manager care that he didn't like animals? It seemed like he could spin it in his favor to say look at how professional he was in his temporary role at OSF. If he didn't particularly like four-legged actors and had successfully cast them in shows, that wouldn't be a blemish on his résumé. If anything, he could sell it as an accolade.

No, if Newell was the killer, he had to have another motive.

I was missing a critical clue.

Was there more to Newell and Anton's relationship? Could they have been lovers? Had they had a nasty secret breakup or a love affair that had gone wrong? Or were they archenemies? Maybe Anton had learned about Newell's dislike of his furry friends and threatened to ruin him. Could Newell have killed Anton because he was worried that Anton would refuse to recommend him or—worse—give him scathing feedback in a reference check for the new positions he was applying for?

Both theories were possible, but that didn't mean that I was necessarily on the right track. I needed to think. I needed to bake.

The kitchen was the space where I could work out big problems. Everything seemed to come into focus when I was kneading bread dough or whisking hot caramel. I sent Carlos a text to let him know to meet at Torte when he was done. Then I went straight to the basement. My staff had already cleaned and gone through the closing procedures, which meant that Torte was spotless and empty. The perfect scenario for letting me think through what I had learned about Anton's murder.

I had been craving pumpkin bread, so I gathered pureed pumpkin, flour, sugar, eggs, warming spices, and mini chocolate chips. For the batter, I creamed together butter and sugar before adding the pumpkin puree, eggs, vanilla, and a splash of buttermilk. Next, I incorporated the dry ingredients—flour, salt, baking powder, and my warming spices. Soon the batter was thick. I dusted the mini chocolate chips with more flour. That would ensure that they wouldn't sink to the bottom of the pan during the bake. I carefully folded them into the batter and then spread it into baking tins.

The ovens had been turned off for the night, so I needed to give them time to warm before I put the loaves in. While I waited for the oven to come up to temp, I grabbed the sketchbook that I used for cake designs and opened it to a blank page.

I made a list of each of my suspects. Newell was at the top of the list. I just wished I could nail down a firm motive for him. While the fact that he didn't like animals and had been hired to cast animals was problematic, it didn't seem like a firm reason to kill Anton.

The oven timer dinged in unison with my cell phone.

I reached for my cell first.

There was a text from Lance.

"911. EMERGENCY. GET UP TO CAMPUS NOW."

# Chapter Twenty-Five

I didn't hesitate. I left my pumpkin bread on the island and sprinted to OSF. Lance was pacing in front of the bricks with his phone glued to his ear. When he saw me, he held up a finger and finished his conversation.

"Thank goodness." He threw his arms up. "You are a sight for sore eyes."

"Lance, what's going on? What's the emergency?"

"There's been a kidnapping."

"You mean Pippa?"

"*You* know?" he scoffed.

"I was with Jax a little while ago."

"And you didn't call moi?" Lance sounded incensed.

"Is that why you texted me?"

"No, no, no." He crooked his index finger. "Follow me." In a fluid motion, he spun around and took the steps that led to the entrance to the Lizzie (as he affectionally referred to the Elizabethan theater) two at a time. He unlocked the arched wooden doors framed with ivy and motioned for me to follow him.

"Is this an elaborate ruse to get me onstage?"

"I'm offended, Juliet. Honestly offended." He didn't say

more. Instead, he threw his shoulders back and marched through the aisles. When he got to the front row, he came to a halt. "See here, O ye of little faith."

He stepped to the side and drew his arm over the aisle seat as if he was a conducting an orchestra.

I came closer. Sitting on the seat was the one and only Pippa, with a note tied to her collar. "Pippa?"

Lance gave me a gleeful grin. "None other than the pampered pooch."

"How did she get here?"

"Read the note."

"Have you already read it?"

He nodded.

"And you put it back on her collar?"

"Read it, darling."

I followed his instructions and removed the envelope. It had a hole punched in the corner and had been tied to Pippa's collar with a piece of twine.

"PLEASE BE SURE PIPPA IS RETURNED TO JAX WOOFARD. I APOLOGIZE FOR LEAVING HER HERE BUT HAVE NO OTHER CHOICE. I KNOW THAT SHE WILL BE TAKEN CARE OF.

SIGNED, NEWELL TAYLOR."

"So Newell is the one who dognapped Pippa?" I asked, confirming my theory.

"Apparently." Lance took the note from me. "Why steal the dog and then return her to the Lizzie?"

"Maybe he had second thoughts?" I suggested. "He could have taken her and then felt bad about it and brought her to the theater, knowing that there are dog lovers around."

"I counter with this." Lance held his finger up as if

preparing to give a lecture. "First, the Lizzie is dark for the season. The odds of anyone stumbling upon Pippa are slim to none. Second, if Newell is the killer, I highly doubt that he would have any regrets about taking a dog since he's capable of murder."

"True." I looked from Pippa to the stage. "How did you find her?"

"A stroke of luck. I was heading home for the evening and happened to hear whimpering. I thought someone was crying, but then upon closer inspection, I realized it was a dog's whimper."

"And there's no sign of Newell."

Lance made a clicking sound. "This is where the plot thickens." He reached into his jacket and handed me his phone. "He emailed me his resignation. One of the jobs he was applying for came through. He's on a plane to New York as we speak."

"Wait, so Newell found Pippa."

"Or took her," Lance interjected.

"Right, took or found Pippa. Returned her to the Lizzie with a note and left for New York? That doesn't sound normal. Why wouldn't he have taken her to the animal shelter? Or called the police? Or at the very least called Jax?"

"So many questions. So few answers." Lance picked Pippa up from the seat.

"Who were you talking to when I showed up?"

"Jax. She's on her way." He patted the poodle's head as we returned up the aisle. "I'm afraid that she might break every traffic law getting here. I encouraged her not to speed, but she was beside herself with the news that Pippa has been found safe and sound."

"I still don't get it. Newell's decision-making is erratic at best. I mean, I suppose that makes sense if he's a killer, but still . . ." I trailed off.

"Unless he isn't."

"How so?"

"Here, can you hold her?" Lance handed me Pippa so he could lock the doors behind us. "What if that note wasn't written by Newell? What if it the killer is trying to implicate him?"

"Okay. Yeah." I petted Pippa, who quivered in my arms. "That's a possibility."

"The killer could be trying every possibility to shift suspicion away from them."

"But how would they have gotten into the Lizzie?"

Lance pursed his lips and stared at me like he was waiting for me to come to the same conclusion he had already discovered.

"Newell worked for OSF but didn't have keys. Trey and Camille also wouldn't have had a way to gain access. And Jax wouldn't have taken her own dog."

"Or would she?" Lance countered. "You're forgetting about her paramour—Perry. The two of them could have come up with this entire scheme together."

"You're convinced about them, aren't you?" Lance hadn't strayed from his theory since we'd started making inquiries. "I don't know. Jax was distraught when she realized that Pippa was missing. I don't think she could fake that."

Lance rolled his eyes. "Please. A few simple acting tips from Perry. Some eyedrops, then cue the waterworks. It's not as difficult as you might believe."

"It was weird that she left Pippa in the cemetery."

"Tell me more about that before she gets here." Lance sat down on one of the large cement benches to wait for Jax's arrival.

I explained everything that had happened before and after finding Wendy on her kitchen floor.

Lance made his signature tsking sound. "This is quite interesting, isn't it? Thomas's warning makes me believe that you and I have done it again. We must be close. There's no other possible explanation."

I wasn't sure I would go that far. There were plenty of other possibilities, but I wasn't going to rule out Lance's theory. "Do you think Jax would have risked something happening to Pippa, though? Even if her acting skills are better than she lets on, I can't imagine her taking any chances with Pippa."

"Murder makes one desperate," Lance said with a knowing frown. "Jax reeks of desperation."

"You're suggesting that she left Pippa at the cemetery intentionally while ransacking Wendy's house?"

"Perhaps. Or perhaps Perry did her dirty work. and then she appeared out of the blue in order to establish an alibi with you. They could be playing a long con." Lance spoke with his hands as he expanded on his theory. "There's a very viable possibility that Pippa was never left alone. Perry could have done the damage at Wendy's, knocked her out, and then run up to the cemetery to watch over Jax's precious poodle while she came down and buttered you up with her sob story. In my mind, this seems more likely than Jax abandoning Pippa, don't you agree?"

To tell the truth, it did.

My gut feeling about Jax had been that there was something off the entire time we were speaking. Not to mention, her motive was much clearer than Newell's. She had been one of my top suspects from the beginning. Was she a clever con artist?

"Do you think they faked the note?" I asked Lance.

"Undoubtedly. Perry has keys to the Lizzie because of rehearsals. Newell didn't. Now, there's also a chance that Newell could have swiped someone else's keys or asked one of the custodial staff to let him in. He has an OSF badge that would give him access, but I know for a fact that he didn't have a set of keys to the theater. Why would he need them?"

"Good point."

A car screeched up Pioneer Street and came to an abrupt halt in a temporary parking space adjacent to the bricks. It had to be Jax.

"Lance, you realize that if Jax and Perry are the killers and they faked Pippa's dognapping, we could be in real danger right now?" I whispered, watching the passenger's and driver's doors open. "Thomas warned me not to get involved."

"Not to worry. I've already thought of every angle. Play it cool. We'll give them a taste of their own medicine and put on a little show of our own. Follow my lead."

He stopped talking as they approached. I wasn't sure this was a good idea. One killer was dangerous enough, but two?

# Chapter Twenty-Six

"Pippa, Pippa, Pippa, my sweet, dear Pippa, you're okay." Jax went straight for Pippa, took her from me and proceeded to kiss the top of the dog's head again and again. Pippa didn't flinch. Jax held her up, inspecting her for injuries. She reached for Perry. "She's okay. I'm so relieved. My baby is okay."

Perry stood in silence. I observed him closely, hoping that a facial tic or a shared look between them might reveal the truth, but he remained stoic.

"Where did you find her? I could kiss you." Jax leaned in toward Lance.

He pulled away and held out his hand to stop her. "No, no. There's no need for that."

Jax squeezed Pippa so tight I was worried the dog might not be able to breathe. "Pippa pup, I've been so worried about you. How did you find her? Where was she?"

Lance nodded to the theater. "She was in the Lizzie."

"How did she get in there?" Jax nuzzled her face on the dog's head.

"It appears that someone put her there." Lance offered her the note.

Jax's eyes widened. "There's a note? Did the dognapper leave her with a note? I don't understand. What am I missing?"

"Read it," Lance encouraged.

Jax handed the note to Perry. "You read it. I'm not putting Pippa down ever again."

Perry read the message for everyone to hear. "That's weird. Why didn't Newell call you?"

Jax rocked Pippa like a mother trying to put an infant to sleep. "I have no idea. Did you talk to him?" she asked Lance.

Lance pressed his hands together. "He was long gone by the time I heard her."

"You heard her?" Jax gasped. "Was she hurt?"

"She was whimpering."

"Oh, Pippa pup." Jax nuzzled the poodle's head. "I'm so sorry, baby. You must have been so scared." She looked up. "Was she scared? Was she shaking when you found her? She shakes when she's away from me for too long. Poor, poor puppy."

I could tell that it was taking every ounce of self-control for Lance to keep from saying something sarcastic.

"She was happy to see me," Lance replied with unusual restraint.

"Why is everyone standing around? We need to alert the police immediately. Newell should be arrested for dognapping. He's not going to get away with this." Jax had shifted from concern to rage. "How dare he try to take my fur baby. How dare he leave her here unattended. Imagine if you hadn't found her? She could have frozen to death tonight. He should be behind bars."

"Alas, he's on a plane," Lance said.

"I don't care." The fury on Jax's face gave me a moment of pause. Maybe she had it within her to kill after all. "I'm calling the police this very minute. Perry, call 911."

"That might not be the best response. I have the Professor's cell. Why don't I call him?" I suggested.

"As long as he gets here in record time. I want that plane stopped and Newell arrested immediately. He's not going to get away with this."

Again, her words sent a shiver up my spine.

I called the Professor, who assured me he would be there as soon as he could.

Jax became more and more agitated as we waited for the Professor. "I knew it was Newell all along. He's been up to absolutely no good. The man hates animals. How dare he do this to Pippa? To me?"

"Try to relax," Perry said, reaching out to comfort her.

She yanked her arm away. "Relax? At a time like this. You relax."

"I'm trying to help." He moved away from her.

"You're making it worse by dismissing the severity of this situation." She cupped her hands over the poodle's ears as if she was worried that the dog would hear what she was about to say next. "Pippa could have been killed."

"But she's fine. That's what I'm saying. I get that it could have been worse, but it wasn't." Perry's logic made sense to me, but Jax refused to listen.

She sat down and clutched Pippa to her chest. "People who would harm a poor, innocent animal like Pippa are the scum of the earth and deserve to die."

Lance caught my eye and raised his brows. "Dramatic much?" he whispered in my ear. "Leave me to this. I have a plan. Just make sure the Professor gets here."

I glanced at my watch. Carlos would be coming to pick me up soon, and my pumpkin bread needed to go in the oven. "Listen, I should get back to the bakeshop. You can handle this until the Professor shows up, right?" I made sure that Jax and Perry could hear me.

"Leave this in my capable hands. We'll chat later, yes?"

"Yes." I gave him a look of thanks. As much as I would have loved to observe the Professor's interaction with Jax, there wasn't much to be done. If Newell was on a plane, the Professor would have to track his flight and alert the authorities wherever Newell intended to land. Short of taking Jax's statement—which I had already heard—I doubted there was anything new to learn by hanging around.

I headed down Pioneer Street. To my surprise, Trey was coming up the hill in my direction. Sprinting and huffing up the steep hill was a better description. The look of fear and panic on his face was illuminated by the streetlamps, which had just come on.

"Trey, what are you doing here?"

He bent over, trying to catch his breath. His hair was completely flat. It reminded me of a deflated balloon.

"Did you run all the way from Wizard of Paws?" I asked.

He nodded as he gulped air like a fish out of water. "I heard about Pippa. I had to come right away."

"You heard that she had been found?" That was odd, because Lance told me he had only called Jax.

"She's been found? You're sure? She's safe?"

Why would Trey have run a mile and a half uphill if he didn't already know that? And why would he come to campus this late at night if he didn't?

"Yes, Jax is with her now."

"What a relief." His breathing had returned to a slower pace. "I can't believe it was Newell. I didn't think the guy had it in him. If anything, he seemed like a coward to me."

"How did you hear it was Newell?" I knew that Lance hadn't said anything about the note. Perry had it read it out loud to Jax in front of us.

"Jax texted. I told you that."

Did he sound like he was getting frustrated with my questions?

"But Jax just heard."

"I know. She texted me. I dropped everything and ran here. I didn't have time to go get my car. It was parked a half mile the other direction, so I got my exercise in for the night."

Maybe I had been overthinking Anton's murder too much, but I didn't believe a single word coming out of Trey's mouth. "That's impossible, because this just happened." I pointed toward the bricks. "Jax learned that Newell had dognapped Pippa a few minutes ago."

"Right. And she texted me." Trey sounded perplexed that I didn't understand.

The thing is, I didn't. I had left them minutes ago. Unless Trey was an Olympic runner, there was no possible way he could have run a mile and a half in that short time. And from his red cheeks and his breathy voice, I didn't think he was anywhere close to an Olympian.

"Why are you looking at me like that? I didn't do anything wrong. I came to help my friend and make sure that Pippa is okay."

"When did Jax text you?"

He shrugged. "I don't know fifteen, maybe twenty minutes ago. Why?"

"The math doesn't add up." I should have stopped pressing him, but he was obviously lying.

"No one ever believes the dude with the spiky hair and tattoos. You want to see the text?"

"If you don't mind, that would be helpful."

He rolled his eyes, but he took out his phone and held it for me to see. Sure enough, there was a string of texts from Jax. Trey wasn't lying about his exchange with her. She had told him to come meet her at the bricks, that Pippa had been found, and that Newell was responsible for her dognapping.

The timestamp on the first message was from eighteen minutes ago.

I handed him back his phone. "Sorry. I guess time went faster than I realized."

"Can I go?" Trey stuffed the phone into his pocket.

"Yeah, they're right up there." I pointed him in the direction of Lance, Perry, and Jax and kept going down the hill.

But I hadn't gotten mixed up about times. Jax had arrived less than ten minutes ago. That meant that she was putting on an act. She knew about Pippa and knew that Newell had taken the dog. I had a sinking feeling that Lance's theory was right. Jax and Perry had to be in on it together. It was a hoax. They must have "dognapped" Pippa themselves and planted her at the Elizabethan with a fake note from Newell.

I had to call the Professor again before he got to OSF. He needed to know that Jax and Perry's response to Lance finding Pippa was one elaborate ruse . . . which could mean they were the killers.

# Chapter Twenty-Seven

I didn't wait to call the Professor. Unfortunately, he didn't answer. Hopefully, that meant that he was already on his way to the OSF campus. I left him a detailed message about everything that had transpired and told him to call me back if he needed anything else from me.

I wasn't sure if I should stick around and wait for him. He would likely check his messages. But then again, if he didn't, he might let Jax and Perry get away. Maybe that was their plan. Frame Newell, make a big production about finding Pippa, and then make an escape. Or maybe they thought the Professor would buy their story. I wondered what police protocol was when it came to a dog-napping. Would the Professor take the note as evidence? Would it be dusted for fingerprints or checked against Newell's handwriting?

Before I could make a decision, my phone rang.

Thank goodness.

The Professor must have gotten my message.

But when I looked down, it was Carlos's face on the screen. "Mi querida, where are you? I'm at Torte and the ovens are on and there's batter in bread tins, but no one is around. Did something happen?"

I could tell from the way his voice quivered and how he rolled his "r"s more than usual that he was worried about me. I felt terrible. "I'm fine, I promise. I'm over by OSF. It's a long story, but I'm on my way to you now."

"Okay. I will watch for you."

That solved my dilemma. I returned to the bakeshop to find Carlos standing by the basement door.

"Julieta, you scared me." His voice was breathy. "I came in and saw the kitchen like this and thought the worst." He wrapped me in a hug and kissed the top of my head.

"I know. It's my fault. Lance texted, and I left without thinking."

"The ovens were on." He released me and studied my face. "This is not like you."

"It wasn't smart of me." I had been trained better than that in culinary school. Commercial ovens should never be left unattended. "I didn't mean to worry you." I told him about Pippa, and Lance's theory about Perry and Jax.

"The Professor should handle this. It is too dangerous," Carlos said, his voice cracking. "I could not imagine what I would do without you."

"I feel the same." I squeezed his hand. "Let me put this bread in the oven. We can have a glass of wine while it's baking, and I'll give you the longer version of everything that's happened."

Carlos looked as if he wanted to say more, but went to open a bottle of wine. I put my pumpkin loaves into the oven and then joined him on the cozy couch in front of the atomic-style gas fireplace in the dining area adjacent to the kitchen. The space was a popular spot for Southern

Oregon University students to camp out on Sunday afternoons with endless cups of coffee while they crammed for midterms.

I leaned against him and relayed the strange mix of my day, including finding Wendy with Detective Kerry and then the dognapping that was beginning to feel more and more like it had been staged.

"None of this makes sense." Carlos swirled his wine.

"Trust me, I know. I've been trying to piece it all together, and I keep coming up with dead ends."

"You do not think that Jax and Perry did it?" he asked.

"I think it's an interesting theory, and I suspect that Lance is right about them faking Pippa's disappearance, but I just can't see either of them as the killing type. Maybe I'm giving them too much credit. I guess I keep coming back to the dragon and the mahjong set. There's something about it that I'm missing, but I can't figure out what."

"It hurts my head to watch your brain work overtime like this." Carlos massaged my arm. "Do you think you can give it a rest tonight? Will you be able to sleep, or should you call the Professor again before we go home?"

I gnawed on my bottom lip. "You know me too well. I don't want to interrupt him right now. He's probably in the middle of trying to sort out what happened to Pippa, but I might try him after my bread is done. If he and Thomas and Kerry are investigating long into the night, they could use some sustenance."

"Like pumpkin bread?"

"A slice or two of pumpkin bread usually does the trick." For the first time all day, I felt my shoulders relax and the tension I'd been holding on to fade away. Carlos had that effect on me. His calming presence had always reminded me of Mom. They both had an easy way of holding space. Never rushing a conversation, rather giving time for the words to flow, for thoughts to gather, for a conversation to grow. It was almost like building the layers of a tiered cake. They understood that the foundation came first. Otherwise the cake would topple over and fall apart.

We sat in comfortable silence for a few minutes watching the flames flicker in the fireplace and sipping our wine.

"I'm obsessed, aren't I?"

He frowned. "Are you?"

"I am. It feels good to admit it and say it out loud. Out loud, to *you*. I can't let Anton's death go. I suppose there's a part of me that feels like if I can come up even with the tiniest shred of evidence or work through even the roughest sketch of a theory as to why and how he was killed, then I'm somehow a piece of the solution. Does that make any sense?"

"Sí." He reached for my hand and laced his fingers through mine. "This is one of the reasons I love you."

"I'm not sure I deserve that." I clutched his hand tighter. His touch had the same calming effect on me. "Tonight is proof. I took off and left the ovens running without a second thought."

"You were worried about Lance. This is a sign of how much you care about your friends and everyone you love, Julieta."

I knew that Carlos was trying to make me feel better, but his tender response made it worse.

"It wasn't a smart move, though, and I like to think of myself as an intelligent and strong woman."

"Julieta, you are in your head. Let it go. Holding on to

our mistakes serves no good. You have taught me this, sí?" He massaged my thumb as he spoke.

The oven buzzed, signaling that it was time to take my bread out. I gave him a light kiss and stood up. "Thanks." Letting go has never been my strong suit. It was a lesson that continued to recur and a glaring reminder from the universe that if we don't take time to examine our patterns and behaviors, we're destined to repeat the same mistakes.

My pumpkin chocolate chip loaves had baked to perfection. I removed them from the oven and set them on the island to cool. Then I made sure to turn off the ovens and cleaned up the kitchen.

I didn't have to package up a loaf to deliver to the police station because a knock sounded on the basement door. Carlos answered it to find the Professor.

"Come in, come in." He ushered the Professor inside.

"I'm sorry to bother you at this late hour, but I noticed the lights on."

I sliced the warm bread and brought it out to the dining area. "Thanks for coming by. I wanted to follow up. Pumpkin bread?"

He took off his tweed jacket and sat on the couch. "That smells absolutely divine. I don't mind if I do."

"Can I get you a glass of wine? I could also make a pot of coffee or a cup of hot tea." I handed him the plate and a napkin.

"There's no need to go to any trouble on my behalf." He folded the napkin into a neat square and helped himself to a slice of bread.

"Let me make a pot of French press," Carlos offered. "I feel like this cold night calls for coffee."

"It looks as though you've already completed cleaning procedures for the evening." The Professor astutely had observed the space in a matter of minutes. I supposed that it shouldn't surprise me. He had been built a long-running career out of being able to assess and analyze situations and behaviors.

"No, it's not a problem," Carlos said, moving in that direction. "I will get it started. You two can talk."

I appreciated that he recognized that I wanted time with the Professor.

"How did it go with Jax?" I asked.

He savored a bite of the bread. "This is delectable as always. I enjoy the spices mingled with the chocolate. It's quite an unexpected melody on the tongue."

"Thanks. Help yourself to more."

"I just may do that." He took another bite and then removed his Moleskine notebook from his jacket, which he had draped over the arm of the sofa. "What can I tell you about Jax?" He flipped through the pages. "I will share that her story doesn't exactly line up."

"Do you think she and Perry could have staged Pippa's dognapping?"

He was pensive, absently running his hands along his reddish beard streaked with gray. "Perhaps. I'm certainly not ruling it out."

"What about Newell? Any update on him?"

"We've tracked down his flight, and authorities will be making contact when he lands. However, if he is attempting a getaway, he's either terrible at it or he's intending to get caught."

"Why?"

"He made no effort to conceal his travel plans. Flying is the worst possible escape strategy. He had to show his identification to board the plane. If he's responsible for dognapping Pippa or for Anton's murder, I would suppose he would have made an attempt to keep a low profile. Again, unless he's looking to be arrested. We'll have to wait and hear from our colleagues when they pick him up at the airport."

"Would he get arrested for dognapping?"

"Jax wants to press charges, which I'm sure will not come as new information to you, but no, our first matter of business is to bring him in for questioning. I do have some concerns, as he was given strict orders not to depart the area without checking with us first. That certainly has me interested in wanting to understand his intentions for booking a flight to New York."

"I'm stumped. I can't figure out his motive."

"I may be able to offer assistance with that." The Professor finished his bread.

The smell of Carlos's French press permeated the room. Suddenly I found myself craving coffee.

"That's the reason I stopped by. Kerry has been at the hospital with Wendy, who is awake and talking."

"That's great news."

"There's more. Her cognition seems to be improving. Kerry is to call me the moment she is able to confirm anything, but she believes that Wendy may be close to remembering who attacked her."

Carlos came toward us carrying a tray of coffees.

"Ah, here's Kerry now." The Professor took out his phone. "I must go. Sorry to have put you to the trouble of making coffee, but we may finally have the proof we need to make an arrest." He grabbed his coat, gave Carlos a half bow, and left.

I watched him go.

Wendy was awake and knew who had hurt her? If only I could follow after the Professor and find out who.

# Chapter Twenty-Eight

Carlos and I sipped his rich French press. "You are wishing you were with the Professor, sí?"

"Am I that obvious?"

"Yes, maybe only to me, but yes."

I laughed and savored the notes of nutty cocoa and spiced fruit. "I feel relieved that Wendy's okay and that it sounds like they may be close to making an arrest. I just wish I knew who did it."

"They will let us know when they can," Carlos said wisely. "It is their responsibility. We should go home and wait for word from the Professor or Thomas."

"You're right."

We finished our coffees and headed home. Ramiro had a late study group and had let Carlos know he wouldn't be home for dinner, but I hadn't realized quite how long the night had been. It was after eight.

"Should I make us something easy for dinner?" Carlos asked, rolling up his sleeves and scanning the fridge for ingredients.

"I can't believe it's so late. Where did the night go?"

"You were in the middle of a very stressful situation. Time goes fast in moments like that." He held out a container of eggs. "Omelets?"

"That sounds great."

I stared at my phone, willing it to ring or vibrate while Carlos whisked eggs and chopped vegetables. Soon the kitchen was alive with the aroma of searing onions and peppers. I was taken back to our early years on the ship, when we would steal away for a dinner on the upper deck under the stars between our shifts. Carlos wooed me with his simple signature omelets and a bottle of sparkling wine. Some of my favorite memories were of midnight meals next to an empty pool as the *Amour of the Seas* cut through nighttime waters. In those days I never minded that I had to be up before dawn to prep for the morning breakfast buffet. Time felt endless and decadent and vanishing all at once. There was something romantic about eating beneath a blanket of shimmering stars in the middle of the Atlantic Ocean.

Carlos fried thick slabs of honey-coated bacon and shredded tangy Parmesan into the omelets. "It is like old times."

"I was thinking the same thing."

"And you were thinking of the murder." He sprinkled the cheese over the eggs.

"True. That too. I keep coming back to the mahjong set. It has to hold the missing piece, no pun intended."

"What does that mean?"

"I don't think that Jax, Perry, Newell, or even Trey ever touched the set."

"So it must be someone else?"

"That's the most logical explanation, don't you think?"

Carlos seasoned the omelets. "This is not my specialty. Eggs, sí. Murder, no."

"I've been replaying everything that happened from the first fateful day that Wendy discovered the warning note in the set. I can't think of any time that Jax, Perry, Newell, or Trey would have had an opportunity to hide the note in the game box, which leaves us with one suspect—Camille."

"The shop owner?"

"Yeah. She had the mahjong set in her possession before Wendy bought it. She was at Wendy's party the night the set went missing. And I'm sure I saw that cloak at her shop before Halloween. It was part of the window display. Then she had it in the stack that she claimed to be donating to the winter shelter. What if she took it to get rid of it? What if she knew that I saw her in the cloak at Wendy's that night? But then again, I saw her with the cloak, so that doesn't make sense. If we go with the theory that the note and Anton's death are connected, she is the most likely suspect for sure."

"Why would she kill him, though? They are strangers, no?"

"Not exactly. She admitted that he had come into the shop a number of times. We also know that he was an art collector and had an extremely valuable piece of dog art. I have a strong hunch that Camille isn't being truthful about how well they knew each other. Here's a theory— what if Anton told her about the piece? Camille would know exactly how valuable it was. She could have killed him to get her hands on it." I paused long enough to catch my breath. "I keep replaying my first conversation with Camille. Wendy and I asked her about the original owner of the set, and she freaked out. Her reaction wasn't normal. At the time, I blew it off, but now I'm sure that she and Anton were much more connected than she wants us to believe."

"Freaked out how?" Carlos flipped the omelet.

"She became really defensive. She broke a teacup. She refused to let Wendy go into the storage area. I can't pinpoint exactly what it was. It was more her entire demeanor. It's been bugging me ever since."

Carlos dished the omelets onto plates and paired them with a fresh green salad. He joined me at the table.

"Thank you for dinner, this looks amazing."

"It is nothing. Humble eggs, some bacon and vegetables. Food the way it is meant to be served."

"Lucky me to be the recipient of your humble food."

Carlos sat next to me. "I don't understand, aren't Wendy and Camille friends?"

"I'm not sure if they're friends exactly. More like close acquaintances. They met through the shop. Wendy's a frequent customer, and because she's so connected in Ashland and has lived here for her entire life, she made it her mission to introduce Camille around town and invite her to events."

"Then it would be even more horrible if Camille is the one who hurt her."

"Agreed. I could be wrong. I could be way off about Jax and that whole crew, but my gut feeling is that Camille is involved. It makes the most sense. Maybe I'm grasping at straws with a motive, but I feel like she had to have known about Anton's collection."

"What is this expression—grasping at straws?" Carlos

dug into his omelet. "I do not understand these American-isms sometimes."

"I have no idea." I laughed, nearly choking on a bite of the savory eggs. "Literally no idea."

"We must look it up." He grinned. "Back to Camille. I don't think you are grasping at straws, as you say. I think your intuition is usually right. Could there be more than his collection? What if she and Anton have had a secret connection that no one knew about?"

I nodded. "You mean like an affair? I suppose it's not out of the realm of possibility, but there's nothing that hints at that. Plus there was such a big age gap between them."

"Stranger things have happened."

"I won't argue with that. An affair gone wrong could be motive, but I just don't see it. Maybe Anton witnessed something at the shop that put him in harm's way."

"Like what?"

I could tell Carlos was invested too.

"If he was a regular, maybe he learned that she was overcharging customers? That could explain why she reacted the way she did when Wendy asked about the origin of the mahjong set. She could have been valuing antiques at more than they were worth."

"Or, what if they weren't valuable at all?" Carlos suggested.

"Mmm-hmm, I see where you're going with that, and I like it. Anton realized that and threatened to reveal her bad business practices. That would give her another motive."

"Sí, but I am with you in that the art collection is even more solid. Money." Carlos rubbed his thumb and fingers together. "Do you know how much his collection was worth?"

"Not a dollar amount, but that one balloon piece could have been worth millions on its own. He supposedly had one of the largest collections on the West Coast." As I said the words out loud, I realized that maybe I should have spent more time considering the connection between Anton's expensive hobby and Camille's shop.

"This seems like a link, sí?" Carlos finished his salad.

"It does, and I'm kicking myself for not seeing it before now." I set my fork down. My hunger had evaporated. This was the shift in focus I had been missing. I felt like there were neon lights flashing in my face, signaling that I was finally on the right track. "What if Anton discovered something nefarious at the shop? Maybe he learned that Camille was overpricing items? Or maybe he witnessed her undervaluing items to customers interested in consignment, only to turn around and sell them for a bigger profit. Or maybe she had a stash of very valuable pieces that she took in and sold on the underground market. What if Anton was at the wrong place at the wrong time? He could have seen Camille doing something illegal, and that's what got him killed. He could have been the one to stash the warning note in the mahjong set."

"Your face is shining like the jack-o'-lanterns," Carlos said.

"I can feel it in my body. I think we're right about this. The question is, what should I do?"

"The answer to this is simple: finish your dinner and go to bed. I know that you will not do this, though. You will not sleep until you have at least spoken with the Professor again. Am I right?"

I gave him a sheepish smile. "Yeah, unfortunately you know me too well."

"Then you should call him. I will clean up." Carlos took my plate.

I appreciated that Carlos wasn't passing judgment. He understood me maybe better than I understood myself, and it was time for me to stop fighting this urge to be involved in bringing Anton's killer to justice.

# Chapter Twenty-Nine

"Juliet, were your ears burning?" the Professor asked.

"Were you talking about me?"

"Indeed. I was giving Thomas and Kerry the gist of our conversation."

"How's Wendy?"

"She's alert and appears to be relatively unscathed." He paused momentarily to answer someone in the background. "Many apologies. I'm not at the hospital. It's quite hectic here."

"I don't want to bother you, but Carlos and I were talking over dinner, and I had an aha moment, and I thought I should fill you in."

"I'm all ears. But speaking of ears, can you swing by the—" A crackling sound came through the phone. "The . . . shop." He cut out again. "I know it's late but—" Static filled the line, and the call dropped.

I tried him back, but he didn't answer.

Carlos tossed a dish towel over his shoulder. "What did the Professor say?"

"I couldn't get through. We were on the call and then it

dropped. He's not answering, but he asked if I could swing by the shop."

"What shop?"

"That's the odd thing. He never refers to the station as the shop." I paced from the table to the stove and back again. "What if he means the hospice shop?"

"Should we go?" Carlos dried his hands and hung the towel next to sink.

"We could at least drive by."

"I'll get my shoes." He moved toward the door.

I grabbed a coat and followed him outside. A cold wind assaulted us as we hurried to the car.

"You should drive. You know the way." Carlos handed me the keys.

"Do you think our theory could be right?" I asked, as I steered down the pitch-black hillside. Wildlife made their appearance at this hour. It wasn't unusual to happen upon a bear or a fox, so I turned on the brights and kept a tight grip on the steering wheel. "What if it is Camille?"

"Why would the Professor ask you to come, though? He wouldn't put you in danger." Carlos voiced what I was thinking.

"Maybe they've already arrested her?" My throat felt like it was narrowing. I swallowed twice and reminded myself to breathe.

It didn't take long to get to the hospice shop. The parking lot was plunged in blackness. None of the streetlamps were on, and every other storefront was shuttered for the evening. If the Professor or any of his team had been here, they were long gone.

"Nothing. This is a dead end."

Carlos held his hands like binoculars over his eyes. "Wait, wait. Did you see that?"

"What?" I came to a stop.

"Over there. On the back side. Drive slowly."

I turned the headlights to low and steered in the direction he pointed.

"There's someone hiding in the shadows," Carlos whispered.

We were inside the car with the windows rolled up. It was unlikely that anyone could hear us. Not that I blamed him for being cautious. I could feel my pulse swooshing in my head.

"Go slow. There. To the left."

My fingers were going numb from clutching the wheel so tight. "I don't see anything."

"Someone is there. I saw movement. They know we're here."

"Should we bail?"

"What can they do? We are in a car. They are on foot." He peered through his hands again.

*True, but what if they have a gun?*

I didn't express my fears out loud. Carlos sounded confident, so instead of panicking and jumping to worst-case scenarios, I would follow his lead. And keep my foot on the gas pedal just in case we needed to hightail it out of here.

"See!" Carlos whisper-screamed. "Right there."

I squinted to see in the darkness. Sure enough, a figure appeared to be crouched near a dumpster in the back of the hospice shop. "What do we do? Should we try the Professor again?"

Before Carlos could reply, two cars squealed into the

parking lot. Another came from the opposite side of the street. We were surrounded by police sirens and blinding white lights.

"Exit your vehicle with your hands in the air," a voice on a bullhorn demanded.

"They're talking to us." I turned off the engine.

We did as we were directed. I tried to keep the person hiding in sight, but it was impossible with the police lights. Dots and squiggly lines blurred my vision.

"Keep your hands in the air while we approach," the voice commanded.

I could hear footsteps as the officers came toward us.

"Jules? Carlos? What are you doing here?"

I recognized Thomas's voice, but I kept my hands in the air until he told us otherwise.

"You can put your arms down. We're not here for you."

We turned to see Thomas, Kerry, and a team of officers.

"The person is over there," Carlos said, pointing to the dumpster.

"Stay put." Kerry put out her hand to signal us to stay away. "Get in the car."

Everything else happened in a blur, like a scene from an action movie. The detectives spread out in formation, cutting off any escape routes for whoever was hiding. I couldn't see much from my vantage point, ducked down in the driver's seat, but I heard the team call commands and warn their suspect to come out or face the consequences.

"Do you know who it is?" Carlos asked. "It's too dark for me to see, especially with the lights." He shielded his eyes.

"Same. I can't tell, but I don't think the person got away. There are too many police officers here."

"We have you surrounded," Thomas said into the bullhorn.

The person didn't move.

"Come out with your hands up and let's talk. No one needs to get hurt."

Again, nothing.

The standoff continued for what felt like an hour but was actually twenty minutes according to the clock on the dashboard. After Thomas's repeated attempts to get the person to come out willingly, the Professor arrived on the scene along with a negotiator. The negotiator escalated the situation, warning that they would use nonlethal tactics next.

The warning worked, because the next thing I saw was the person standing with their hands in the air before being handcuffed and taken to an awaiting squad car.

"Who is it?" Carlos craned his neck from side to side to get a better look.

"I can't see."

The Professor tapped on the window and motioned for me to roll it down. "I thought you would both want to know that we have arrested Camille for murder."

"It was Camille?" I asked. "Is that why you asked me to come here?"

His brow furrowed. "I didn't ask you to come here. I asked if you could come to the bakeshop. Your mother forgot her purse, which has our house key. I left her at the hospital with Wendy and was going to swing by Torte before taking her home."

"The *bake*shop. Oh my gosh. The bakeshop."

"Am I missing something?" He looked from Carlos and then back to me.

"You cut out when we were talking. I heard 'shop' and wrongly assumed you meant the hospice shop."

"Ah, I see." He gave me a small nod.

"So Camille is the killer. Was it because of Anton's art collection?"

"It appears that way. I can't expand further for the time being, other than to say we found tangible evidence amongst Anton's collection that directly links Camille to his death."

"I can't believe it was her. This entire time I was sure that his murder had something to do with his profession and the puparazzi, not collecting rare art."

"I'll be able to give you more details soon." He kept one eye on the activity behind him. Red and blue lights cut through the darkness. More light glowed from within the hospice shop where officers were already combing through evidence. "It does appear that Anton is the person who stashed the note within Wendy's mahjong set. Camille has not admitted to anything and has a lawyer en route as we speak."

"We won't keep you. Thanks for letting us know. I'll sleep easier tonight, and I promise that neither Carlos nor I will say a word until we hear from you." I reached for my purse. "By the way, here's a key to Torte; I have a spare at home."

"Excellent. Rest easy, and I'll be in touch when I can."

I turned the car on again, feeling equally relieved and deflated. Anton was dead because of Camille. I was glad that justice had been served but heartbroken that she had resorted to murder. I was also sad for the Professor, Thomas, and Kerry. They would likely be working through the night, making sure that not a single detail was left unfinished. They would want to ensure that the case against Camille was solid when they handed things off to the district attorney.

"They arrested Camille. She's the killer." Reality had yet to sink in. My voice sounded weird, like it wasn't coming from me.

"Sí." Carlos clicked his seat belt. "Our theory was correct. She killed him for his art collection. Who would do something so senseless?"

"It's horrible, isn't it?" I steered the car out of the lot, toward home.

We didn't say much on the short drive. I had a feeling that like me, Carlos was trying to process what we had just witnessed.

Back at the house, Carlos nodded toward the stairs. "You should go get some sleep, Julieta. They have made an arrest; you can stop worrying."

"True."

"Then why are you looking like that?"

"I don't know. I feel bad. I thought I would be more relieved, and don't get me wrong, I am, but I guess now that it's real and we know that Camille killed him, like you said, it feels so senseless."

"Sí, it is. It is terrible." Carlos left the dishes and came closer to console me. "But we have done everything we can, and now it is up to the police to finish this."

"Yeah." He was right. There was nothing more to be done tonight.

The news of Camille's arrest did not make sleep any

easier. I thought I might drift off, but instead I lay awake for two hours, staring at the ceiling and wondering how she had done it. How had she stabbed him in the middle of the parade and post-parade activity? Had she planned it, or was it a crime of passion? Maybe they'd gotten into an argument in front of Torte, and in the heat of the moment, she had lunged at him.

Was it intentional? Or could it have been an accident?

Long after midnight, I finally dozed off briefly, only to awaken to dreams about giant balloon dogs and dragons roaming Main Street.

# Chapter Thirty

Typically I woke without the aid of an alarm, but back-to-back late nights and worry had finally caught up with me. Moonlight danced off our bedroom window, but I knew there was no chance I could get back to sleep, so I got dressed and slipped downstairs without waking Carlos. There was no need to subject him to my baker's hours.

I didn't bother making coffee. I could do that at Torte.

More questions about Camille's motive and how she had done it swam in my head on my short walk to the bakeshop. Hopefully the Professor would make good on his promise to fill in some of the gaps. I knew he would if he could. It would only be a question of how much he could share with the public at this stage of the case.

When I arrived at Torte, I immediately brewed a pot of Andy's heady fall roast and made myself a bowl of steel-cut oatmeal with cranberries, toasted almonds, a splash of cream, and touch of honey. I sat at the island to enjoy my breakfast and review what needed priority in terms of custom orders and preparing for our Sunday Supper.

Oatmeal was the perfect comfort food. It was soft and creamy with tangy bites of cranberry and a nice crunch from the toasted almonds. We didn't typically have oatmeal on the menu, but this cold November morning called for it. I also wanted to make Swedish cardamom buns and an assortment of hand pies. When Sterling got in, I could task him with savory breakfast and lunch specials.

I got to work on the cardamom buns once I had finished my oatmeal and poured myself a second cup of coffee. They would need time to rise. My first task was to activate my yeast. I warmed water, added a touch of sugar and packages of yeast. While that began to ferment and bubble, I gathered flour, more sugar, cardamom, butter, whole milk, and sea salt. The dough was relatively simple to make. Whenever we featured the sweet and slightly spicy buns, they sold out within minutes. I wanted to make sure that we had enough product to last through the lunch hour, so I tripled the recipe.

I brought the milk to a slow boil over medium heat on the stove. Then I secured the dough hook to our industrial mixer and added butter, sugar, flour, cardamom, and the yeast mixture. I let the mixer do the grunt work, giving it just enough time to let the dough come together.

Once a nice, round ball of dough had formed, I floured a section of the island and finished the rest of the kneading by hand. After my arms were sufficiently burning from kneading, I covered the dough with a towel and set it aside to prove.

The secret to the flavor in these buns was three layers of cardamom. First, the cardamom in the dough, then a buttery cardamom filling, and I would finish the rolls with a cardamom-infused egg wash.

I went to the walk-in for more butter and eggs. Then I combined butter, sugar, and cardamom on low until it created a granular paste. This wasn't a filling that should be whipped until it was light and airy. The pasty quality would allow it to stick to the dough and create a bite of piney, warm, sweet cardamom in the center of each bun.

Rolling the buns was the most challenging part of the bake. I rolled the dough out into a long rectangle, then I dotted the filling throughout the dough and used an offset spatula to smooth it out evenly. I felt like a seamstress as I used a pizza cutter to slice long strips and then begin to twist and tie them together. Soon I had rows and rows of buns waiting to be brushed with the egg mixture and sprinkled with sea salt.

I probably should have quadrupled the dough, because the smell of the unbaked buns was making my stomach rumble. I couldn't imagine how aromatic the kitchen was going to become once they were toasting in the oven.

I arranged them on parchment-lined baking sheets and set them to bake. Waiting for them to be done was going to be torture. Or at least on par with waiting to hear more from the Professor.

*Don't go there, Jules.*

Bethany showed up early, which didn't allow me to get sucked back into the unrelenting list of questions.

"Morning, Jules." She took off her puffy jacket and hung it on the rack near the basement door.

"Good morning to you. You're the first one here."

Bethany smoothed the front of her long-sleeved T-shirt that read BAKE UP AND SMELL THE COFFEE. "The shirt says it all."

"You're up early and ready to smell the coffee, huh?"

"Sort of." She glanced upstairs. "Is Andy here yet?"

"No, you beat him, which is quite impressive."

"We're supposed to do some coffee pics before the espresso bar gets crazy. I told him I didn't mind coming early, but wow, it's a shock to the system. I can't believe how much of a difference an extra forty-five minutes of sleep makes."

"If it will help, I already made a pot of coffee."

"Can I take it in IV form?" Bethany tapped her arm. "Hit me with it."

I laughed as Andy breezed inside. "Hey, boss." He greeted me with a morning salute and then noticed Bethany pouring herself a cup of coffee. "Put down the mug and walk away from the coffeepot."

She looked from the diner-style mug she was holding to the coffeepot. "Why? What's wrong with it?"

"I didn't make it." Andy tossed his coat on the rack.

"You are such a coffee snob," I teased.

"Takes one to know one, boss." He winked. "Come with me, Bethany, I'll hook you up with the good stuff."

"That hurts." I pretended to wince.

"Look, Jules, we all know that you are the ultimate pastry goddess, and I'm well aware that you and Mrs. The Professor hold Torte to the highest standards when it comes to artisan coffee, otherwise you wouldn't have hired me." He waited for a reaction from me or Bethany before continuing. "But I also know that once you get baking and wrapped up in projects—or other stuff—that you might continue to drink copious amounts of coffee without paying attention to how long a pot has sat."

"Me? Never," I protested. "I might not have your roasting prowess, but I would never stoop so low as to let a pot sit too long."

"I'm watching out for Bethany's pristine tastebuds,

okay?" He practically dragged Bethany upstairs. I had a feeling his teasing had little to do with me and everything to do with wanting to impress Bethany.

He wasn't wrong about coffee, although I would have argued that I was equally uptight about brewing a perfect cup. The chemicals in coffee break down as it cools, which gives a pot that's been sitting on a burner too long a bitter aftertaste. We never let our house blends sit long in the dining room. Andy was right about me, though. If I was baking in the kitchen, I might let a pot go slightly longer than it should. I was willing to give up a touch of perfection in favor of more caffeine. That might signal that I had a problem, but as vices went, caffeine wasn't the worst one.

My buns finished baking. I pulled them from the oven and transferred them to cooling racks. The smell was otherworldly. It took every ounce of self-control not to bite into one and burn my tongue.

Mom saved me from myself by showing up unexpectedly.

"Good morning. To what do we owe the pleasure?" I placed the last tray on cooling racks.

"Doug had to get an early start. I hear you already are in the loop about what transpired last night. You know how it is with a high-profile arrest like this. They worked until late, late last night, and now this morning it's miles of paperwork." She went to the sink to wash her hands. "I decided to tag along with him and have you put me to work. Tell me what you need, and I'll get to it." She bent her fingers, letting the tiniest hint of pain flash on her face.

Her joints tended to get stiff, particularly on cold

mornings like this. She blamed genetics and years of kneading bread dough and doing detailed piping work with her hands.

"How's your arthritis?" I asked, removing my oven mitts.

"Manageable." She flexed her fingers as if to prove her mobility. "See? I do my daily stretches, and every once in a while, I take an anti-inflammatory. You worry too much. I'm still a spring chicken."

"You are. You are younger in spirit than almost anyone I know. Plus you look amazing for going on sixty. What are we going to do for the big six-oh, by the way?"

"Doug has all kinds of extravagant ideas. Like I told him, I don't need a big party. Dinner with you and Carlos and Ramiro would be lovely."

"Consider dinner done, but I'm with the Professor; a new decade calls for something extra celebratory, don't you think?"

She rolled up her sleeves and reached for a recipe card. "Simple is my style."

"Fair enough." I wasn't going to press it. If Mom wanted a birthday dinner with just us, that was fine by me. She liked to put on events rather than be the center of attention. I had inherited that same tendency from her. Although I understood why the Professor wanted to make a big deal about her birthday—she deserved adoration and being made to feel special, not only on her birthday but every day. She did so much for everyone else without ever asking for anything in return. Maybe he and I could come up with a happy medium. Something in the middle that didn't involve inviting everyone in town to a party, but perhaps a couple of surprises.

"These rolls smell heavenly." She leaned down near the trays and wafted the scent toward her.

"They've been torturing me, and the irony is that I'm not even hungry. I made oatmeal for breakfast."

"Cardamom will do that to you." She tapped the recipe card. "Should I start on chocolate velvet cakes?"

"That would be great." I touched the top of one of the rolls to see if it was cool enough to cut into tasting bites. It still needed a couple of minutes. "I can't believe that it was Camille. Did the Professor say more last night or on the drive in this morning?"

Mom unwrapped squares of semisweet dark chocolate for the velvet cakes. "I'm shaken by it, Juliet. I can't believe it myself, and I can't believe that she hurt Wendy."

"All because of a note in the mahjong set."

"No, did Doug not tell you that?"

I shook my head. "He didn't go into much detail. He was in the middle of questioning her and waiting for her lawyer."

"Right. It wasn't the note that she was looking for." Mom broke sections of the chocolate and placed the chunks into a saucepan. "She needed the set."

"Why?"

"Doug is theorizing that Anton was onto her. They found the missing tile in amongst his things, along with photos and notes. He had apparently been watching Camille. They had worked out an arrangement where he was storing some of the pieces in his collection in the back of the shop. He realized a few things had gone missing and must have suspected that Camille had taken them, so he began keeping a log of what he witnessed at the shop."

"You mean like spying on her?"

"It sounds that way. I don't know how, but he must have discovered that her business practices were not on the up and up. Everything is documented in a journal that Thomas and Kerry found at his apartment. Doug wonders if Anton saw something transpire that sent him on his investigative path, or if he just put two and two together when he realized a few of his collectables had gone missing."

A path that got him killed. I thought about some of the choices that Lance and I had made. We were lucky we hadn't met the same fate.

"In any event, Doug believes that Anton discovered just how rare and valuable the dragon tile was. Camille swapped it with a fake plastic piece, but that one tile alone was worth close to fifty thousand dollars."

"What?"

Mom brushed chocolate from her hands. "Yes, the missing tile was leather and wood with traditional Chinese calligraphy. It belongs to a rare Berluti set that was made in partnership with Benwu Studio, a Chinese designer. The current owner is willing to pay upwards of fifty thousand dollars for that single piece in order to complete their set."

"And Camille knew this?"

"This and more. Doug and the team are barely scratching the surface of what she's been pocketing."

"Wait, so Wendy's set on its own isn't particularly valuable. That's why Camille cut her a deal? Because she wanted the Berluti tile?"

"Doug is still gathering proof and hoping that Camille will be more cooperative, but yes, that's his working theory. Anton left pictures of the tile and of Camille in the act of swapping the pieces in the back room."

"Do you think he confronted her?"

"That's what Doug is trying to determine at the moment. There isn't a money trail, so he doesn't believe that Anton attempted to blackmail her. Doug is disappointed that Anton didn't come to him sooner. He wonders if that was the final straw. Maybe Anton told Camille that he was going to inform the police."

"Does this mean that Wendy gets the money?"

Mom sliced butter into one-inch slats and added them to the saucepan with the chocolate. "She should. She's the rightful owner of the set where the tile was found."

That was a glimmer of good news.

"Do they know how Camille did it?"

"They believe they've found the murder weapon. An antique letter opener that can be traced back to the store. Camille certainly had the opportunity to take the letter opener. Doug assumes that she stabbed him in the middle of the action. There was so much going on—noise, costumes, people dancing in the street. The team thinks that she stabbed him repeatedly and then casually strolled away. The worst part is that had someone found him sooner, his injuries may not have been fatal. He lost too much blood."

That made me feel worse.

"I can see guilt on your face, honey. This isn't your fault. There's no way you could have known that he was even in front of the bakeshop. You and Carlos acted immediately. He was already gone by the time you found him."

"I just feel terrible for him."

"Me too." She gave me a sad smile. "I'm thankful that

Doug figured it out and that Camille is in custody, but it is so senseless."

"And for money."

"Apparently a lot more money. The tile wasn't the only item she had stolen from her customers and intended to re-sell to profit for herself."

"What will happen next?"

"They have a solid case, but I don't expect to see him much today. They'll be working diligently to make sure they have what they need to get a conviction in court."

The rest of the team arrived, and the conversation switched to baking and our Sunday Supper. Like Mom, I was relieved that Anton's killer had been arrested, and I hoped that knowing that Camille couldn't hurt anyone again would provide some much-needed closure.

# Chapter Thirty-One

The next few days flew by. Wendy was released from the hospital so the mahjong group threw her a welcome home gaming breakfast, complete with Torte pastries and Andy's custom November roast. She was in relatively good spirits when I arrived with a large pastry box and a carafe of coffee.

"Special delivery," I said, knocking on the door, which was partway open. This time it was because Janet, Mom, and Marcia had put everything back in its place in Wendy's house and brought bouquets of flowers, candles, and bath salts for her.

"Come in, Juliet." Wendy was propped up on the couch with three pillows behind her neck. A large bandage covered the top of her head, but her cheeks had good color, and her eyes looked bright and clear. Cooper rested at her feet.

"How are you feeling, and where should I put these?"

Wendy motioned to the coffee table. "Within arm's reach would be good. They said I'm not supposed to move much for the next few days."

"I'll bring plates and cups out here," Mom offered.

Marcia lit the gas fireplace. "That's cozier, isn't it? Do you need anything else, Wendy?"

"You all are spoiling me. I need to get a concussion more often."

"Don't say that," Janet scolded. "You had us so worried."

"I'm fine, I swear. And now that Juliet brought coffee and pastries, I couldn't be any better."

Mom returned with cups. I poured everyone coffee and opened the pastry box.

"Oh, everything looks so delicious. How do we pick?" Wendy asked.

"When you're recovering from a head injury, I believe the answer is one of everything. That's why I brought a knife." Mom pulled a kitchen knife from behind her. "I can cut pastries in half or even quarters."

"I love that idea." Wendy took the coffee from me. She patted the edge of the couch. "Sit, sit."

I obliged. The other women pulled chairs closer, encircling the couch. It felt symbolic. This what friends did—they nestled you in when you were at your worst. Not that Wendy was at her worst, but she'd certainly been through a terrible ordeal.

Marcia dipped a scone into her coffee. "I can't believe it wasn't Jax. I was so sure she did it."

"You weren't alone," Mom said. "I think we all suspected her."

Janet nodded in agreement.

"Get this. She stopped by the hospital with Perry and Trey. They brought Wendy those flowers." Marcia pointed to a huge arrangement of sunflowers in the center of the coffee table. "Then they came to visit me and brought me a similar bouquet. Jax apologized profusely for her behavior. She said she got caught up in the thrill of potentially having Pippa on the stage. She had no idea it was going to get so out of control. Now she wants to partner up for some playdates with Pippa and King George."

"That's good to hear," I replied. "What about Pippa's dognapping and Newell? Every sign pointed to Jax staging the dognapping herself."

Marcia nodded. "You were right about that. It was her last-ditch effort to get more attention for Pippa. And poor Newell was none the wiser. He landed and was immediately taken into custody. He was as shocked as the rest of us, and he had a solid alibi to back up his statement."

"Wait, so we know for sure that Jax staged Pippa's dognapping?" I couldn't believe she had done it. "She's a better actress than Pippa. I thought that whole evening was weird. Leaving Pippa in the graveyard and everything, but she was so distraught, she had me convinced."

"Don't quote me directly, I'm only passing on what I heard, but yes," Marcia answered. "I heard that Jax confessed. She roped Trey and Perry into helping her stage the dognapping. Remember, I told you that she had them both wrapped around her finger. She and Perry pretended like they weren't together, probably because they figured it would be obvious that they were in cahoots to bring Pippa down. Not that they had a single soul fooled. According to what I've heard, Trey was at the cemetery with Pippa, then Perry let them into the Elizabethan. Pippa was probably only alone and safe in the theater for five minutes before Lance showed up. They wrote the note. They set the entire thing up. Jax was hoping that it would make front-page news and that everyone in town would feel sympathetic, and that would force Newell's hand. He would have to give Pippa George's role if public opinion was on her side."

"Wow." I couldn't think of anything else to say. Although that did explain my interaction with Trey the night of the dognapping. He had gotten to the bricks quickly because he was part of the scheme. That made so much more sense. There was no possible way he could have made it from Wizard of Paws to the theater between the time Pippa had been found and Jax had called him. I also wondered if that's what he and Jax had been discussing when I interrupted their conversation the other day. It was like a hundred puzzle pieces were finally starting to fit together.

"It makes logical sense that Perry would help her," Marcia said, pausing to take a drink. "From what I've heard, it sounds like Jax was trying to hold George's dye job over Trey's head. Perry added the dye into the conditioner bottle when Trey wasn't looking. He was blameless in the incident, but Jax used his weakness—the shop and his customer base—against him. She threatened to tell everyone that she and Perry saw him dye George's tail. That's how she got him to agree to help her stage the dognapping."

"Jax really would do anything to get Pippa onstage," Mom said, shaking her head in disbelief.

"It worked in Camille's favor too," Marcia continued. "The police were tied up having to track down Newell on the opposite coast and also looking into whether Jax, Perry, and Trey could have set up the whole thing, which bought her more time to pack up and get out of town and dispose of any other evidence that may have linked her to Anton's murder. It's a good thing she didn't get far. I worry who else she might have hurt. The woman obviously is disturbed. How could she kill Anton and hurt you, Wendy, for money? No collectible is worth someone's life."

"Who knew we were dealing with such a coldhearted killer?" Wendy shuddered.

"We should change the subject. This probably isn't good for your recovery. You're supposed to be resting," Mom wisely noted.

"Are you kidding? This is exactly what I need to recuperate. Good friends, good coffee, good pastries, and best of all, good gossip." Wendy smiled. "Did you hear the other bit of gossip?"

"No, do tell," Janet said.

"I'm coming into some money. Thanks to Thomas, who has been following the trail," she said to Janet. "It may take a while to sort out, but he and Kerry sounded very confident that eventually I will receive payment from the owner of the set."

"That's great news." I reached over to take a piece of blueberry buckle coffee cake.

"We're going to have to have a big mahjong party when the money comes in," Wendy said with a twinkle in her eyes.

"I know a caterer." Mom winked at me.

"Count me in."

Wendy stirred her coffee with a spoon. "Thank you all for being here for me and everything you've done. Putting the house back together, this, everything. I'm so lucky to have friends like you."

"We're glad you're okay." Marcia patted Wendy's leg. "We've all been so worried about you. I can't get over

Camille knocking you out. How did she do it? That is, if you're up for talking about it. If you're not, that's absolutely fine."

"The doctor said it's good to talk about it. It will help strengthen my short-term memory." Wendy shifted positions, using one of the throw pillows to support her neck more. "It was fuzzy at first. The details of how she hit me still are too, but what I remember is that she called and asked if she could swing by. She said some new information had emerged about the owner of the set and she wanted to share that with me. I didn't think anything of it at the time. When she stopped by, there was something about her energy that put me on edge. It's nothing specific, but she seemed different. Angrier. More determined, maybe?"

"She was on a mission to harm you," Mom offered.

"Yes, although I wonder if she would have if she had found what she wanted." Wendy massaged her neck. "I should have lied. I should have clued into what was happening. She said she needed to see the set, and I explained that it was missing. She got really upset and began yelling—telling me that she knew I was lying and that I needed to give it to her immediately. It was such a shift of character. It took me aback."

"But I thought she stole the set at your happy hour party," I interrupted. "Then I saw her at Torte with the cloak she'd used as a disguise."

"She was too brazen. That's one of the reasons she was caught," Wendy replied. "But there was another message inside the set. Another note from Anton. I have no idea what happened to it. I never saw it, but the police think that note is what officially linked her to his murder. That's why she had to find it before they did. So she stole the set the night of the party, tore it apart, but couldn't find the note. She must have assumed that I took the note and I knew that she killed him. The irony is that I didn't."

"Then she attacked you?" Marcia asked.

"I think so. I remember going into the kitchen and offering to get her a glass of water or make her a cup of tea to help her calm down. It sounds silly replaying it now, but at the time, I wasn't thinking that I was in danger. I thought she just needed a moment to compose herself. That's when she must have hit me. The next thing I remember is waking up in the hospital room."

"And then she started tearing your house apart to try and find the note," Janet suggested.

"That's what Doug thinks." Wendy winced as she readjusted her position again.

"I think we should change the subject," Mom said. "Let's start planning this celebratory party."

I glanced at my watch. "I need to head back to work, but just let me know what you want in terms of catering, and we'll make it happen."

"Thank you again, for everything." Wendy blew me a kiss.

I left them to their planning and returned to Torte feeling lighter. My questions had been answered. Camille was in custody and Wendy was healing. It was time to put Halloween behind me and focus on all the good things ahead.

# Chapter Thirty-Two

By the time Sunday rolled around, news of Camille's arrest had calmed down. Things returned to normal, or at least closer to normal. We went about our usual slow, Sunday morning routine, baking egg custards and serving flat whites and creamy chai tea lattes. After the brunch crowd dispersed, we shifted focus to preparing our potion-themed feast.

Bethany and Steph layered custards with edible sparkles. Sterling and Andy looked like mad scientists as they experimented with dry ice for the bubbling punch that would be the centerpiece of the table. It was as if a spell had been cast over the kitchen as the team crafted white bean dip, hand-smashed guacamole, and beer and cheese sauce for the appetizer course. Marty scooped savory meat filling into hand pies, and Rosa carried tapered candles and black tablecloths upstairs.

"Hey, Jules, you want to taste my skeletal stew?" Sterling asked, ladling a scoop of the hearty stew into a bowl.

"It smells incredible, but the name is sending shivers up my spine."

"That's the idea with this magical feast, right?" He

handed me the bowl. His pork and tomatillo stew had rustic cut Yukon gold potatoes, carrots, and fire-roasted Anaheim chiles. He had topped it with fresh herbs and a sprinkling of Spanish cheese.

"This is absolute perfection. It's like a warm hug in every bite." I savored the melodic spices blended with the tomatillos and shredded pork. "It's magic."

"Glad you like it." Sterling couldn't conceal a prideful smile.

He should have felt proud of his abilities. He continued to impress me every day. His talent and unique take on food rivaled that of any professionally trained chef.

"The flowers are here," Rosa called from upstairs.

I went up to help her rearrange the dining room and decorate for the dinner. We served our Sunday Suppers family-style at one long, shared table. The goal was to encourage conversation and new friendships. It was one of the many reasons that the event tended to sell out quickly. People loved coming together around the table to share a meal and laughter. That was more important than ever after Anton's death.

"You want to do all black, right?" Rosa asked, unfolding the dark tablecloth.

"Yes, we're leaning into the gothic vibe, as Bethany calls it," I replied, grabbing one end and helping her stretch it out over the table. Janet had made a dramatic bouquet with black irises, deep purple calla lilies, and Bordeaux tulips.

Rosa arranged gold and silver plates, and I set the flowers in the center of the table. Then we used an assortment of candle holders for the black and purple tapered candles, leaving space for the punch bowl that would be filled with Andy's secret concoction and dry ice.

To finish the theme, we strung black and purple twinkle lights from the ceiling and turned the overhead lights off so that the dining room was lit only by the glow of the candles and the dazzling dainty lights above the table.

"Oh, it's spooky and beautiful," Rosa said, standing back to appraise our work.

"It feels like Hogwarts and *Hocus Pocus* and maybe even a set from *Hamlet*."

She smiled. "Should I bring up wine, or will we only be serving Andy's potions?"

"Wine, too." I pointed to the office. "Carlos brought a couple of cases over from Uva."

Rosa got the wine, and I took a last sweep of the kitchen. The appetizers had been plated and ready to serve. Marty's flatbreads and house-made chips would make excellent vessels for the variety of dips.

"Those are ready to go upstairs," Sterling said. "I'll bring up the cauldron of stew and salad when you give the signal."

"Dessert course is done, too," Steph added. "Deadly and decadent. You might warn guests to eat at their own risk."

"They're going to love this dark rye over my bread body," Marty bellowed, giving Bethany a grin. "That one's for you."

Bethany bowed in gratitude. "Don't worry, I'll put that on a shirt for you immediately."

She helped me arrange platters of her milk- and dark-chocolate brownies, which she had cut in the shape of skulls and dusted with powdered sugar.

"How's everything with the coffee guy upstairs?" I asked.

Her dimples sunk inward as she tried to hide a smile. "The coffee guy?"

"Seems like you two have been spending more time together since you've been back."

"We have, but why are guys so hard to read, Jules?"

"I would be a rich woman if I could answer that." I reached for a second platter. "Are things not going well?"

"No. I don't know. Maybe." She snapped a couple photos of the dessert trays on her phone. "I thought we kind of had a vibe going. He wanted to do some coffee and chocolate pairings, which I sort of assumed was an excuse to hang, but then he literally talked about coffee all night."

"Give him time," I suggested. "Coffee might be his love language."

Bethany twisted her face. "So what you're saying is that I'm going to have to make the first move?"

I shrugged. "Or bake him a batch of your droolworthy chile chocolate brownies and see where things go from there."

She picked up the first plate. "No time like the present." With that, she winked and headed upstairs.

Guests had already begun arriving when I returned to the dining room with platters of appetizers. Lance and Arlo were among the first guests, which was slightly surprising, since Lance usually preferred to make an appearance.

"Darling, this is absolutely divine," Lance said greeting me with air kisses. "My tastebuds are tingling with excitement. You're not going to serve us anything that actually might harm us, are you?"

"I don't think so."

"I once had a potion drink at a swanky rooftop bar in LA that was spiked with Pop Rocks," Arlo said. "It was so cool to have your mouth exploding with each sip. Slightly unnerving at first, but once I realized the fizzy feeling was from candy, it was pretty cool."

"We should have thought of that."

"Next time." Arlo excused himself to go talk to Carlos about the latest soccer match.

"So, do tell, how are you feeling by now?" Lance asked.

"Do you want some punch?" I motioned to the steaming punch bowl on the table.

"Drinks can wait. I want to hear if you know any more about Camille's fate?"

"No. The last update I heard was from the Professor. He seemed to think they have a solid case against her, but I haven't heard more. Why? Have you?"

"Mostly the same. I did see that her arraignment is in two days. I'm thinking of going. Want to join me?"

"I don't know."

He cut me off. "Wrong answer."

"What?"

"We must go, darling. It's our civic duty."

"Why?"

"I don't know. It feels important, though."

"Okay."

"There is news from my neck of the woods." Lance moved closer to the table and helped himself to a glass of the bubbling punch. "Jax and Perry came into my office to offer me a full confession. Perry went so far as to withdraw his name for the lead in *A Play About a Dragon*, but I absolutely refused."

"You did?" I took a glass that Lance offered. The punch had a nice bite from the cranberry and lemon base and an herbaceous finish from the rosemary. Touches of ginger ale and cinnamon completed the sensory experience.

"Never fear. I gave him a stern lecture and fair warning that should he attempt another prank like that, or sneak into any building on campus after hours, that he would be immediately replaced by his understudy."

"That sounds fair."

"You'll love this." Lance plunged a sprig of rosemary into his drink. "Jax has had a change of heart. Rather than attempting to get her ill-trained poodle onstage, she's going to complete a dog-training course and get certified herself."

"She's taking over Anton's role?" I asked.

"In sorts, yes. Trey suggested it. He's agreed to partner with her, as he did with Anton. No one can deny that out of everyone we know, Jax should have a career working with those four-legged furry beasts."

"Now she can obsess over her own dog and other people's pets." Although Lance was right. That sounded like a perfect career path for Jax.

"As long as it stops her from her pitiful begging, it's fine by me." He clinked his glass to mine. "Do tell, now that we've put this case behind us, what's next for you, my pastry maven?"

"Honestly, I'm not sure. The holidays of course, but I feel like there's some change coming our way." I bought myself a minute by taking another sip of the punch.

Lance put his arm around my shoulder. I half expected him to make a flippant remark. His voice turned husky. "We're already changed, Jules. Look at us. Look at this." His gaze drifted to Arlo and Carlos. "We're living our best life. Now the challenge becomes how we manage not to squeeze all the best parts out of it."

"What do you mean?"

"We can't hold too tightly to the past. If we had, we never would have made space in our lives for these loves, for these beautiful people gathered here together tonight. But change is the only thing we're promised in this life. Change is the constant. We have a choice as to whether we embrace or resist what's ahead."

"Why would we resist?" I didn't like his tone.

There had only been a handful of times in our friendship when Lance had truly let his guard down and let me in. This felt like one of those moments.

He removed his arm and sighed. "We're at a crossroads, darling. Families, partners, jobs."

"You're not thinking of leaving Ashland, are you?" A tiny quiver spread through my stomach. "Is Arlo moving on?" Arlo had been hired as an interim manager. No one had mentioned whether or not his contract would get renewed. I guessed I had just assumed it would.

Lance tapped my chin. "Chin up. No, I'm not leaving, and Arlo will only be allowed to go over my dead body. I've been in talks with the board to secure his position permanently. I'm simply stating the obvious." His stared at Mom and the Professor, who stood hand in hand at the foot of the table chatting with friends. "I sense retirements on the horizon. Perhaps some expansions?" He raised his eyebrows from me to Carlos. "Changes in the plaza.

There's new blood coming in. New partnerships in progress. I love our Ashland, yours and mine, but we can't keep it only to ourselves, can we?"

I still wasn't sure what he was hinting at. "Does this have anything to do with why you've been hanging around the Merry Windsor so much lately?"

He guzzled his punch. "You know I love and adore you, yes?"

I furrowed my brow. Where was he going with this? "Lance."

"It's nothing. I'm feeling mushy, that's all. Ask Arlo. I'm really pushing some boundaries with the lineup for next season, and I suppose I feel a tad vulnerable about it."

We got interrupted by more guests. I knew there was more that Lance wasn't saying, but that would have to wait. My attention was diverted to Mom and the Professor, who were peppering Ramiro for details about his upcoming state soccer tournament. I wandered in their direction.

Ramiro was growing into his broad shoulders. He had shot up in the last few weeks.

"You're towering over Mom now," I noted.

Mom tilted her neck. "Story of my life. I'm forever going to be staring up at this kid now."

Ramiro patted her shoulder. "I cannot help it. You all feed me too much good food."

"My advice," the Professor said with a touch of radiant grin. "Follow the wise words of Carroll Bryant, 'Growing old is mandatory. Growing up is optional.'"

"I'll toast to that." Mom lifted her mocktail. "Age is purely a state of mind, and speaking of state of mind, how are you feeling about State? I'm delighted that you're going to State with your team, and as long as we won't be too much of an embarrassment, Doug and I can't wait to come cheer you on."

"I've already purchased my Go Grizz sweatshirt," the Professor said.

"I don't know what to expect. We take the bus to Portland and stay in a hotel there for three nights. It should be fun, but Coach says that the teams we're going up against are solid. Our toughest competition of the year."

"Win or lose, we'll be rooting for you." Mom squeezed his waist.

My eyes misted. Seeing them dote on Ramiro made my heart swell, for them, for Ramiro, for me. This was my chosen family. Early grief and loss left its indelible mark and it had also cracked me open to making space for new connections. It was almost impossible to think about how small my circle had been on the *Amour of the Seas* and how coming home to tiny Ashland had vastly expanded that circle.

Gratitude and the heat of bodies warmed my cheeks. The wine and punch were flowing. People nibbled on Marty's black rye bread dipped in creamy beer and cheese sauce, and swapped stories around the table. Everyone applauded when Sterling delivered a cauldron of rustic, spicy pork stew. Bowls were passed around family style as happy laughter filled the dining room.

Lance lost any hint of the wistfulness he'd displayed in our conversation as he regaled everyone with ghoulish stories of hauntings of the Lizzie while Steph and Bethany brought up trays of layered Madagascar vanilla, cappuccino, and spiced pumpkin potion custards; dark chocolate miniature cakes, dripping with ganache; and an assortment of skull-shaped brownies. Andy offered guests evening coffees spiked with Baileys Irish Cream and our house-made whipped cream.

At one point I caught Carlos's eye across the table. He gave me a knowing smile. We didn't need words. I knew he was soaking in the moment like me. Things were starting to shift. Our future plans were becoming clearer, and while I was excited about what was to come, I was also nervous. Changing the dynamic would inevitably mean things would be different. Not that different was bad. Different was, well, different.

But for tonight, I sunk into the moment, happy for everything that I had in Ashland—Carlos, Mom, the Professor, Ramiro, so many friends, and Torte. It felt like magic because it was.

# Recipes

## Pumpkin Cupcakes with Cinnamon Cream Cheese Frosting

**For the pumpkin cupcakes:**
½ cup (1 stick) unsalted butter, at room temperature
1 cup granulated sugar
1 cup pumpkin puree
1 teaspoon ground cinnamon
½ teaspoon ground nutmeg
¼ teaspoon ground allspice
2 large eggs
1 ½ cups all-purpose flour
1 teaspoon baking powder
½ teaspoon salt
¼ cup sour cream

**For the cinnamon cream cheese frosting:**
½ cup (1 stick) unsalted butter, at room temperature
8 ounces cream cheese, at room temperature
4 cups powdered sugar

1 teaspoon vanilla extract
1 teaspoon cinnamon

## Directions:

*To make the cupcakes:*
Preheat the oven to 350°F and line a muffin tin with paper liners. In a large bowl, cream the butter and sugar together until light and fluffy. Add the pumpkin puree, cinnamon, nutmeg, and allspice to the bowl and mix until well combined. Beat in the eggs, one at a time. In a separate bowl, whisk together the flour, baking powder, and salt. Gradually add the dry ingredients to the pumpkin mixture, mixing until just combined. Stir in the sour cream until the batter is smooth. Divide the batter evenly among the prepared muffin cups, filling each about ⅔ full. Bake for 18–20 minutes, or until a toothpick inserted into the center of a cupcake comes out clean. Allow the cupcakes to cool completely before frosting.

*To make the frosting:*
Beat the butter and cream cheese together until light and fluffy. Gradually add the powdered sugar, vanilla extract, and cinnamon, mixing until smooth.

## Chicken and Stars Soup

### Ingredients:
2 tablespoons olive oil
1 cup diced carrots
1 cup diced onion

1 cup diced celery
2 cloves garlic, minced
8 cups chicken stock
1 teaspoon dried basil
1 teaspoon dried oregano
1 teaspoon dried thyme
Salt and pepper, to taste
2 cups chopped cooked chicken breasts
1 cup stelline pasta
½ cup light sour cream

**Directions:**
Add the olive oil to a saucepan over medium-high heat. Then add the diced carrots, onion, and celery to the pan and sauté for 5–7 minutes until the vegetables are softened. Add the minced garlic and cook for another minute until fragrant. Pour in the chicken stock and add the dried basil, oregano, thyme, salt, and pepper. Stir in the chopped cooked chicken breasts and bring the soup to a low rolling boil. Cover the pan and turn the heat to low. Let the soup simmer for 30–40 minutes until the chicken and the vegetables are tender. Add 1 cup of stelline pasta to the soup and continue cooking for 8–10 minutes until the pasta is tender and cooked through. Right before serving, stir in ½ cup of light sour cream to finish the soup with a creamy tang. Serve hot!

## Devil's Food Cupcakes

**Ingredients:**
½ cup vegetable oil
1 cup granulated sugar
1 teaspoon vanilla extract
2 large eggs
1 ½ cups all-purpose flour
1 teaspoon baking powder
½ teaspoon salt
4 ounces dark chocolate, melted and cooled
¼ cup buttermilk
2 teaspoons espresso powder

**Directions:**
Preheat the oven to 350°F and line a muffin tin with paper liners. In a large bowl, whisk together the vegetable oil, sugar, and vanilla extract until well combined. Add the eggs one at a time, whisking well after each addition. In a separate bowl, whisk together the flour, baking powder, and salt. Gradually add the dry ingredients to the wet mixture, whisking until just combined. In a small bowl, mix together the melted dark chocolate, buttermilk, and espresso powder until smooth. Add the chocolate mixture to the batter and stir until well combined. Divide the batter evenly among the prepared muffin cups, filling each about ⅔ full. Bake for 18–20 minutes, or until a toothpick inserted into the center of a cupcake comes out clean. Allow the cupcakes to cool completely before frosting.

## Halloween Cookie Bars

**Ingredients:**
1 cup (2 sticks) unsalted butter, at room temperature
1 cup brown sugar
1 cup white sugar
1 cup creamy peanut butter
1 teaspoon vanilla extract
2 large eggs
2 cups all-purpose flour
1 cup rolled oats
1 teaspoon salt
1 teaspoon baking soda
Assorted leftover candy bars, chopped
Orange and black M&M's

**Directions:**
Preheat oven to 350°F and grease a large glass baking
dish. In a large bowl, cream together the butter, brown
sugar, and white sugar until light and fluffy. Add in the
peanut butter, vanilla extract, and eggs, and continue
mixing until well combined. In a separate bowl, sift together the flour, oats, salt, and baking soda. Gradually add
the dry ingredients to the wet mixture, mixing until just
combined. Fold in the chopped leftover candy bars and orange and black M&M's by hand. Spread the cookie dough
evenly into the prepared baking dish. Bake for 25–30
minutes, or until a toothpick inserted into the center of
the bars comes out clean. Allow the cookie bars to cool
completely in the pan before cutting them into squares.

## Carlos's Humble Omelet

**Ingredients:**
3 eggs
Salt and pepper, to taste
1 tablespoon butter or oil
¼ cup diced onions
¼ cup diced bell peppers
2 strips of honey bacon, cooked and chopped
¼ cup shredded Parmesan cheese

**Directions:**
Crack the eggs into a bowl and whisk them together. Season them with salt and pepper. Heat a nonstick skillet over medium heat and melt the butter or add the oil. Add the diced onions and peppers to the skillet and sauté them for 3–4 minutes until softened. Pour the whisked eggs over the onions and peppers in the skillet. Let the eggs cook for 1–2 minutes until the bottom is set and the top is slightly runny. Sprinkle the chopped honey bacon and shredded Parmesan cheese on top of the eggs. Use a spatula to carefully fold the omelet in half, covering the bacon and cheese. Cook the omelet for an additional 1–2 minutes until the cheese is melted and the eggs are cooked through. Carefully slide the omelet onto a plate and serve hot.

## Andy's Trick-or-Torte Latte

**Ingredients:**
1 shot of espresso or strong coffee
½ teaspoon vanilla extract

2 teaspoon raspberry syrup
2 teaspoon blackberry syrup
1 cup milk (Andy uses oat milk)
1 teaspoon matcha powder
1 teaspoon beetroot powder
Sprinkles

**Directions:**
Pour the espresso into a mug. Add the vanilla extract, raspberry syrup, and blackberry syrup to the mug and stir to combine. Heat the milk and whisk in the matcha and beetroot powder. Pour the milk mixture into the mug with the espresso and syrups. Top with sprinkles. Serve hot!

## Apple Decadence Cake

### *Gluten Free, Dairy Free, Nut Free*

Recipe by Miri Pizann

**Ingredients:**
**For the cake:**
Dry

- 270 grams gluten-free one-to-one flour (I used Bob's Red Mill Gluten Free 1-to-1 Baking Flour)
- 1 ¾ teaspoons baking soda
- 200 grams brown sugar
- ½ teaspoon kosher sea salt
- 2 teaspoons ground ginger
- 1 teaspoon ground cinnamon

- ½ teaspoon ground nutmeg
- ½ teaspoon ground allspice
- ½ teaspoon ground cloves
- Pinch of cardamom

Wet

- 1 cup of dairy free milk (I use Oatly oat milk)
- 2 large eggs, at room temperature
- 4 ounces vegan butter (1 stick), melted (I use Earth Balance Soy Free Buttery Sticks with the pink label)
- 1 teaspoon vanilla extract

**Apple Filling**

- 2 Granny Smith apples, peeled, cored, and diced
- 33 grams granulated vanilla sugar (plain granulated sugar also works)
- 1 tablespoon arrowroot flour

**Caramel Sauce**

- ½ cup dairy free milk (I use Oatly oat milk)
- 1 tablespoon unsweetened SunButter
- 2 tablespoon honey
- 2 tablespoon maple syrup
- ¼ teaspoon kosher sea salt
- 1 ½ teaspoon tapioca starch
- ½ teaspoon vanilla extract

**Vanilla Bean Buttercream**

- 4 ounces vegan butter (1 stick), softened
- 4 ounces shortening, softened
- 1 tablespoon vanilla extract

- 1 pound powdered sugar
- 1 teaspoon ground vanilla powder

**Directions**

Lightly coat the inside of two 8-inch cake pans with pan release and set aside.

Combine all the dry cake ingredients (flour, baking soda, sugar, sea salt, and spices) in a large bowl and break up any clumps.

In a separate bowl, combine the wet cake ingredients (dairy-free milk, eggs, melted vegan butter, and vanilla). Pour the wet into the dry and stir or whisk to combine.

Set the batter aside to rest for 30 minutes. Do not skip resting the batter. While the batter is resting, preheat the oven to 350°F and make the apple filling.

Combine the diced apples, sugar, and arrowroot flour in a medium pot until apples are coated. Stir over medium heat. The apples will release juice and create a sauce. Stir until sauce is clear and gooey, and the apples are tender. Set aside to cool.

Once the cake batter has rested, divide it evenly between the two prepared cake pans.

Bake for 30–35 minutes, rotating the pans at the halfway point. Cakes are done when they spring back from a light touch and a toothpick in the center comes out clean.

Cool the cakes for 5 minutes in the pans, and then allow them to cool completely on a rack.

While the cakes are cooling, make the caramel sauce by combining all the of caramel ingredients in a small saucepan. Whisk intermittently over medium-high heat until the sauce is bubbly. Lower the heat to medium and whisk constantly for 45–60 seconds, until it is thicker but still pourable.

Remove the caramel sauce from heat, set aside, and allow to cool.

While the cake and caramel sauce are both cooling, make the vanilla bean buttercream. Start by using an electric mixer to cream together the vegan butter, shortening, and vanilla extract. Scrape down the bowl as necessary.

Slowly add the powdered sugar and mix on medium until well combined and fluffy. Add vanilla bean powder to taste and for visual aesthetic.

Add 1 tablespoon of water and mix in completely. Continue adding 1 tablespoon at a time until you have the consistency you prefer.

Once the cake is cool, apply a crumb coating of buttercream to the top of the first (bottom) layer. Put a thick ring of buttercream just inside the edge of the cake and put all of the apple filling inside the ring, spreading it out to lay flat. Drizzle the apple filling with half of the caramel sauce.

Put the second layer of cake on top and put the crumb coating on the top and sides of the cake. Frost with the remainder of the buttercream, and decorate with the caramel drizzle.

**Read on for an excerpt from
A SMOKING BUN—
the next installment in Ellie Alexander's
wonderful Bakeshop series—
coming soon from St. Martin's Paperbacks!**

# Chapter One

They say you should embrace the seasons of life. It wasn't hard to do in the constant flux of the ever-changing landscapes of the lush Rogue Valley. I simply needed to use Mother Nature as my guide. She had a way of reminding me to pause at the sight of the pinkish sun rising over the Siskiyou Mountains or delight in the sweet bundles of birdseed that someone left along the fenceposts in Lithia Park to feed the dark-eyed juncos.

Beauty was literally all around me. My problem was more about centering on the moment. To be fully present and not spiral into imagined worries and plans for my future. As we leaned deeper into winter, I had been mildly successful at embracing my new quest. It helped that my husband Carlos was here to stay. He had opted to make my hometown of Ashland, Oregon, his too. Having him in our little hamlet in the Southern Oregon mountains filled me with a level of joy I didn't know was possible. Plus, Ramiro, his son from Spain, had been living with us for the last five months.

We enjoyed a leisurely holiday break, cozying up in front of the crackling fireplace as snow drifted down from a dark December sky, dusting Grizzly Peak and blanketing Ashland in a soft coat of white. There were family meals, sledding afternoons, game nights, baking copious amounts of Christmas cookies, and weaving in Spanish traditions, like making Ramiro's favorite treats, "roscos de vino." The festive donut-shaped biscuits were made with a touch of sweet wine and nuts. Their icing sugar coating made them look like they had been dipped in snow. I had made a batch for our family bakeshop, Torte, and customers had raved about the cookies. They also wanted to know what gave the "wine rolls" their unique flavor and consistency. A baker should never reveal her secrets, but in this case, I explained that the cookies were made with ground sesame seeds and a splash of Anisette liqueur. Thanks to Ramiro, "roscos de vino" had a permanent place on Torte's winter menu.

Ashland's Elizabethan charm was heightened in December and January when snow covered the Tudor-style rooflines in the plaza. There was a sleepy vibe in town, with the Oregon Shakespeare Festival dark until early spring and only a handful of tourists who came seeking snowy adventures. It was one of the things I enjoyed most about living in the Rogue Valley, the shifting rhythm of each season.

With the holidays behind us, we were shifting gears to get ready to ring in the new year and welcome houseguests in the form of Ramiro's mom, stepfather, and little sister. They had graciously agreed to share Ramiro with us for a year so that he could do an exchange program in Ashland. I'd been nervous at first about connecting with Sophia, Ramiro's mom, but after weekly Facetime chats with her and Luis and Marta, I couldn't wait for them to arrive. We had spent two days after Christmas preparing the house and packing the pantry with everything we might need to entertain our international visitors.

The Torres family was arriving in time to celebrate the New Year with us before they continued south to California for more adventures. Sophia and I had been emailing almost daily. I sent her updates on Ramiro's soccer scores, pictures of him baking at Torte, and check-ins about how her only son was doing halfway around the world. Our friendship had blossomed over the miles. It was almost like having a pen pal, and Sophia's genuine gratitude for something as easy as texting her a quick pic of Ramiro in his homecoming tuxedo gave me new insight and appreciation into how hard it must have been for Mom to let me take off on my own global travels.

The morning their flight was due in, Ramiro bounded down the stairs and poured himself a cup of coffee. It had taken me a little while to adjust to his Spanish habits, like breakfast espresso. Not that I was ever one to turn down a strong cup of coffee.

"Today is the day, Jules." He beamed as he added a glug of heavy cream to his mug. "I cannot believe they are finally coming." He sounded more excited than he had been Christmas morning.

"I know. It's going to be so much fun to have them here and show them Ashland. Are you sure about the snowshoe tour? It won't be too late for Marta?"

"She's twelve. She's going to love getting to stay up past her bedtime."

"As long as you're sure." I had booked a midnight snowshoe on Mount Ashland or, as locals called our ski hill—Mount A. The trip would take us from the lodge around the rim of the mountain to a warming hut where we would enjoy hot drinks and a late-night feast under a full moon and a starry sky. I had wanted to make the trek for years, and Ramiro's family visit seemed like the perfect opportunity. The brochure had sold me with its description: "Experience the serenity of winter while experts guide you on a snow-packed trail under a romantic starry sky."

The snowshoe trip sounded like the perfect way to kick off the Torres family's visit. Sophia had told me they loved the outdoors, and aside from spending time with Ramiro and us, they wanted to see Oregon's rugged landscapes.

This was where my tendency to overthink and overplan might have gotten the best of me. I had arranged for another snow outing for the next day. It was Mount A's annual Downhill Dummy competition—an event I had wanted to participate in in recent years but hadn't made the time. Last summer, after Carlos and I had taken a vacation to travel through Europe with Ramiro, I promised to do more things for myself. Running a bakeshop, winery, and pop-up summer ice-cream stand had been fulfilling, but in the process of growing my little Ashland empire, I might have focused too much of my attention on work. My intention for the New Year was to find a better balance between work and play.

Ramiro living with us had given me the perfect excuse to change that and embrace all that Southern Oregon had to offer. The Downhill Dummy was one of those things. Entrants dressed up dummies in various outlandish costumes and makeshift vehicles, attached them to skis and snowboards, and sent them hurling down a ski jump. The winner took home bragging rights and a free ski pass for the year.

Andy had been begging me to sign Torte up for the competition for years. So when I approached him about entering the Downhill Dummy this year, he did a backflip in the middle of the dining room—literally—and promised me that he would work with Bethany, Steph, and Sterling to come up with a killer dummy.

I had no doubt about my team's creativity, and I was eager to see what they would construct. They had asked if I wanted to be involved in the build or be surprised. There was no question; I had to be surprised.

I removed a container of peppermint cream from the fridge and offered some to Ramiro.

"I can't wait to show your family everything the Rogue Valley has to offer, but I'm pretty sure I've overbooked us. Sorry. You know me."

He brushed a long strand of dark hair from his eyes and added a splash of cream to his coffee. "It's fine, Jules. They're not ninety. They want to see where we live, and it's not like we can't cancel if it's too much, right?"

"Right." How was he wiser than me as a teenager?

"A moonlight snowshoe and snacks around a bonfire," Ramiro said, helping himself to a cinnamon roll. "It's so American. They'll love it."

"Good. And then we're going back up to the mountain the next day for the Downhill Dummy, assuming everyone isn't too tired." I filled my coffee cup with water and placed it in the microwave to heat for a minute.

"Si. We can't miss it." He laughed and pressed his finger to his lips. "I am sworn to secrecy by Andy, but I will tell you the Torte dummy is so, so good."

"I can't wait. How's the soccer team's dummy coming together?" I removed my mug from the microwave, dumped the water on a potted peace plant resting on the window above the farm-style sink, and then poured myself a cup of coffee. It was a trick I had learned in culinary school to make my morning cup of Joe stay hotter for longer.

"It's pretty great." He plopped into a chair, letting his lanky limbs rest at his sides like long noodles.

Unless he had been good at hiding his emotions, he had seemed comfortable since the start of his stay with us, but as the months had gone on, he had become even more at ease. At first, he would ask if he could have a snickerdoodle or open a bag of Tortilla chips. Now he helped himself to whatever he wanted. This was his home, and I loved that he felt empowered to raid the refrigerator and invite friends over after school.

"So they really launch the dummies down a ski jump?" He licked frosting from his finger.

"They do. It's utter carnage." The Downhill Dummy had been going strong since I was in high school. It was popular with skiers, snowboarders, and the general public since no athletic skills were necessary to be a spectator.

"The goal is to get the most air, but the real winners are the dummies with the most outrageous crashes." I checked the pantry to make sure I had everything I needed for dinner. The Torres's flight got in later this afternoon. I intended to start my day at Torte and leave early to meet Carlos and Ramiro at home before we caravanned to Medford to pick them up at the airport.

"Like a crash test dummy for cars?" He took another

bite of the cinnamon roll, oozing with melty cream cheese frosting.

"Exactly. The bigger the crash, the better. Body parts, well, dummy parts, will be flying in the air." I twisted my long blond hair into a ponytail and kicked off my slippers.

"Cool."

Carlos came in through the back door with an armful of almond firewood. "Good morning." He took the wood to the living room to stack near the fireplace and returned to join us for coffee. "Julieta, do you want a ride to the bakeshop? I can take you and then go finish the list of errands."

"No, that's fine." I glanced out the steamy kitchen window to our backyard where the Manzanita and Madrones looked as if they had been crumb coated—a term we used in the bakeshop, meaning frosted in a thin layer of buttercream. "It's a brisk winter morning. Perfect walking weather."

Ramiro rubbed his arms. "It's freezing. If I were going to school, I would take a ride."

We had timed it so that the Torres family was visiting during the last part of Ramiro's extended winter break. Classes would resume after they had returned to Spain. As for Torte, it was also our slowest time of the year. That meant my team could take the lead while I took time off to spend with the Torres family. I would still check in but had penciled myself out of daily shifts.

"You two have fun on your errands." I took my coffee to the sink and turned to Carlos. "I might have you pick me up at Torte, depending on how the day goes, but I'll text you."

Carlos stood to kiss me. His dark eyes had a way of always making my knees go slightly weak. This morning was no exception. As he pulled me toward his body, I could feel the heat radiating off his skin and smelled a faint hint of chopped wood. His lips brushed mine before he released me with a flirty grin. "Have a good morning, Julieta, and let me know if you think of anything else we might need."

I surveyed the kitchen. Thanks to Carlos, it was better stocked than the industrial kitchens we had worked in on the *Amour of the Seas*. Food was our love language. Having houseguests meant welcoming them with round-the-clock meals and snacks. Carlos had prepared a variety of homemade bread to make pintxos—skewered baguettes with smoked salmon and cheeses along with bocadillo de jambon—ham sandwiches prepared with thin-sliced Serrano ham, cheese, olive oil, and tomatoes. Our cabinets were filled with staples to make soups and stews and pasta. We had enough food to feed a small army. And that didn't include everything I would bring home from the bakeshop. "I think we have enough food to feed the entire neighborhood or, better yet, all of Ashland," I teased.

I gave them both hugs and went to bundle up for my walk to the bakeshop. Frosty air greeted me outside as I made my descent down Mountain Avenue. A crunchy layer of light snow coated the sidewalks. Smoke puffed from chimneys. Holiday lights and Christmas trees still dotted the front windows of a few houses that wanted to stay in the spirit a bit longer. The campus of Southern Oregon University was utterly still, aside from a flock of turkeys huddled under a giant oak tree, as I passed the extensive grounds.

Once I turned onto Siskiyou Boulevard and headed past the Carnegie Library, I could make out the soft glow of light illuminating the plaza. Storefronts had warm winter displays of cashmere blankets, candles, books, and assorted teas. Like some of the houses in my neighborhood, many shops and restaurants had opted to leave their exterior twinkle lights on for another few weeks. Christmas trees and garlands had been replaced with crystal champagne glasses, sparklers, and lanterns to welcome the new year.

I crossed past the information kiosk and stopped to take in Torte's front window display. Decorating the windows and interior was another task I had handed off to my highly capable staff. Rosa, our front-of-house manager, and Bethany, our cake designer and lead baker, had partnered on many occasions to create compelling window displays to entice customers inside.

Once again, their vision for the New Year took my breath away. White birch trees entwined with glittery white lights stood in each corner of the window. Oversized paper snowflakes hung from the eaves, and an assortment of white winter wonderland cakes were perched on glossy ceramic stands. Pale shades of silky buttercream in porcelain, ivory, and pearl made the cakes look iridescent.

The display was equally inviting and drool-worthy. They had sprinkled vanilla bean macarons and miniature cupcakes with shiny foil wrappers on the base of the window. Everything looked like it had been painted with a cloud of luster dust. I smiled as I used the handrail to navigate the slippery brick steps that led to the basement entrance.

I unlocked the door, flipped the lights, and turned on

the atomic fireplace in the dining area adjacent to the open-concept kitchen. Working in the space that Mom and I had designed was one of the highlights of my day, but there was no debating that the basement was a good five to ten degrees colder than upstairs.

Before I started baking or making a pot of coffee, I heated the ovens and started a fire in the exposed brick, wood oven. That would help ensure my team didn't have to spend half the morning blowing on their fingertips to keep them warm.

Once that task was complete, I gathered ingredients for the first bake on my morning task list—persimmon sweet bread. It was similar to banana bread but with a winter twist of persimmons, cloves, nutmeg, and cinnamon. The fruit offered a rich, earthy flavor to a breakfast bread.

I began by creaming butter and sugar together. Then I added eggs, a trio of warming spices, a touch of rum extract, honey, and persimmon pulp. Once I had a fluffy batter, I alternated between adding splashes of buttermilk and my dry ingredients—flour, salt, and baking soda. The batter was thick and smooth. I couldn't resist swiping a taste before I spread it into greased tins. Spicy notes came through, along with a touch of vanilla.

The final step for the bread was to thinly slice persimmons and arrange them on top of the batter to form a pretty pattern. Persimmons were harbingers of winter; their date-like flavor, soft sweet fruit, and bright orange color made them versatile and festive for baking.

As I was sliding the loaves into the oven, Andy came in through the back door. He was dressed in multiple layers with his ski parka, a pullover sweater, a puffy retro vest, and fingerless gloves. Ski passes dangled from his zipper while he tugged off his hat and tried to tame his hair. "Morning, boss. It's a cold one out there."

"That's why I'm baking bread." I grinned. "However, I didn't start the coffee. I decided I would wait for the A-team to arrive."

"I'm glad you did because I have a winter roast that I want you to try." He removed a plastic tub of beans inside his coat like a magician pulling a rabbit from a hat. "Stay put; I'll be back in a flash."

He darted upstairs. I loved seeing his enthusiasm when it came to coffee. He had decided to make a significant life change and drop out of college to pursue his passion. Thankfully his family supported his career shift. His grandma had helped him set up a roaster on her property, and Mom and I had been committed to sending him to courses and workshops on roasting techniques. Next on our list was to take him on a tour of some of the growing regions where we sourced our beans.

I could hear beans pulverizing in the grinder, followed shortly by their intoxicating scent.

Steph, Sterling, and Marty arrived shortly after Andy. It was hard to believe that we'd been working together for as long as we had. Turnover on the ship and, quite honestly, in most professional kitchens was a big problem. Fortunately, my team was like a second family. Everyone had their own roles and autonomy. Marty was the most recent hire. He focused on bread and pizza dough. Sterling had taken over savory items and had the official title of sous-chef, although I felt it was time to offer him a promotion.

Steph worried me the most. Not because of her talent or work ethic but because she had recently graduated from

Southern Oregon University, and her talent for cake artistry was unmatched. I didn't want Torte to hold her back,
but I also wasn't ready to let her go. Yet another reminder
of how lucky I was to have my relationship with Mom. I
needed to ask her how she had managed her own grief
when I had gone away.

I tried to push the thought aside as we went over specialty and wholesale orders.

"Bethany is delivering cakes to the Green Goblin later,"
Steph said, tying on a candy apple red Torte apron. "We
crumb-coated them last night, so they'll be ready by noon."

"This old dude is ready for bread duty." Marty rolled
up his sleeves. "Things are fairly slow for our wholesale
orders. So many restaurants are taking a much-needed
winter's nap."

He was right. Several businesses in the plaza opted to
close shop for a few weeks in January or even for the entire month. This was the one time of the year that small
businesses owners could get away for a little respite or
even complete tasks that couldn't be done during the rush
of summer tourism or the holidays, like taking inventory
or mapping out quarterly sales goals for the next year or
even just giving the space a deep clean or a fresh coat of
paint.

"Are you making more of those buns you did yesterday?" Sterling asked. He had grabbed an apron too, but
instead of tying it around his neck, he opted to wear it
folded around his waist with a dish towel tucked into
one side. "They were so popular I thought I could make
spiced chicken and a veggie chickpea mixture to stuff in
your buns."

"Stuff in your buns," Marty chuckled. "You make it; I'll stuff 'em."

"What about a soup for the day?" I asked.

Sterling opened his sketchbook containing snippets of poetry, recipe ideas, and doodles. "How does a spiced Moroccan chicken stew sound?"

"Delish." I gave him a thumbs-up. "Yes, please."

Andy came downstairs, balancing a tray of coffees with one muscular arm. "Okay, here you go. These should taste like snow."

"Snow?" Steph curled her lip, perfectly lined in a shade of violet that matched her hair and eye shadow. "Doesn't snow taste like nothing? It's just frozen water."

I had come to love and appreciate her sarcasm.

Andy shook a finger at her. "Hey, no lip from you. It doesn't taste like actual snow. I meant it should remind you of a snow day. I think I'm calling it a winter warmer."

"Then you should have said a snow day," she bantered in return, twisting fluted tips onto a piping bag filled with blushing pink buttercream.

Bethany breezed in. "Sorry I'm late. I stopped by the grocery store to see if they might have any sprinkles. I know it's a long shot, but I ran out of the gold glitter after working on the window display last night, and I thought maybe with New Year's Eve, they might."

"Any luck?" I asked.

She shook her head, tugging off a rainbow parka and matching hat. "Nope. I struck out."

"I'm going up to Medford later to pick up Ramiro's family at the airport. I can swing by our supplier. Unless you need them sooner."

"That would be great. They're for an anniversary cake the couple picks up this weekend." She pointed to her purple sweatshirt with a silhouette of a rolling pin and the words LET'S DOUGH THIS on the front. "Check it out. It's a good one, yeah?"

"Love it," Andy replied with enthusiasm. "Love it. Love you. Love, uh, wait. What? What did I say?" His cheeks warmed, matching the color of Steph's buttercream. He cleared his throat. "As I was saying, I have a winter warmer for you to try. Hopefully, it will bring back fond memories of canceled school and sledding."

"What is it?" Bethany came closer.

"It's my spiced winter roast with white chocolate and a trio of orange, raspberry, and housemade cranberry syrups. I think it's a nice blend of the sweetness of raspberry with the tart cranberry and citrus notes of the orange. There's a housemade marshmallow to top it off." He passed around the drinks, avoiding Bethany's dewy gaze. "White chocolate can go way too sweet fast, so you'll have to tell me what you think."

I took a sip of his creamy latte. It tasted exactly as he described, and it felt like it was meant to be savored from a cushy chair in front of a crackling fire in a mountain lodge. "This is a snow day."

Andy grinned. "You like it?"

Everyone agreed. He returned to the espresso bar to add it to the daily special menus along with Sterling's soup and stuffed buns. Marty turned his attention to bread dough. Bethany and Steph began batches of muffins and cookies to stock the pastry case.

I teamed up with Sterling to chop onions, carrots, and celery for the buns. Mirepoix, the humble French flavor base, was the foundation for nearly every savory dish that came out of our kitchen. The unfancy veggie combination practically disappears after performing its part, but without the trio, soups and stews would lack depth and end up bland.

Sterling rolled up the sleeves of his slate gray hoodie, revealing tattoos from his elbow to his wrist. He smashed garlic cloves with the edge of a knife blade, removed the peels, and began finely dicing them.

"What next?"

He flipped a page in his notebook to the recipe. Like any good chef, there were notes in the margins with ideas for enhancing the recipes. "For the filling, I want to do tomato paste, turmeric, smoked paprika, chili powder, ginger, coriander, and salt and pepper. I made an update to add black sesame seeds to the tops. I'll brown some ground chicken for the meat option and then substitute that with chickpeas for a vegetarian version."

"Sounds delish."

"How do you feel about fresh peas?" He tossed the veggies in a pan with some olive oil.

"Love them, why?" I opened the spice drawers and began gathering everything Sterling had requested.

"Do you think it would be too much to incorporate peas? On the other hand, they could give a nice hit of sweetness and pop of texture."

"Let's do it." I handed him a container of turmeric.

While he made the filling, I rolled out a batch of Marty's dough and then cut it into circles. Next, we spooned two to three tablespoons of the chicken-and-chickpea mixture into each ring and then sealed them by flipping the sides and pinching them together.

We placed them upside down on a parchment-lined baking tray and brushed them with an egg wash. Sterling finished each bun with a sprinkling of black sesame seeds for color and texture and slid them into the wood-fired oven to bake.

My persimmon bread had cooled enough to slice. I cut it into two-inch servings, arranged it on a tray, and put it in the pastry case upstairs. I touched base with Rosa, who managed the dining room, before I left for the airport.

Seeing Torte running so smoothly and my team working together like a stage director had choreographed us made my heart happy. I knew the bakeshop would be in good hands over the next few days while I entertained and got to know Sophia, Luis, and Marta. I hoped that they would love Ashland as much as I did. How could they not? It was an idyllic time to visit, with nothing much going on other than ample time to get to hang out and really get to know each other. Little did I know that I might be very wrong about that.